NATIONAL BESTSELLER • BOOKER PRIZE FINALIST

"...rdi's characters are so sharply drawn that they bite."
—CHRISTINA SCHWARZ,
THE ATLANTIC MONTHLY

INDEPENDENT • BOOKSELLER • RECOMMENDATIONS

Book Sense 76 Pick

The Hiding Place

a novel Trezza Azzopardi

Praise for *The Hiding Place:*

"Elegant and auspicious . . . Because Azzopardi's writing is unsentimental, even the cynical and skeptical will find themselves moved by the Gauci family's heartbreaking saga. Highly recommended." —Eleanor J. Bader, *Library Journal* (starred)

"Azzopardi's novel vividly conveys the violence and grief of family life gone awry. [A] poetic, perceptive look at a family's disintegration." —Francine Prose, *US Weekly*

"[Dolores] tells her story in fragments, which come to life through a child's perceptions: slightly tilted, incomplete, yet remarkably perceptive. Like the gritty world they inhabit, Azzopardi's characters command a ragged, sharp-edged dignity in this haunting debut." —*Kirkus Reviews* (starred)

"*The Hiding Place* is an accomplished and courageous debut. The setting is original, and Azzopardi's approach to her characters is expressionistic. In its sheer strangeness and poetic charge, the novel sometimes recalls *Wuthering Heights*." —Rupert Shortt, *The Times Literary Supplement* (London)

"Intense . . . [Azzopardi's] credible and compelling descriptions of family life could easily pass for memoir." —Leo Carey, *The New York Times Book Review*

"Trezza Azzopardi has accomplished something extraordinary in this poignant debut novel: She has truly captured the brutality that can kill the innocence of childhood." —Paula Friedman, *Atlanta Journal Constitution*

"[*The Hiding Place*] proceeds at a cracking pace, full of neat but unobtrusive gestures at the horrors beneath." —DJ Taylor, *The Guardian* (UK)

"Rich, poetic . . . Brave youngest daughter Dol narrates this heartbreaking tale of secrets and lies, fires and misfortunes. Think *Angela's Ashes*, the chick version." —Cathi Hanauer, *Glamour*

"Azzopardi's voice throughout is strong, insistent and entirely convincing." —Robin Beeman, *San Francisco Chronicle*

trezza azzopardi

the hiding place

GROVE PRESS
New York

First published in 2000 by Picador, an imprint of
Macmillan Publishers Ltd., London, England

'I've Got You Under My Skin', words and music by Cole Porter © 1973 Chappell-Co Inc/Assigned To Buxton-Hill-Music Corp, Warner Chappell Music Ltd. Reproduced by permission of IMP Ltd.
'You Make Me Feel So Young', words and music by Mack Gordon & Josef Joe Myrow © 1946 Twentieth Century Music Corp., USA/ Bregman-Vocco & Conn Inc., USA. Reproduced by permission of IMP Ltd.
'Buonasera Senorina', words and music by De Rose/Sigman © 1950, renewed and assigned to Major Songs Co. and De Rose Music.
'Needles and Pins', words and music by Sonny Bono and Jack Nitzsche © 1963 EMI Catalogue Partnership, EMI Unart Catalogue Inc, USA. Worldwide print rights controlled by Warner Bros Inc, USA/IMP Ltd. Reproduced by permission of IMP Ltd.
'Is you is or is you ain't my baby?', words and music by Billy Austin and Louis Jordan © 1944 by kind permission of Universal/MCA Music Ltd.
'Ain't Nobody Here but Us Chickens', words and music by Whitney and Kramer © 1947 by kind permission of Universal/MCA Music Publ. Ltd.

Printed in the United States of America

FIRST GROVE PRESS PAPERBACK EDITION

Library of Congress Cataloging-in-Publication Data

Azzopardi, Trezza.
    The hiding place / Trezza Azzopardi.
        p. cm.
    ISBN 0-8021-3859-4 (pbk.)
        1. Cardiff (Wales)—Fiction. 2. Maltese—Wales—Fiction. 3. Poor families—
Fiction. 4. Gamblers—Fiction. 5. Girls—Fiction. I. Title.

PR6051.Z96 H53 2001
823'.92—dc21
                                                                00-046424

Grove Press
841 Broadway
New York, NY 10003

02 03 04 05   10 9 8 7 6 5 4 3 2 1

For my mother

acknowledgements

Thanks to Derek Johns and Linda Shaughnessy at AP Watt, and Mary Mount and Peter Straus at Picador.

Special thanks to Rita Isaacs and Andrew Motion.

Extra special thanks to John Kemp for tirelessly retrieving the songs; David Hill for reading it, reading it, reading it; and Stephen Foster, for leaving it alone.

part one

waiting

Despite the fact that Carol Jackson has to sit in a pram, she and her mother are going out together, while mine is downstairs whispering with a perfumed woman in an animal skin.

I watch as the pram disappears round the edge of the street. Mrs Jackson's stick legs and slippers are the last bits to vanish, but if I move my face further left into the crack of the window, I might still see them. I don't do this. I lick the glass I've frosted with my breath, to get a clear view up the hill to the betting shop, and wait for my father, like I'm told.

When my mother's friend Eva slipped in through the back door, I expected her to stay put. But she followed us up the stairs. She stood on the landing in her ocelot coat, with one hand closed upon the other. My mother stationed me at the glass.

Do three Our Fathers, and if you can't see him by then, come down, she said. Eva laughed. Her body bent forward and she flipped the air with a glove she'd fingered off in the doorway.

Are you sure it's alright, Mary? she asked, rapping across the floorboards in her heels.

He'll be ages yet, said my mother, moving her away from the mattresses and the faint smell of urine, and taking her back down the stairs.

My father doesn't like it when Eva comes round. He says she drinks too much. My mother says Eva's the only friend she's got left. When my father goes to the betting office, they sit downstairs and talk, and both of them drink too much. Sometimes I can hear them laughing. But when Eva came up to my room I panicked, because there's really no more space for anyone else in this house.

~

This is my bedroom, and Luca's, and Fran's, and my mother's. The four of us sleep here, and at the back of the house live Celesta and Rose, my other two sisters who I don't really know. They have pinned a notice on the door which I can't read but which I know says, KEEP OUT. THIS MEANS YOU! I think it means me. I imagine they're serious.

We are Celesta, Rosaria, Francesca, Luca, Dolores. I'm the last, and like Rose and Fran I am shortened in my name: I am Dol. This is so my mother can get us all down for breakfast in one breath. There is one more of us, Marina, who comes after Celesta, but she's not here any more, which is just as well, because how would she fit in?

My father has the last bedroom. It's called the Box Room, but it has no boxes in it, at least none that I can see. It's always open, as if he's saying he doesn't really live there, or is pinched by the size of it, or wants us to know he's still alive at night by letting us hear him snore. I never go in there by choice, but sometimes I stand at the door.

My bedroom is full of beds. It's practically a ward. There's also an old fold-up, which has lost the ability to do what it suggests. It lounges on its side against the far wall, as if it's waiting for another child to fill it. I share the big bed with my mother and my sister Luca. We lie on either side of her in our winceyette pyjamas, like two brackets stuck with fluff. I never consider that this might be my father's place.

Fran sleeps on a slim divan in the corner. It's not because she doesn't want to sleep with us, but because she always wets

4

the bed. I do too, sometimes, and so does Luca. It's easy to tell who's to blame; the mattress is patterned with flowers, and stains. My mother doesn't understand why we do it, children of three, six, eight, and we can't explain.

Our Father, who art in Heaven . . . I've done two as far as I know, which is only up to Daily Bread, so I stop and watch. I think I see his shadow on the hill, but as the shape trots down I laugh because it's just a dog.

There's only space for one more thing in here, and that's the chest, which is also a bed of sorts. My mother keeps her old handbag in it, busting with photographs of lots of people I don't know. They're always getting married and standing on a step, so the two are linked forever in my head. There are others, too, of me and all the rest, black and white, cracked and creased, sliding on each other inside the dim nylon pouch, inside the handbag, inside the chest.

I slept in the chest, when I was newborn. My mother told me how she wrapped me in a shawl at night and hid me from my father.

He would've smothered you, she said, without malice but with a strange sense of pride, as if I were a Rescue kitten she had taken in.

I think about the little baby in the chest, and my father, creeping into the bedroom like a pantomime giant. He's lifting his legs very high, placing one shiny hobnail boot slowly in front of the other. He has a pillow concertinaed in his hands; he's sniffing the air for signs.

But wouldn't he have heard me? I say, and my mother smiles.

Not when I shut the lid. You didn't make a peep.

~

My mother's laugh below and the chink of a bottle reminds me I am on lookout. He's loping down the street, almost home, and I run to whisper in my mother's ear. Eva drags her coat off the chair, pockets the bottle of rum, and moves to the back door. She lifts the latch and lets herself out. The air is frosty. My mother breaks off some blackened parsley from a pot next to the step, and folds it into her mouth.

Go upstairs now, Dol, and do your puzzle, she says. I must keep out of my father's way.

~ ~ ~

That was a time before I was four. The house is still here, and now I am here, standing at the window of the bedroom we shared. A veil of grime is drawn across the sill. My mother would never have allowed it.

The Jacksons have long gone, moved to a new estate called Pentwyn Farm. It says so on the front of the bus which takes you there. Their house is empty now: one top window is boarded up, the other gapes; a smash of black glass juts from the frame like a broken bone. A stone's throw. The other houses in the row are nailed with identical sheets of gunmetal grey, decorated with ribbons of graffiti red. There are a few people left on the street, but I don't know any of them. There are no cars at the kerb.

I'm standing at my window, and I'm the last. All the rest have gone. All the sisters have gone. I'm waiting for them to stage their comeback.

one

Six-to-four the field, six-to-one bar!
Shouting the odds, the TV and my father, low down on the living room floor.

C'mon, baby! he yells, beating his flank with his fist. With the betting slip in his teeth, he gallops down the last furlong of the rug, to the home straight of the lino. Words bolt from the side of his mouth: Yankee Piggott Photo-finish. I don't understand any of it: I think my father's English leaves a lot to be desired.

He curses: Jesus Christ.

At the end of the race, his face is very flushed, an inch from the set. He's watching the lines and dots as if Barney's Boy will suddenly leap through the screen. Ripping pink shreds of paper from his mouth, my father tears up his slip and spits the remains on the rug. Then he starts in on the *Sporting Life*, holding it out in front of him, rending it between his fists until he's tearing air. I know at these moments that he would tear me too, for the slightest thing, and I crawl ever so slowly behind the couch, until he's put on his donkey jacket and slammed the back door.

He isn't just like this about horses. My father will gamble on anything that moves. He won't do Bingo or fruit machines or snow on Christmas Day, but horses and pontoon and poker and dogs. My father's love is Chance. Look at that roulette wheel! Bet red, bet black, bet red, bet black. If he could place his bet Under Starter's Orders he would still change his mind over every fence. The Form makes no difference, the words don't make sense, and the odds at Joe Coral have no bearing on his stake.

He has always been this way, according to my mother. She made her own bet on him, in November 1948, in the church of St Mark's, in a white lace gown.

~ ~ ~

This is what happens just before I am born: it's 1960. My parents, Frankie and Mary, have five beautiful daughters, and a half-share in a cafe overlooking Cardiff docks. Salvatore Capanone, my father's oldest friend, owns the other half. The sailors on shore leave pour in through the red door to eat, and find a girl. My family lives above the cafe. They have two rooms; one long one, divided into bedroom and lounge by a thick toile curtain depicting scenes of the French aristocracy, and an airless back room which they call The Pit, because you have to climb down into it. My sisters inhabit The Pit, and my father has put a gate up in the doorway to stop Luca, who's only two years old, from climbing up the steps and falling down again. Luca swings her fat leg over the gate whenever my mother isn't looking, and falls from that instead.

There is a third room, one more flight up. It has a square wooden table covered with worn green felt, and four vinyl-backed chairs stacked one upon the other. In the far corner is a window where a blind conceals the day. My mother never goes into this room; it's not hers to use.

There is no kitchen. Every morning my mother trudges downstairs to the cafe to fetch food for my sisters to eat, which they do, sitting in a long line on the couch and watching the Test Card on the television in the corner, while she moves her washing from surface to surface, doing her impression of someone who is tidy. My father's old sea chest is the only storage space, filled with baby clothes. I'll be wearing them soon. My mother knows this, but she doesn't want to air the clothes because my father doesn't. Also, she's determined that I'm a boy this time, and so a lot of the shawls and bonnets and little woollen coats will be redundant, being mainly pink.

Celesta, who's eleven going on forty, is helping to get Marina and Rose ready for school. They look like two turnips in their cream-coloured balaclava hats, and Celesta doesn't want to be seen with them. She wears a straw boater with a chocolate-brown ribbon, bought for when she goes to Our Lady's Convent School. She won't start there until next term, by which time the boater will have a distinctly weathered look, but at the moment she wears it all the time, even in bed. Fran has just begun at primary school. She draws angry pictures of bonfires using three crayons at a time. My mother pays no attention to this, having to deal with Luca now, and the prospect of me later.

When the other children leave, my mother squashes Luca into her hip and goes downstairs to the cafe. She unbolts the front door, slipping off the heavy chain which swings against the wood, and paces the narrow aisle between the tables. At the furthest end, where the daylight doesn't stretch, are two booths and a long counter. Close to its brass lip sit a single smeared tumbler and a half-empty bottle of Advocaat. The air is sweetish here. A sleeveless Peggy Lee is propped against the gramophone in the corner – Salvatore has had a late night.

My mother eases Luca into her high chair, and as soon as she is down, with the rush of cold around her thigh, she screams. She won't stop until she has something sticky on bread, or until my father comes back from the market and swings her in his arms. Luca can't understand why she isn't allowed to practise running. Salvatore used to let her, when my mother had to go and fetch Fran, or hunt the Bookies for my father.

Frankie and Salvatore are a strange brace. My father is smooth and lean, well cut in his well-cut suit. His partner is softer, larger, with milky hands and brimming eyes. Every morning Salvatore puts a clean white handkerchief in the pocket of his apron to deal with the tears which will flow through the day. He blames the heat of the kitchen, rather than his childless wife or the plaintive tones of Mario Lanza. The air is full of music when Salvatore cooks. He plays Dino and Sammy, endless Sinatra, and his favourite, Louis Prima, who reminds him of somewhere not quite like home. The records are stacked in the plate rack on top of the counter, the plates haphazardly stowed beneath. Salvatore glides through the days and nights, dusting flour into the grooves of Julie London, wiping her clean with his napkin. And then he wipes his eyes.

There is a delicate division of labour in this business. Salvatore is a better cook than Frankie, for whom the flames of the kitchen are too much like his vision of Hell. So while Salvatore cuts his fingers, brands the soft flesh of his forearm on the searing stove, and sings and cries, Frankie wears his suit and does things with money upstairs. But Salvatore likes it this way, he gets to see people.

~

At first, convinced that it would tempt the passers-by, Salvatore made stews and bread and almond cakes dusted with sugar. He wedged the red door open with a bar stool, wafting the smell of baking out into the street with his tea-towel. He wrote a sign, DELICIOUS FOOD, in a careful hand, and tied it with parcel string around the rusted frame of the awning outside. But Mack the Knife spilt out on to the pavement, upsetting the barber shop owner next door, the sign ran in the rain, and soon Salvatore brought the stool back to the bar. The pigeons in the yard grew fat on unbought food.

Never mind, said my mother. It takes time.

Now he cooks for the sailors, who want egg and chips or bacon in starchy white rolls, and the cafe is busy. Sailors bring in girls, and girls attract trade. Salvatore fries everything in the flat black pan on the stove, his thinning hair stuck to his head with steam. The combed strands come unglued throughout the day, falling one by one in lank array over his left ear. He pretends to be a widower so that the night girls will pity him. In fact he is married to Carlotta, who is respectable, and will not enter The Port of Call, our cafe. Or as Carlotta calls it in her broken English, That Den-o-Sin.

~

Salvatore loves my mother and my father and my sisters. He is part of the family. And he will love me too, when I am born. Until then, he has to make do with Luca, who shrieks from her high chair the moment my mother's back is turned. Salvatore watches from a safe distance as Luca's arms jolt up and down in an urgent plea to be lifted. He would free her, but he daren't. The last time he did, she ran like a river to the end of the cafe and caught her head on the edge of a table. She stared at it, astonished, while her forehead bulged and split. The knock held her silent for two days, so silent, my mother thought she was damaged: it was the only time Luca was quiet.

Now when my mother has to go out, she traps Luca in The Pit with soft toys to keep her happy for the five minutes she thinks she will be away. Luca throws them at the furthest wall, screaming like a bomb.

In search of my father, my mother is blunt and shaming. She no longer has the time to be discreet.

Have you seen Frankie? Len the Bookie? In The Bute, are they? Righto.

She tracks down her husband, to the arcade, the coffee house, the back room of the pub. When she finds him, she is vocal. My father complains.

This is business, Mary. Keep out of it.

The other men look down and grin into their shirts. And when my father does return, my mother points to Luca's head.

That's down to you, that is.

Sufficiently shamed, or just tired of losing, Frankie starts a clean sheet. He stops betting; he has finished with it for good. But when my mother tells him about me (at six months the evidence is mounting), he takes the money he's accumulated through *not* gambling and opens a card school in the top room of the cafe. He wins, and wins. And suddenly I am luck personified.

We'll call him Fortuno, he says, rubbing my mother's stomach as if she's harbouring the Golden Egg. My mother has other ideas.

~ ~ ~

In the top room, all four chairs are occupied. There is a haze of cheroots, a sweat of onions, the stink of eggs in oil. My father has staked everything on the winning of the game. Away in the infirmary, I'm wailing at the midwife as Frankie decides to Twist. My mother is straining with the labour of prayer. Over and over.

Oh God, let it be a boy.

When the midwife pulls me out, she conceals me. I am shunted from scales to blanket to anteroom. She closes the door on my mother.

If you have to tell her anything, tell her it's a boy, says the midwife to the nurse.

Salvatore's wife Carlotta, waiting in the corridor with her big black handbag poised on the bulge of her stomach, catches just this one phrase – tell her it's a boy – and makes a phone-call to the cafe.

Salvatore is watching the card game from the doorway upstairs, peeping through the curtain of beads which hangs from the lintel. They cascade from his shoulders like Madonna tears. He doesn't hear the telephone; his mind is in anguish for the game he's not allowed to play. His eyes are fixed on the Brylcreem glint which crowns my father's head. Salvatore's right hand rests stiff across his heart, his left holds a spatula, which oozes slow drips on to the red linoleum floor. He should be downstairs making greasy meals for the thin night girls, but Salvatore cannot concentrate on bacon and eggs when his business is at stake.

~

Salvatore likes his partner Frankie, even though he's lazy and not always dependable, and he adores the night girls downstairs. The young ones perch on the stools, their bouffant heads nodding in time to the music on the gramophone; they are stiff-lacquered, clean-scented. The older ones smile, now and then flinging an arm across the booths to display their latest Solitaires. Or they sit in silence. They draw their wet fingers round the rim of their glasses, in an effort to make the last rum last.

Rita, Sophia, Gina. Salvatore recites the girls' names in his sing-song voice. These women are really Irene and Lizzie and Pat. They close around the green metal ashtrays, depressing the buttons with their jewelled hands, watching the debris swirl into the hidden bowl below. When they do leave, the imprints of their bored thighs remain a while upon the shiny leatherette. They never say thank you and they never look back. Salvatore always forgives them. He wipes his hands down the breast of his apron, and sings through the night, while Frankie gambles in the room above his head.

~

Tonight, Salvatore wants to watch. Here we have my father, the giant Martineau, Ilya the Pole, and crooked Joe Medora. This pack of men is busy.

Sal . . . telephone, says Joe, not looking up.

Salvatore rolls reluctantly downstairs.

Joe Medora wears a slouch hat, a silk scarf anchored at the neck, a Savile Row suit. He's an archetypal villain who makes sure he looks the part. He angles his cigar into the side of his lipless mouth, staring over his Hand. He's seen all the films; no gesture is wasted. He is patient.

It's my father's move. Jack of Hearts, Five of Clubs, Four – winking – Diamonds.

It's a boy! cries Salvatore, beating back upstairs. Bambino, Frankie!

And my father, who is Frankie Bambina to his friends, poor unlucky Frank to have so many daughters, Twists in reckless joy, and loses the cafe, the shoebox under the floorboards full with big money, his own father's ruby ring, and my mother's white lace gown, to Joe Medora.

At least I have a son, he thinks, as he rolls the ring across the worn green felt.

~ ~ ~

My father stands above my cot with a clenched fist and a stiff smile. He rubs his left hand along the lining of his pocket, feeling the absence of his father's ring and the nakedness of losing.

At the end of the ward, Salvatore's face appears in the porthole of the swing door. Carlotta's face fills the other, and for a moment they stare separately at the rows and rows of beds and cots. Carlotta lets out a shout, Mary! Frankie!, and sweeps towards my parents. Salvatore raises his hand in salute, but takes his time, pausing to exchange greetings with the other mothers.

A fine baby, Missus!

What a beauty! Boy or girl?

Twins? How lucky!

There aren't enough babies in the ward for Salvatore, perhaps not in the world. He bends over each one with his big smile and his hands clasped at his back.

Carlotta spreads herself on the chair next to my mother's bed and rummages deep into her bag. She makes small talk, not trusting herself to mention me, or the cafe, or the future. My father stabs his teeth with a broken matchstick he's found in the other pocket of his trousers, and sucks air, and says nothing. No one looks at me. Then Salvatore approaches the foot of my mother's bed and opens his arms wide to embrace my father. Both men lean into each other, quietly choking. Carlotta produces a dented red box from her bag, prises off the lid, and offers my mother a chocolate.

Please have one, Mary. They're your favourites.

Mary is in a state of mute blankness. A girl baby, yet again. In her head, she wonders what to call me – she's exhausted her list of Saints' names on the boys she never bore, and is sick of all the arias in the names her girls have got. Dolores drifts up in miserable smoke.

Salvatore rests a hand upon my mother's arm and gazes into my cot. The pink matinee jacket is fastened too tight around my neck; it reeks of mothballs. Wearing his best suit for the visit (which is also the one he wears to funerals), Salvatore smells the same as me. He lands great kisses on my forehead and holds me up for inspection, cajoling my mother.

See, Mary! So pretty!

My mother fixes on the flaking paint of the radiator, and wishes we would all go away. Frankie, too, has had enough of Cooing and Aahing. He puts his hand on Salvatore's chest and shunts him back down the ward. He presses so hard, Salvatore feels the buttons of his shirt indent his skin.

Mary is in shock, my father tells them. Better leave her alone.

This is nothing compared to the shock she'll get when she finds out she's homeless, and her wedding dress adorns a bottle-blonde from Llanelli.

~ ~ ~

I am a week old when everything changes. My parents move into a run-down house at one end of a winding street. The other end is dead, sealed by a high wall spun with barbed wire. Joe Medora owns our new house, and our old cafe. The rent increases on a whim: when Joe gambles on a loser, it goes up. But it can go up when he bets on a winner, too.

My father is put in the Box Room: it is a cell. Celesta and Marina and Rose have the back bedroom. One window overlooks the road, where Rose leans out to spit on unsuspecting heads. Marina springs up and down on her bed, tearing off the wallpaper in long strips, while Celesta puts her fingers in her ears, reads *The Book of Common Ailments*, and convinces herself that she is dying.

The front bedroom becomes Our Room, my mother and Fran and Luca and me. Fran has the bed in the corner, and Luca has exclusive rights over my mother, who puts me in the chest. When she's convinced that I'll survive the night, I'm allowed to share the bed.

~

Carlotta is recruited in these difficult times, apparently to look after us children. She's really here to make sure my mother is a Good Wife who doesn't desert her fallen-on-hard-times husband: my mother might at any second run away with, say, the Coalman. This is prescient, but not in the way Carlotta thinks.

For now, Salvatore still works at the cafe, renamed The Moonlight Club in sputtering neon, and he leaves his friend Frankie alone. But he thinks about us, he worries about me, and he asks Carlotta every night for a report.

Getting big now, Carlotta says, stretching her arms out like a fisherman to show how I'm growing.

Salvatore is not entirely convinced, and once a week he sends Carlotta with a parcel of food, stolen from his shifts at The Moonlight. He feels he is entitled; after all, he's still a partner in the business. Except these days, working with Joe Medora, he feels more like a slave.

While my mother takes to her bed and stares at the ceiling, Carlotta cooks up a steam in the little kitchen. She makes baked pasta with blackened edges, solid slabs of home-made bread. Everything she provides is sharp and hard, as if to counteract the softness of her body and the thick roll of her voice. My mother thinks of little, but she listens. She hears the sticky cough of the woman in her kitchen, and imagines Carlotta dipping her feelers in the cooking pot, testing the saltiness of the ham.

It is about this time that I am burnt.

two

They're defying gravity.

Nebuchadnezzar, King of the Jews, Bought his Wife a Pair of Shoes . . .

Celesta's hands are plaiting air: the tennis balls skim her palms, fly, beat on the red brick; hand, brick, hand, brick. She is concentrating. If Celesta could only take her eyes off the arc she is weaving, she would see Rose upended in a handstand: her scuffed shoes pressed flat against the wall, her fat legs splayed, her black hair hanging like pondweed from beneath the bell of her skirt. Marina's eyes flit from Rose to Celesta and back again, carefully studying the moves. She won't try anything yet: she'll examine every angle first.

Through tartan wool, Rose sees the world the wrong way up. The houses on the street fall out of the sky; a dog trots blithely along the grey cloud of pavement.

Look at me! Celesta! Look!

Celesta twirls and claps and catches; the balls hang in the air just long enough for a spin to the left. She ignores Rose and her blood-rush face.

Rose rights herself, squints at the grit embedded in her palms, spits on both hands and wipes them on her skirt. She inches along the wall, feeling the vibration of each bounce through the brick, and stops. Rose is intent for one minute, then suddenly snatches at a mid-flight ball, interrupting the pattern of hand, air, brick. The ball flies into the gutter. Celesta is patient. She retrieves it, inspects it, and resumes her game.

You, are, a Pain-in-the-Neck, she says, in rhythm.

~

They all ignore Luca: she is tethered to the pram. The harness is blue and has a lamb frolicking on the front, which Luca has drenched with dribble. Two metal hooks clip on to two rusted rings at either side of the hood. She pulls at the rings, and yells, and smears her face with her sticky fist. Fran has been told to watch her; but Fran has gone Walkabout. She's got a box of England's Glory in her pocket. Inside are three pink-headed matches. She's heading for The Square.

We live at Number 2 Hodge's Row. Between Number 9 and Number 11 is an alleyway which leads on to a hopeless patch of asphalt called Loudoun Place, but which everyone calls The Square. Fran goes there a lot, sidling along the alleyway until she reaches open space. The Square is a rectangle of nothing. There used to be swings and a see-saw, but now all that's left is an iron climbing frame and a strip of battered grass. Fran explores. She likes it: better than wiping snot from Luca's nose; better than sitting on the low kerb and watching Celesta play that impossible game: better than waiting for Rose to find an excuse to hit her.

There are treasures here, stashed along the edge of The Square where scrub grass ends and gravel begins. Fran studies the ground minutely, her boots marking a careful path between the dog-shit, broken bottles, coils of rusted wire, fluttering chip-papers. The asphalt shimmers with shards of glass; green, blood-brown, clear as ice. She collects the best shapes and places them carefully in the pocket of her gymslip. Today, Fran has the matches. She strikes one and holds it to her face. A rush of phosphorous stings her nose. Crouching now, she strikes another. Fran loves this sweet, burning scent.

She licks the sandpaper edge of the matchbox. A tang of spent fire.

Under her bed, Fran keeps a red oblong box. It used to have chocolates in it, and smells like Christmas when she prises off the lid. But now the plastic tray holds all her jewels from the Square: jagged slips of sapphire; worn lumps of emerald; a single marble with a twisted turquoise eye. To mark my arrival, she has begun a secret collection which she stows in a cigar box my father has given her. Not glass this time, but an assortment of cigarette stubs she picks up, when no one is looking, from the pavement outside our house. Tipped or untipped, flaky grey, or smooth menthol white. Some are crushed flat with the weight of a heel, others are perfectly round and lipstick-smeared. Fran holds each butt to her nose before she hides it away.

~

I'm stuck in the house with my mother: at one month old, I'm sickly and I must be kept warm. My mother brings the chest down from the bedroom and puts me in it, smothers me in layer after layer of mothballed blankets. She drags a bucket of coal from the outhouse to the kitchen, bumping it against her knee until she gets to the hearth, where she pauses for breath. She bends down, rattles at the grate; it looks like an age since a fire was lit in the kitchen: the ash which should be smooth and fine is clogged with stray hairs, clots of dust. Turning the strips of newspaper neatly in her hands, she thinks: Joe's man will call for the rent today, that kindling's a bit damp, bet the chimney needs sweeping. The chest scrapes across the tiles as she pulls it, pulls me in it, nearer to the hearth; two long thin scars, like a tram track, will remain to show what she did. My mother puts me at an angle in front of the fire: the sight of the flames will amuse me.
She turns to the table, hacks at a loaf of bread and sings in her sharp, tense voice,

Don't you know, Little Fool, you Ne-ver can Win
Use your Men-talitee, Wake up to Re-alitee . . .

~

Upstairs, my father is making music too, whistling through
his teeth as he pulls a tie off the rail in the wardrobe, catching
sight of himself in the mirror as the wardrobe door widens.
He looks Lucky. Today, Frankie's choice is a black tie with a
thin seam of gold running through it. He sweeps the length
between finger and thumb, smooth and cool as water, then
ducks his head, flips the tie around his neck, folds back the
stiff white collar of his shirt. He pauses in front of the mirror,
pushes the door open to get a better view. It annoys him, this
glass; flecked and tarnished with oily orange patches beneath
the surface – even in close-up, he can't get a clear reflection.
Frankie pauses. He hears my mother downstairs, shouting
from the front door.

Celesta! Kids! Dinnertime!

My father pulls on the jacket of his suit, casually stretches out
his left arm, then his right, turning the exposed cuffs over the
sleeves. A pair of gold cufflinks, embossed with the rising sun,
is now the only jewellery he owns. He lifts them from the
polished surface of his dressing-table, chinks them in his palm
for a second, and then puts them back. He doesn't feel *that*
lucky. He takes his hat from the bed-post, pads downstairs,
avoids my mother's eyes. She weaves between the children in
the kitchen as he makes for the living room mirror.

I won't tell you again, wash those hands. Will you see
Carlotta today, Frankie? Leave that. Eat your dinner. Frankie?
Frankie, mouths my father as he steps up to the glass. Frankie,
he goes, flipping one end of the tie into a smart loop, taking
up the slack, adjusting the knot, nice and tight.

Do you hear me? shouts my mother.

He's going out, says Celesta, straddling kitchen and living
room doorway and staring at my father. They share the same

black eyes, hard as steel, and a stubborn squareness in their faces. Celesta holds a plate of sandwiches high in the air, out of reach of Rose and Marina. My father grins at her in the mirror. She grins back, then suddenly retreats into the kitchen as the clamour rises behind her.

Wash your hands first, Celesta yells, slapping at Rose and Marina as they snatch at the bread. And again, Mam, tell them to wash their hands.

Wash their hands, says my mother automatically.

It's getting very hot in this kitchen, what with the fire and the heat of my mother's bad mood. She wedges the back door open with a chair, sending a blurt of wind racing through the house. The flames in the fireplace swoon in the draught. A door slams upstairs.

My mother mixes up a bowl of something grey for Luca, rapidly beating milk into powder. Her fury travels down the spoon and into Luca's dinner. I am breast-fed: I get rage straight from the source. My mother's also angry with herself: she needs Carlotta to visit with one of Salvatore's parcels; some corned-beef pie maybe, or a bit of roast chicken. Her words are thrown to anyone who will catch them.

Never thought I'd want to set eyes on her fat face again, she says, thinking of Carlotta as she forces Luca into her high-chair. Celesta laughs, thinks it's a shocking thing to say about your kid, even if it's true.

And where's Fran? asks my mother, an afterthought.

~

My father moves from the mirror to the sideboard, stops his breath as he pulls open the drawer. His eyes stay on the doorway, watching the shadows on the kitchen wall while his hand slides over bills and chits and a soft bundle of knitting. All promises forgotten now, Frankie thinks only of the Race. His fingers trip along the stitches, the sharp point of the needle, and down to the cool metal surface of the Biscuit Tin. Then his hand inside, and the unmistakeable greasy slip of money beneath his touch. Frankie feels the edges of the notes – not much, enough – catches them up fast and folds them over, straight into his pocket. It takes five seconds. With his tongue hot on his lip, he pushes the drawer back into place, and starts up his whistling again.

Do you hear me, Frankie? Will you see Carlotta?

My mother appears at the doorway with one hand on her hip, waving a spoon in the other.

And where do you think *you're* going?

She has noticed his smart suit. And the hat.

Frank?

An accusation.

Out, he says.

~ ~ ~

There are eighteen cafes on Bute Street, and my father doesn't own any of them. Not any more; not since me. My parents argue about whose fault it is. She blames him, he blames me, and I can't blame anyone yet. But I will. I'll lay it all at Joe Medora's door, when I'm ready.

Except Joe Medora has so many doors. He owns nearly everything round here: two boarding-houses on the Terrace, and our home, of course; and four cafes on Bute Street – the latest being The Moonlight.

My mother has to pass the cafe every day. She's got herself a job at the bakery next to the timber-yard. It's a factory more than a bakery, churning out hundreds of thick white loaves which my mother drags from the ovens with a long metal pallet. She does the nightshift, so whether she's setting off for work or coming home at dawn, she can't pass The Moonlight without noticing that the lights are on and there are people inside. Sometimes, not often, she can smell cooking, and she gets a yearning for one of Salvatore's almond tarts. She hears music too, a lonely voice in the early hours; but mostly she hears the jangle of money rolling over and over in Joe Medora's pocket. She spits a dry curse at the window as she passes.

~

My father takes the same route now, cutting over the street, down the alley, and across The Square. Fran sees his shape approaching from around the broken fence, his head cocked to one side in the sunshine, and she hides from him. For a second she wonders if he's come to march her back home for dinner, but Fran senses that there's something different about him today. She sees how his hair catches the light, a slice of pure silver dancing on the black, and the hat in his hand beating lightly against his thigh; she hears his whistle wandering on the air. It's like watching a stranger. Fran ducks, crabs along the track of dirt near the railing and hides behind the hedge.

My father doesn't expect to see her, so he doesn't: his eyes are fixed straight ahead, conjuring the sleek brown frame of the horse he will gamble on. Just one bet, that's all. Court Jester. Two-thirty.

Frankie strolls past the Bute Street cafes, nodding now and again at a familiar face, or raising his hatted hand in a greeting. This is Frankie's Patch. Most of the restaurants and cafes are owned and run by his friends: seamen from the Tramp Trade who came to rest and stopped for good. And my father has also stopped, for now, although like most of the other Maltese, he won't settle in the city – he can't escape the salt-scent of the docks. When he talks about his ship coming in, meaning a winning streak, an odds-on favourite, a dead cert, he also feels, like glitter in his blood, the day when he will take a folded stash of money and simply disappear.
This is not that day. This is the day I am burnt.

~ ~ ~

She was sure. She was absolutely certain. But now the money has gone. My mother wrenches the drawer and it slides too quickly, tumbling from her hands on to the floor, and with it falls the spilling mess of paper, magazines, a brass bell, a broken picture-frame, the abandoned knitting in baby-blue. She claws on her knees through the bills while the Tin sits wide open beside her. Perhaps she put it somewhere else. She casts her eyes around the room to the fireplace: two framed photographs, my father's long black comb with its pointed end jutting over the tiled lip, and in the centre of the mantelpiece, a glazed chalk fawn with a mocking smile. The dull orange Rent book nestles behind it, thin and empty.

Celesta! she calls, wildly scanning the floor, Have you been in this sideboard?
Celesta stands over my mother with Luca in her arms and a look of dismay on her face. She drops Luca into the armchair, crouches down on the floor.

No. It's Him. Again.
As if my mother needs telling. Celesta rises to shunt the empty drawer back in its gaping hole. She gathers the heap of papers from the floor and forces them back.

Use your Men-talitee, my mother sings suddenly, with a bitter laugh. It frightens Celesta, this noise.

What you gonna do, Mam?
My mother doesn't answer directly. She's listening for the thud of a fist on the door.

Haven't a clue, she says, to the ceiling. Not a clue.
Then to Celesta,

Take the kids out for us, Cel. Get them out of the way for a bit.
Celesta leans over to pull Luca's coat off the chair. She kneels in front of her, pushes one baby hand into the sleeve, pulls the coat around the back, bends Luca's arm into the other.

C'mon, she says to Rose and Marina, Let's go and find Fran.

~

My mother drags the chair from the back door and sits on it. We both stare into the orange fire. She contemplates the sink, the square table strewn with crusts of bread, the gas cooker with its beckoning oven: she could put her head in there. Instead, she bends, puts her hands between her knees. There's an ache in her leg where the falling drawer had caught her. She stares down at her calf and the rising blue in her flesh.

~ ~ ~

Frankie passes Domino's Resto, then Tony's Top Cafe, then the Seamen's Mission. He passes the barber's shop with its striped red awning rippling in the breeze. Next to it is The Moonlight, its new neon sign at a right-angle to the wall. It smells of fresh paint here, and sure enough, on the red door there's now a glossy silhouette of a woman in a tight dress and stiletto heels. Frankie doesn't falter, doesn't turn his face to the window: he looks straight ahead towards the black square of shadow like an oil-spill under Bute Street Bridge. Just got time for a soda before meeting Len the Bookie.

~ ~ ~

My sisters go searching for Fran. The sun has gone, whipped away by the sharp wind, and in its place, a bolt of cloud. It scuds over the top of the wall at the end of the street, smearing the last of the blue sky with a hard metallic grey. Rose cradles two of Celesta's tennis balls in the crook of her elbow, dawdles behind the train of pram, Celesta, Marina. She pauses at the corner, watches her sisters cut sideways down the alley, waits, then turns to the wall next to Number 9.

Rose throws hard, first one ball, then the other: she catches the first but not the second, which angles off the brick, rebounds against the door of Number 4, and finally deflects with a clud off the window of Number 1. Home of the Jacksons. It rolls in silence along the pavement and drops into the gutter. Rose stands waiting with her fist wrapped around the other ball and her legs set to run. She runs.

~ ~ ~

Len the Bookie sits in the cafe with his back to the window: he needn't bother, no one can see in since the glass got smashed six months ago. The proprietor has mended it with a rough square of hardboard. He's written a notice on the side which faces the street:

MIKEY'S BAR

Open Late For Tea's Coffee's Reffershment

Len's refreshment, depending on who asks, is a lemonade soda. Mikey has tipped in a thimbleful of something which is supposed to be whisky. The tall beaker sits on the table in front of him, pale yellow, lethal, a tart froth breaking slowly on the surface. Len leans slightly to one side now to avoid the wind pushing in around the shifting board at the window. He hears a sudden burst of rain, like horses' hooves, sputter at his back. He reaches inside his pocket for his notebook.

Len is not a noticeable man. He's small and thin as paper, his smooth brown head fringed with remnants of hair. He rests his notebook in his lap: a row of carefully pencilled lines dissect each page; a series of tiny numbers crawl in steady formation from the tip of his pencil. As he writes, his free hand scratches absently at the bristles on his cheek. He has only two remaining digits on this hand; forefinger and middle finger. He managed to save his thumb. He used to gamble himself, but now he's found a safer occupation.

Never Bet with the Syndicate, my Friend, is his only piece of advice. He gives it with a wave of his carved fist.

The door of the cafe bangs open and shut.

Hoy! Lenny! says my father, pinching up the fabric of his trousers as he bends to sit with the man.

Frankie, says Len. Long time no see.

~ ~ ~

My mother stands on the front doorstep with the Tin in her hands and the lid hanging open like a shout. Martineau is

27

collecting today. Mary shows him that there is no rent to be had this week. They both stare into the shiny inner; Martineau with his heavy lashes cast down like an apology; my mother's reflection distorted into a cold silver fury. My mother wishes Frankie dead. It's not just rent money: it's bills and housekeeping and family allowance; it's debt money; it's her wages. It's everything.

Martineau, soft, holds out his big hands and tries to take it from her, but my mother throws it. It hits the pavement with the sound of an oil-drum being slapped.

Let's go inside, Mary, he says, We'll talk about it. Maybe Joe can wait a week, uh?

He'll have to, won't he? You go and tell him. Tell him to take a running jump.

~

The wind breathes through the swinging back door, circuits the kitchen. One rush of air is all it takes for the single coal to tip out from the fire, falling to rest on the frayed edge of the runner. It settles: lets out a wisp of smoke, a lick of curling light around the coal, and then a sudden sweep of gorgeous blue. Like the crooked eye of Fran's marble, the flame twists in the draught.

And this same wind moves on to the living room, escapes past my mother at the front of the house, and blows the door shut behind her. She sways on the step, surprised to feel the wood so solid at her back. She wraps her arms around her body and stands her ground.

~

I'm all alone now. I'm watching. The blue flame ebbs and flows, ebbs and flows, sneaking along the fringes of the runner, lighting each strand like touchpaper. A bright coil of orange turns, widens, presses itself against the polished wood of the chest. It's so pretty.

~

28

Martineau bends to pick up the Tin, and over his stooped back my mother sees Alice Jackson at the window opposite. The woman raps twice on the pane, points her finger at my mother. I want a word with you, she mouths through glass.

Mary, pleads Martineau, We are friends.

We're not – we can't be. Not now you're Joe's flunkey.

The door of Number 1 swings open and Alice Jackson steps into the street, retrieving the abandoned tennis ball from the gutter outside her house. Alice moves towards my mother with a grim fix on her face. My mother ignores her, turns away; she's trapped now between Martineau and this woman she doesn't know. She moves quickly, forgetting me, forgetting me, pacing up the street ahead of Martineau. The man is crouching; he's trying to make himself smaller. He looks like he's dodging the wind.

Frankie's taken the money, Tino, she says. The words fall out behind her and are lost. What am I supposed to do?

Mary knows what she *could* do. She could go to Joe herself; she could plead. But the thought of him heats her insides like a swarm of wasps. There is another way.

Alice Jackson stands at our closed front door with her arms folded over her chest. She clutches the tennis ball against her ribs and watches as my mother flings her arms open, cutting down the alley with the big man at her back. Alice Jackson sniffs something burning on the air. Turns her head to one side, sniffs again.

~ ~ ~

Frankie stirs his coffee with a long metal spoon, leaning his elbow on the bar in The Moonlight like he's never been away. Salvatore hears what he has to say, but he can't look at him, so he scrapes at the enamel stove with a blunt knife.

Stars of blackened cheese skid away from his touch. Salvatore holds his tongue until my father has ended his monologue of woe: then he straightens, launching into the silence.

Okay, so you lose on a horse. Then what you do? You go home? No. Too sensible for you, eh Frank. Frankie, he don't want to go home! Frankie want to win, yeah?

Salvatore talks and scrubs, plunging his hand into the bowl of filmy water, chiselling fiercely with the edge of his blade. Rainbow bubbles cling to the black hairs on his wrist. He stops, points the knife at the ceiling above his head,

Joe Medora don't want to see you − I don't want to see you,

then waves it in front of my father's eyes.

Take your face somewhere else.

For my father has come to beg. He will beg Salvatore for a loan, and he will beg Joe Medora for extra time with the rent. He stays silent, waits for the storm in Salvatore to pass, and listens to the rain belting off the pavement outside. The going was too heavy, thinks Frankie, watching a replay of the race in his mind. It's not monochrome in his head: the racecourse is green, the horses always chestnut brown, the bobbing jockeys brilliant in Silks. He puts the race away before he catches sight of Court Jester loping home in fifth.

Frankie puts his hand in his trouser pocket, pulls out the chit from Len the Bookie and slaps it on the counter. He turns the lining inside-out, catching the debris in the palm of his hand and depositing it neatly in a gritty mound beside the crumpled docket. A half-crown rolls away from the flecks of tobacco and dust.

Go home, my friend, says Salvatore, hearing the lonely clatter of the coin. He gives the money back to my father and wipes the fluff off the counter with the corner of his apron.

It was a sure thing, Sal, says Frankie, pocketing the half-crown.

Sure thing. Sure. Ciao, Frankie.

Frankie looks steadily at Salvatore, turns and walks slowly away from the bar.

Frankie – il cappello! shouts Salvatore, gesturing to the hat on the counter. Frankie isn't listening. He winds between the booths, heading not for the exit but for the narrow door marked Private which will lead him up the stairs to his old home, to his old life – to Joe Medora's new office. He'll find out for himself if Joe doesn't want to see him. Salvatore smooths the felt brim of the hat with his fingers: his eyes track Frankie's footsteps across the ceiling.

~ ~ ~

Our yard door is locked, so to get round the back of the house, you have to climb over the side wall and drop down on to the flags. Those in the know, when they're out slipping the lead off someone else's guttering, use the outhouse roof as a sliding brake. A foot on the lintel, one hand gripping the frame, then the other hand, and down with a silent jump. Fran has another way of sneaking in: she pushes aside the fencing at the rear of Number 4, sweeps the slat back into place, and throws her leg over the low chicken-wire that separates our backyard from the Rileys'. Fran sees the smoke leaking out from under our kitchen door, and stands amazed.

There is a rush of action, shouting in the street. Alerted by their mother, the Jackson boys come bouncing off our outhouse roof like a pair of experts. They knock Fran sideways on the concrete path. Martineau surfs down after them, slices his palms on the broken slate, and lands with a crack on his knees. He moves the boys away and puts his shoulder to the hot wood of the kitchen door.

My mother, on the wrong side of the wall, hears her baby burning on the inside.

~

Our kitchen thick as tar. A sudden suck of air that punctures heat, and the fire becomes fury. Flames spill in a river across the floor; scalding oilcloth, blistering wood, boiling the blankets on my bed. The boys shield their foreheads with their arms and flail about like drunkards, tipping over chairs and shouting. They are devils out of Hell. It is burning burning burning – and then Martineau lifts me with his great scored hand and hauls me out to daylight.

~

By the time the fire engine arrives, we are all in the alley, the yard door is battered open, and the Jackson boys are the heroes of the hour. They pat each other's shoulders and brush bits of cinder from their clothing. They are all arms now, describing the heat to their friends, pointing to the flames gulping at the window. Martineau bends and grips his mossy knees, breathing in shallow bursts. From under his fringe, he watches my mother. She stands in the pouring rain, her head raised to heaven: she won't look at me. She carries me loosely, this charred little thing, as if I have fallen from the sky. She is sure I am dead. When the ambulanceman holds out his red blanket, she drops me into it like a swathe of kindling.

Later, undressing Fran in the back bedroom of Carlotta's house, my mother finds two dingy cigarette butts and the box of spent matches. Her heart turns mad with blackness.

tinder

My right hand is fine. There's little damage, and the fingers are quite beautiful, in the ordinary sense of them actually being there, bending, flexing, pointing things out to strangers who stop in their cars and wind down their windows to ask directions.

But the left hand. People who don't know me stare when they see it. They look away, then sidelong at my face in search of further evidence. There are scars there too: if they get close enough they could find them. But not many get that close: an outstretched hand, my left one – it's enough to ward them off.

I lost the fingers. At one month old, a baby's hand is the tiniest, most perfect thing. It makes a fist, it spreads wide, and when it burns, that soft skin is petrol, those bones are tinder, so small, so easily eaten in a flame.

But I think of it as a work of art: a closed white tulip standing in the rain; a cut of creamy marble in the shape of a Saint; a church candle with its tears flowing down the bulb of wrist.

I go back, and try to piece together how it was. I think there must be a design. I can picture Len the Bookie and his bet with the Syndicate (how soon my fist would echo his); the sight of my mother hopeless in the rain; Martineau behind her, clasping his casket like Balthazar. And I think of my father, standing all the while in a room across town, knowing nothing, oblivious: always betting more than he can afford to lose.

three

In the top room of The Moonlight Joe Medora sits at his desk. He is busy. He ignores the dull applause of footsteps on the stairs, but Ilya the Pole, stationed at the window behind Joe's head, is twitching like a hare. Frankie knocks on the door, swings in, jutting his head through the widening crack. He parts his lips to speak, but wavers at the sight of Joe's bent head, the faint scratch of Joe's pen, the ribbon of smoke curling upwards from Joe's cigar. Frankie peers through the heavy air, seamed with bitter blue, at Ilya in the far window. Stuck now in the doorway, Frankie's at a loss. His left hand holds the brass knob in a twist, his right rests flat against the frame: both have started to sweat. He half expects Salvatore to come up after him, but Frankie can only hear the faint beat of music from below, and what he thinks is the shush of Joe's hand as it crabs across the paper. It's his own breath making this noise.

Frankie eases his hold on the sweating doorknob, cutting the silence with a shriek of spring. He steps into the room. Joe Medora glances up, then down again at the page in front of him. At least he hasn't told Frankie to go away; nor has he raised his finger in the air, summoning Ilya to escort him off the premises. Frankie weighs it up: he'll wait.

A burst of rain on glass. The blind at the window scuppers

in the draught; a soft bang, silence, then another bang, and down in the city, the low keening of a fire engine. If Frankie were listening he would hear it, but Frankie is all eyes, taking in his old den, now transformed into Medora Territory.

The square deal table with the worn green felt has gone; so too have the vinyl chairs. Instead, a fat sofa is positioned opposite the door, lustrous red and buttoned, and beside it, a glass table with a fan of *Playboy* magazines and the folded pink of the *Sporting Life*. Frankie's gaze wanders – to Joe's desk filling the far corner of the room; to the lone upright chair against the wall where Frankie could, if he was invited, sit down and rest his watery legs – until he fixes on a huge portrait of Persimmon, poised, watchful, framed in gilt above Joe's head. Frankie stares at the horse and the horse stares back: Persimmon wins this contest.

~ ~ ~

I'll look after the kids, Missus, you go on.
Alice Jackson tries to coax my mother towards the ambulance, but she won't move: she's afraid of what she'll find. Celesta shifts Luca higher on her hip, catches Alice Jackson's meaningful look. She wipes the rain from Luca's head and steps into the small space the crowd has left around my mother.

We can go over to the Jacksons' for a bit, Mam, she says, wanting her to say, No, you're all coming with me. But my mother doesn't hear. She wends through the fold of women standing on the corner of the street, stops when she sees the yawning door of the ambulance and the man inside bent over me. A fireman drags a hose along the pavement. She watches this. He waves his arm out in front of him like a swimmer, shouting at the knot of children to clear a way. They're elated, dancing on the spot, lifting the heavy hose and swinging it between their legs. Another fireman cranks a handle on the platform, and the hose jumps to life. The children leap aside, shrieking.

Our house is a mess, the insides sodden, a stink of plastic in the air. The kitchen is a crusted hull. The Jackson boys have set to work, and despite the angry shouts of the firemen, they loop wet tea-towels round their faces and salvage what they can. They haul the skeletons of our chairs into the yard, where the black legs snap like matchsticks and splinter on the flags. Then the boys are back for the table, then the steaming fold of carpet crumbling softly in their grip. Finally, they bring out the scorched chest and dump it in the yard.

Martineau reaches into it and lifts an edge of blanket, still soft and pink, but the piece pulls away like a cobweb in his hand. His chin is black with smuts: he feels an ache in his throat. He carries the fragment in his bunched fist, moves past the women and towards my mother. A man in a blue overall shakes his head at her and points his spanner at the house.

And the gas was off. You sure?

She's not sure of anything. She holds the empty Tin to her breast, her fingernails clawed beneath the rim, and clicks the lid; open-shut, open-shut. The women pat her on the shoulder on the way back to their homes, as if by touching her they're warding off bad luck. Martineau watches the ritual, feels a light tap on his own sleeve, and looks around. The woman beside him is tall and blonde, and through the noise of the children, the women, the firemen, the police, she is quietly asking him something. Martineau registers her green eyes, and that she's wearing the most extraordinary coat – white fur covered with dark splotches. For a moment he thinks it is spattered with cinders.

What? He looks at her hard.

I *said*, What's her name? She points at my mother.

Mary, says Martineau.

Righto. Well, Mary's probably going to want some night things – for the hospital – when you can get in.

She assesses the house, the situation,

And where's that husband of hers? He'll need to be told.

Martineau puts his head down in shame for Frankie, notes the golden straps of the woman's sandal biting across the bridge of her foot, and her toenails, lustrous coral shells under her nylons, and the way this same leg jiggles up and down on the spot as she speaks. She's so close, he can smell her lipstick. He takes it all in.

Are you a neighbour? he asks.

Eva Amil, she says, and with a quick jerk of her head, We're at Number 14.

She smiles at him and waits. Martineau waits too: he can't remember if she's asked him another question.

So – will you tell her husband then? Eva speaks very slowly through her smile. Do you know where he'll be?

I'll find him, says Martineau.

Eva lifts Luca from Celesta's arms, hooking her on to her own shoulder, and prises the Tin from my mother. She hands it to Martineau as he edges past. Eva's free arm circles my mother's waist.

Mary, isn't it? Come on, love, let's get in.

The women climb into the back of the ambulance.

~ ~ ~

Joe's cigar burns neglected in the ashtray; his cut-glass whisky sits untouched on the blotter. Such richness! thinks Frankie, swallowing at the sight of the liquor. He studies the action of Joe's careful writing: it bothers him, and for half a second he doesn't know why. Then he sees it: on the little finger of his right hand Joe is wearing a ruby ring. The jewel sparkles in its setting. Recognizing it makes the sweat prick in Frankie's armpits: he clenches, unclenches his fists. His father's ring on Joe's finger! He won't look at it. He'll shut his eyes.

But Frankie can't not look at the film running in his head. He remembers how they met. A Friday in February 1947 – no – 1948, when he was barely twenty.

~

38

Frankie has never been so cold in his life. It's not the feeling you get on board ship, when the squall punches your face, stabs at your teeth, when your whole head is a sharp pain. That's proper cold, melted into nothing by the heat of work and the next day's sunshine. Nor is what he feels anything like home, where winters are short and February not so cruel. Frankie thinks of Sliema, of the sandy lane winding up to his village, with the sky a soft grey and the rain so fine it's hardly felt at all.

This cold is a slow ache; it makes your skin sore, it makes you want to crouch double. And it's been with him right from the start – it crept up as the *Callisto* docked in Tiger Bay, and snuck like a thief into his bones. Now it's here with him in the basement room he has rented, coating the walls with frozen sweat, clinging to his clothes in a spray of bright droplets. Frankie's two days in Cardiff have been spent below ground. The snow on the road outside is terrifying. He has never seen such a thing before; he thinks the sky has fallen. Frankie hasn't been able to muster the courage to walk into the city. His chest hurts. He sits at the table below the whited window, smokes, pours coffee from the little pan he stole from his grandmother's kitchen, and watches the legs of passers-by as they pick their way along the street. The men move purposefully, the wide fabric of their trousers pinned to their legs in the gale. Frankie is more interested in the women the teetering slip and skid of heels, followed by a high-pitched shriek, has him craning up at the pavement outside. All he can make out through the stiff weeds where the railings used to be are the mottled shins of a girl sliding away fast.

The whole city seems fast to him. On Tuesday he left his ship, and today, Friday, he has a home and a new life. No one cares who he is or where he's come from, and no one wants to know his business. This should please Frankie, who escaped the slow turn of his farming life for the glamour of the sea: who hated the constant mewling of his grandmother, the coins in her pocket clanking her to church three, four times a day (as if she might miss a miracle, or, in her absence, find that Faith had left the country). In the end, Frankie left instead. His last sight was of Carmel, his little sister, waving madly from the harbour, and behind her, Sliema rippling in a hot mist.

~

Frankie knew what to do when he came into port: register, find a place to stay, then cut another passage on the sea. And despite the air like needles up his nose and the wind full of shrapnel, he was excited. He squinted up at the tallest buildings, and down the wide streets to the alleyways off them teeming with people; saw steam from the opened door of a bakery like a giant's breath out; stood amazed at the procession of silent cars gliding through the snow.

At the door of the Seamen's Mission he joined the line of sailors and saw a familiar face – a Greek stoker from his own ship. Frankie raised his eyebrows in greeting, but the man was busy in talk and looked through him. He cast around for anyone else he might know, listened hard for the sound of his own language; it was a mostly silent queue. The men stood clutching their kit-bags and suitcases, or blowing on their hands until they were safely through the door.

When it was his turn, he was questioned, his papers were scrutinized, and he was told to sign a sheet. Without raising his head, the man at the desk put his thick finger on a line.

Francisco Gauci? Sign there.

Frankie picked up the pen, his hand puce, and scrawled a numb X. The man finally looked up.

Let's see if it matches, he said, unfurling Frankie's papers one more time. A younger man at the next desk glanced over, sniggered.

It's the Genuine Article, alright. Maltese are you?

Frankie understood this last bit. Nodded gratefully.

You'll want to see Carlo Cross, then. He'll fix you up. Not related are you, by any chance?

Another snort from the next desk. Frankie didn't understand the joke, but knew it was at his expense.

And don't forget to report to the police, said the man. And seeing Frankie's worried face, softened.

Just routine, son. Your first visit to Wales, is it?
and Frankie, who knew enough of what was being asked, nodded again and said,

Yes, first time in England.
At last the man smiled at him.

As he turned to leave, a small fat figure barred his way and spoke to him. In the rattle of his words, Frankie recognized the tell-tale rhythm of Sicilian-Maltese, and the signs he couldn't hear but simply knew: that emphatic jerking of the head, and the hand gestures – first two kissing beaks, now cupped together in a fleshy round. Carlo Cross, the fat man, had a room for him if he wanted. Frankie wanted.

~

And Carlo brought him here, gave him a chit to sign – another frantic X – for the purchase of the furniture and the rental of the room. He threw Frankie a long iron key for the back door, and told him, in English-Maltese, the rules:

No women in here, capisce, my friend? Leh tifla! Issamma – listen. You know English? No women. Cash only to me. Capisce?
with those hands doing the bird and nest, then moving fast when Frankie handed over the roll of strange notes. Carlo peeled some off, returned the rest, and left Frankie to himself.

It wasn't what he expected. He had imagined a boarding-house full of other seamen, nights of drinking and smoking and playing cards. In the morning (in the sunshine that seemed to exist only in Frankie's head), he would walk out with his new friends – his *habib* – and find the bars he's heard of, take coffee, eat cake. He hasn't chosen Cardiff by accident: he's heard there's a great clan of Maltese here, with more arriving every day. There is money to be made at sea, he's been told, and this is the place to spend it.

Tiger Bay – the Valletta of Britain!

his crew-mate had laughingly told him as the ship dropped anchor. And it was supposed to be a *warm* port.

~

The memory makes Frankie jolt. The coldest winter, ever. He shifts his weight from one foot to the other. Ilya grins suddenly, amused by the sight of my father's discomfort. They both know that Joe Medora could make him stand there all day. It is a battle which Frankie can't win; he must stay calm. He sets his eyes on the past.

~

Frankie sat beneath the window, dabbed at his nose with his handkerchief, studied his new home. The ceiling sloped down steeply in one corner, with a bed wedged in the gap below. The first night, he couldn't sleep for the traipse of feet on the stairs above his head, so close to his ear they seemed to be stumbling over his face.

There is another bunk he could use, shoved against the wall in the narrow space between the front door and the back. But the front door has a gaping mouth for a letterbox, and Frankie shudders at the way the through–draught frets the edges of the pillow: he would rather lie down in the corner with the noise. And in time, he will learn to ignore the din of men who call so late on the women in the flat above. He will learn to slide sideways from his bed in the mornings, and not bang his head.

Frankie doesn't ponder the fact of the beds, he assumes that one of them is intended as a makeshift couch. He has put his cardboard suitcase on it, has hung his clothes in the tilting wardrobe, and placed his shoes, newly polished, under his bed. He thinks he is the only tenant here.

Yesterday, shuddering with cold, he walked out and found a corner shop, pointed at a sack of coal and coasted it back, gliding and skidding, to his door. He carried the coal in handfuls through the scullery and piled them up in the grate, put newspaper on top, added some broken bits of a crate he'd found in the yard, then lit a blaze and watched it die. He started again from scratch, properly, and after an hour Frankie sat in the warmth, loving it: holding his hands out and letting the heat shine through them, toasting his left side, then his right. The room shrank to a bag of fog. Steam breathed off the walls; the ice on the inside of the window melted to a long pool on the sill, then poured suddenly onto the floor. Frankie gave up and opened the window a crack to let in some air. Now it won't shut tight again.

This morning someone banged on the front door. Frankie didn't have any friends to call on him, and he only had the key to the back door. By the time he had scrambled down the alley and round to the front of the house, whoever it was had gone, leaving a neat set of footprints, down the steps then up again, which Frankie measured with his own: the caller was a small man.

Now he dips into his suitcase. He's looking for something to staunch the snow that's fluttering steadily in through the letter box. Frankie finds the leather pouch where he has stored his keepsakes, and removes them one by one: the pink immortelle that Carmel put into his hand when he told her he was leaving; a pair of painted wooden dice; and a portrait of his mother. Frankie stole the photograph on the night before he left, creeping past his grandmother's bed and lifting it from the shrine she had built to her daughter. He was tempted to take the other things: the plain black mantilla his mother had worn to church, the leather-bound Communion Book, the rosary. He decided on the spot, in the darkened alcove next to his grandmother's snoring body, that he was done with all that stuff.

Not for the first time he thinks of his Nana, her grief at finding him gone. He hadn't dared to look at these things on board ship for fear they would be stolen, so now Frankie gets a shock: there is a twist of patterned lacework crushed into the bottom of the pouch that wasn't there before – his Nana's handkerchief. Frankie pulls at it, and a dart of brightness spins out of the lace and through the air. It beats a peal on the concrete floor, skirts an arc to the front door, and twirls down in a hoop of light: red–gold, red–gold, then red and gold as it slows. The door scrapes open. A small, handsome man bends and picks up the ring which Frankie has only just found and nearly lost. He slips it over the first knuckle of his forefinger: holds it out into the space between them. Frankie looks into the stranger's eyes, raises his own hand, and pulls on the other man's finger. For a long, long second they remain this way.

Nice ring, says Joe Medora finally.

Was my Papa's, says Frankie, feeling right at home. He tugs gently at the ring, frees it, slips it on his own left hand. He smiles at his new friend.

~

Habib, thinks Frankie, my very good friend. And how typical that Joe should have had the key to the *front* door. Carlo Cross! When Frankie realized that he was meant to share the room, he renamed him Carlo Double-Cross. But he was secretly pleased. Joe would be company: they would get along fine.

Did he speak out loud? He opens his eyes, blinks up at the portrait of Persimmon. It looks just like any other horse, like Court Jester, even. He remembers why he's here: why this room isn't his, why the cafe downstairs isn't his, why the ring . . . it makes his body twitch. He could really do with sitting down. He can look at Medora, but not – no way – at the ring Joe is wearing. Frankie stares now at Medora's face, cut into light and dark under the spell of round tungsten – so sharply, Frankie can just make out the black dot of a piercing

44

in Joe's left ear. He reaches up, checks his own earlobe between finger and thumb, and goes back down the twelve knotted years of knowing him.

~

Pretty, Frankie, eh?
The girl pretends not to notice Joe's loud aside. Halfway down the street, she turns round and looks back at them before disappearing into one of the tall houses on the terrace. Joe lifts the cigarette from between Frankie's fingers and takes a long draw, closing one eye against the smoke. They are sitting on the white steps at the front of the house, squinting into the pale Spring sunlight. For an hour, they have been watching two men playing a Crap game against the wall. Now they are watching them argue. Frankie takes the wooden dice from his pocket and smiles enquiringly at his friend. Joe's hand covers Frankie's own; he shakes his head.

No, no, my friend. See them – no-good bums!
As he says this, a dull thud makes them look up. One of the men is on the floor. He props himself up on his elbow, and yells at the other, kicking out with his legs. His mouth opens very red as he shouts: Frankie can't tell whether it's spit or blood. Joe lights another cigarette, and they both study the opposite end of the street until the fight is finished. They watch four small boys in a cluster here, gathered round the body of a dead gull. The boys prod it with a stick, poke at it with the toes of their shoes. They break away and group again, screaming and laughing, until a woman leans out from a window high above them and calls out in a foreign tongue. Joe gets up and carefully dusts the seat of his trousers with his hand.

They look good, this pair of men. They are meticulous, sleek. Crisp white shirts, black pants with sharp turn-ups, black suit-jackets, a perfect knot in the tie, and mirror-polished shoes. They are brown and young, and they shimmer with luck. Frankie wears the ruby ring on one hand and a pale yellow signet ring on the other. Joe is ostentatious, showy. He has a diamond earring, a matching tie-pin, a glint of gold when he smiles.

Frankie stands a good head above Joe: for this reason, the latter gets a new hat with a wide band running round it.

A Fedora, Frankie!

says Joe, carefully brushing the brim on his sleeve, picking off invisible flecks of lint,

What a music. Fedora. Fedora. They name it after me!

They laugh, and Frankie feels an unaccountable need to buy a new hat for himself.

~

Their lives weave quietly together. They have a pattern: a late breakfast at The Hayes, followed by a stroll to the market where Frankie buys food. He handles and sniffs and scowls at the produce until the stall-owner loses patience, or Frankie gives up in disgust. While he does this, Joe goes for a talk with his 'Boss' in the pub across the road. They often have an errand after this meeting – to collect a debt, drive a girl to a hotel, deliver a parcel: sometimes, all they have to do is sit on the street and watch. They are paid handsomely for what seems like nothing at all. Joe promises to put in a word for Frankie when his English has improved, perhaps get him a permanent job in the business. Easy money, says Joe, rubbing his finger and thumb together. Easy money, parrots Frankie, making the gesture.

Late at night, Joe teaches him all he knows, his voice gliding like a dream over the basement.

Ain't Nobody Here but Us Chickens,

Ain't Nobody Here adall,

and in a short time, Frankie can echo back:

Kindly Point that Gun the Other Way,

an' Hobble Hobble Hobble off and Hit the Hay!

Frankie learns a lot like this. He watches the small red point of Joe's cigarette sweep to and fro in the blackness,

and ponders the 'Is You Is or Is You Ain't' that is his latest
lesson.

~

    Is you is or is you ain't my Baby? C'mon, Frankie!
shouts Joe, a thin glaze of sweat on his forehead,
    Sing, habib!
Joe nips neatly across the floor of the basement, bending Pearl
like wire in his arms. She is Joe's new lady-friend. Frankie
fumes with envy. He sits on the bed, hardly able to keep his
legs from jumping, and watches them dance. They spin close
to him, Joe dipping Pearl so that her head falls almost into
Frankie's lap. He glimpses her wide-open mouth and her
tongue very pink, and then she's swept to the other side of
the room, screaming at Joe to stop.
    Will you let up now, Joey! Let up I say!
Her accent reminds Frankie of the rusted springs under his
bed. She wears a thick sweet perfume; she is very blonde; she
sparkles all over with the sharp glass of diamonds. For the first
time, it feels hot in the basement. Pearl wears her blouse low
at the front, showing the dark slash of her cleavage. This
makes Frankie love her: all he can think about while he's
watching them dance is how much he would like to put his
tongue in there and lick.
    And Frankie will not be fixed up with anyone else. Joe
knows women; he introduces them to his friend as if he's
handing him a gift. They are thin, blonde, so very Pearl-like,
but they have a way about them which keeps Frankie distant;
they look at him like a hungry dog might eye a bone. Until
Mary.

~

Frankie doesn't want to think about Mary. He unravels the
rope a little further, to one frayed morning in May.

~

Joe's bed has not been slept in for over a week: there has
been a lack of singing in the basement. Frankie is still half-

asleep when Joe shunts open the front door, swinging a large brown suitcase in his hand. Without a word to Frankie, without even looking at him, Joe begins to remove the fragments of his life from the walls and surfaces of their home. Lying horizontal, one hand under his head, Frankie tracks Joe's movements across the room: watches him lift his framed picture of Rita Hayworth as if to weigh it, then put it carefully back on the shelf. Joe ducks through the curtain into the scullery, and Frankie hears the clink of the two glazed china cups as they are swivelled off the hooks. Joe comes back, wraps the cups in one of his shirts, moves out of sight again, and returns with a pan and a plate. He packs methodically. To Frankie, these actions seem to go on for ever: they feel timeless in the creeping light.

Where you going? he asks at last.

Got to go, Frank, says Joe, head deep in the wardrobe. He draws out a suit on a hanger and folds it into his case.

The Boss has got me a place,

and suddenly Joe is animated, looks at Frankie for the first time, rushes the words through while he can,

. . . it's a beaut, habib, down on the main street over Luciano's. Two bed apartment. All furnished. Inside toilet, man! I get to run the club. No rent, Frankie!

Frankie's hand flutters under the bed. He finds his pack of Woodbines, scrapes a match along the rusted iron of the bedpost. It flares with a brief fizz. He lights up.

Two bed, yeah? says Frankie, holding out the new cigarette to Joe.

Joe's arms stretch wide and his shoulders sag. It could be the beginning of an argument.

Frankie. Frankie.

Frankie puts the cigarette between his own lips and slides to a sitting position, placing his bare feet on to the floor. He drags his own suitcase from the dust under the bed and flings it open on the floor between them, takes a puff on the cigarette and holds it up again for Joe to share. Joe chivvies,

Frankie. It's not for you, this thing.

What is for me, says Frankie, carefully picking his way through these unsung words,

I go back to sea?

Joe with his suitcase open, Frankie with his suitcase open. Joe's head tips to one side, and he lets out a sudden short laugh. Frankie grins up at him.

You want in? whispers Joe, his fingers in a scissors for the cigarette.

I want in, Frankie says, holding it out to his friend.

~

Frankie sits on a chair beneath the window. Joe places a clean white handkerchief across Frankie's shoulder, takes up the half-empty bottle of rum from the table, shakes it, then pulls out the stopper with his teeth. He puts his thumb over the rim of the bottle, tipping it upside-down with a swift jerk of the wrist, and presses a wet print against Frankie's ear. Splashes fall on Frankie's shoulder and the floor: a thin sweet smell fills the room. Joe swigs on the rum, passes it to Frankie to hold.

Leaning close now, out of sight for a second, Joe jams the cork behind Frankie's left earlobe. Frankie can feel Joe's breath on the back of his head. With his free hand, Joe removes his tie-pin and sucks on the tip, feeding the point of it directly through Frankie's flesh and drawing it out again, slowly. A slight snagging as the pin is pulled free from the cork: a shift of cold air. Frankie feels a rush on his neck and hopes it's only pain and not blood, feels his earlobe tugged sharply downwards between Joe's finger and thumb, hears Joe part his lips. With one stab, Joe forces the tiny yellow diamond – a replica of the one in his own ear – through the throbbing hole. Frankie stares immobile at the bottle gripped between his knees, and further down, to the quivering droplets of rum on the concrete floor. Feels the sting but doesn't move. Feels his eye begin to water.

Joe crumples the handkerchief and casts it into the fire. He puts his hand on Frankie's shoulder.

Not much blood, habib. It's finished.

~

Frankie can't sleep on his left side for a week. It has nothing to do with his new bed, or the vibration of jazz music from the club below, or the sound of Pearl's hot cries from Joe's bedroom. Frankie's ear is a sticky mess. He inspects it for a few days, and then suddenly can't look at it, but from time to time he finds his hand there, testing for soreness. He stands at the door of Luciano's and greets the guests, his fingers curled around the lobe: it makes him look thoughtful. Pearl notices, sets about the wound with iodine, and Frankie's ear begins to heal nicely.

He is pleased with the way people treat him these days: they know his name, they want to shake his hand. He imagines it's because of his new suit and his new job. Women he's never met before gaze eagerly at him over their drinks, hoop their arm through his when he's standing at the bar, leave him folded messages at the door. And Joe, stuck with Pearl, looks at him differently too. You owe me, says the look.

~

You owe *me*, says Frankie in his head, Waiting like an errand boy for your say-so.

Those days before he knew; before Mary, when there was everything to be had, and when he thought, stupidly, how he and Joe would have it together. Frankie decides to leave, taking a long breath and turning slightly – then jumps at the loud ringing of the telephone on Joe's desk. Joe ignores it, signing the bottom of the paper with a fast zig-zag flourish as the phone rings and rings. He folds the page slowly, sliding it into an envelope; takes a lick at the flap, his tongue darting out with a glimmer which remains on his lips. In the lamplight, they are razor-thin and wetly red, like two slivers of the ruby. The ringing stops.

Bring up a glass before you go,
he says to Ilya, passing him the letter over his shoulder. Joe gestures at Frankie to sit. He finally looks at him, but before Frankie can even open his mouth, Joe sets out his own proposal.

four

It's been an hour since the doctor spoke to my mother. She sits in the hospital corridor and matches her thumbs, chipped pearls, turning one on the other in an endless circle. She has looked at *Reveille!* and *Woman's Weekly,* her eyes skipping the surface of the pages as she listens for her name to be called, or worse, for the doctor to come back and silently rest his hand on her arm. And she has studied intently but without comprehension the notice on the wall above the Reception Desk.

Visitors are Politely Requested Not to Smoke

Everyone in the waiting area is smoking: the floor is a rash of cigarette stubs, the tiles pockmarked with greasy black circles and the smirch of dropped ash. Luca crawls beneath my mother's chair, swiping her hands across the debris as she goes, leaving a trail of drool in her wake.

Eva clacks through the swing doors, skinning the wrapper off a new pack of Players. She taps one out for my mother.

I've rung The Moonlight, Mary. There's no answer.

She sparks the flint of her lighter, bends her head sideways, and sucks on her cigarette. She holds out the flame for my mother.

Does he work there, then? she exhales, Your husband?

Eva understands so little, it makes my mother want to cry.

She looks at this blonde woman: she doesn't know where to start.

~ ~ ~

Mrs Jackson does as promised and looks after my sisters. What this really means is that she lets them use her backyard. Her husband's trade is rag and bone, so their garden is a sculpture park of bent metal and rotting wood stuck with six-inch nails. Two armchairs sit facing each other in a clump of weeds, leaking springs and coils of horsehair. A disused rabbit hutch at the bottom of the garden is home to one worn-out pigeon, who spends most of the time stalking back and forth across the thick crust that has accumulated on the floor of the hutch. When Celesta approaches it, the bird flies up in a frenzy, banging itself against the roof in a spume of grit, mites and feathers. She puts her hand on the wire grille, and bends down to look; in the dark, one round terrified eye looks back. Celesta picks up a long grey feather from the slick of mud at her feet and gives it to Fran.

Rose and Marina sit opposite each other on the chairs and play I-Spy.

I Spy With My Little Eye, something beginning with . . . T!

Marina looks around the yard for inspiration. She sees a television set perched in the long grass.

Telly?

Nope.

Marina tries Teacup and Toilet and Table-leg. Rose kicks her feet against the fabric at each wrong answer, sending squirts of dust into the air. Marina can't see anything else beginning with T.

I give in, she says.

Turd! screams Rose, pointing at a dry white lump peril-ously close to Marina's foot.

And again,

Turd! Turd!
showing Marina the assorted brown swirls hiding in the grass.
The two girls giggle with disgust, and begin a game of Sharks,
leaping from surface to surface in an attempt to avoid the
ground. Rose does her impersonation of a sergeant-major,
bawling at the top of her lungs,

Jump, Private Gauci! Jump I say! I'll have your guts for
garters! Attennn-shun! And Marina stands to attention, wob-
bling gently on the squeaking springs.

Fran won't play this game: she always gets court-martialled.
She is drawn to the wooden pallets leaning against the outhouse. She crawls behind them, crouching in the dark triangle
of space between the moist brick and timber. Raindrops
cling to the surface of each plank; the wall at her back is
glazed with slime; two yellow eyes stare at her from low
down on the ground. Fran has met this dog before, out on
the street. She puts her clenched hand out to his nose, as
our mother taught her to, and after a moment he gives it a
bored lick. He is quaking and smells of rotting earth. Fran
sits next to him, manoeuvring his heavy brown head on to
her lap; the dog lets out a low grumble as he settles into her
warmth.

Fran runs her hand along the rough matting of his coat. If
he were her dog she would give him a good brushing. She
puts her face on his muzzle. And a bath. Through the gaps
in the planks she watches her sisters: they'll be at her for
something any minute now. Your Fault are the words she
hears most, although she knows, she knows it never is. Fran
puts the feather Celesta gave her into her mouth, holding it
like a cigarette, and inhales, exhales. She tries it out on the
dog, sliding the quill between his pink chops, but he shakes
his head vigorously, gives another low groan and settles again
in her lap. Fran turns over the flap of his ear, and whispers
into the pink of it.

London's burning London's burning London's burning London's burning.

~

Celesta stands on the doorstep and shivers in the rain. She watches Marina and Rose playing their new game: they bounce on and off the soaked chairs, falling into the weeds.

Tally ho! Bombs Away!

Soon their legs are smeared with mud and seeded grass. Celesta tries to sort it out in her head, what they will do for tea tonight, where they will sleep. Inside the house, the Jackson children crowd the living room: the big lads with their legs hanging over the sofa and their strange appraising looks; the girls so hard and thick-set, with their ratty hair; the grey-faced toddlers crying. Endless children, too many for Celesta to count – but they match us in number.

~

Shit's sake, Donny, your end, your end!

The yard door swings open: Mr Jackson is home from work. He crabs in backwards, dragging an upended slab of iron which used to be someone's fireplace; Donny, his partner, is attached to the other end. Marina and Rose jump together into one armchair, watch silently as the two men grunt and curse and scrape their way across the flags.

My fucking toe, Don. Let up! Slipping, boy, watch now!

The fireplace drops with a clang on the concrete, and the two men stand above the ringing and stare at it. Job done, Arthur Jackson wipes his hand along his forehead. A tide of rusted orange melts slowly down his brow. He turns his blue eyes on Celesta.

Hello there. You from across the road?

Celesta tries to smile at him but can't manage it: his voice is soft now, not at all what she expected. Tears leap behind her eyes.

Come for tea? he says, patting her lightly as he shifts past her on the step. He moves into the house, followed by Donny. They make a big play of wiping their feet on the matting inside the door; Arthur like a stallion about to charge, Donny's hands pressed against doorframe as if he's jumping into the Abyss. His boots are no cleaner at the end of this performance. Celesta hears Arthur Jackson's voice behind her, echoing in the bare hall.

We've got guests then, Alice?

Alice appears from the living room. There follows a tangle of whispers and gestures. The boy Donny loiters in the kitchen, twisting his rat face on Celesta, then back to Alice and the story she is telling. Celesta squirms under scrutiny. She keeps her back to all of them, but Alice's drone still reaches her, the words running up her spine:

Out with some bloke . . . *abandoned* that child . . . God knows where *he* is . . . Celesta suddenly remembers Carlotta and Salvatore. She calls to her sisters to get their coats.

~ ~ ~

They've put a thick gauze dressing on my hand – it reaches up to my armpit, nearly – and another sheath in layers across my face, each one thin as an insect's wing. Everything is nice under this: soft and dreamy. I wish my mother could have a bit of it; she is so stony and sharp and clear, sitting there on that plastic seat. She's holding my hand, what will become known as my 'good hand' – as if the other one was somehow wicked and got punished for it – and she's listening, as much as she's able, to the doctor. I've lost a fair bit of hair too, but as there wasn't much there to start with, no one seems bothered. They say a new baby's hair falls out anyway, a few weeks after it's born. What's left of mine will, that's for certain.

My mother looks round the ward: we're all babies here, but she doesn't care about any of the others, not even Luca, who is in the corridor wrestling with Eva's gold locket.

Eva doesn't have much feeling for small children yet (and certainly doesn't know their strength: she will find a deep red score on her neck later, where Luca succeeded in ripping the chain from her throat and stuffing it into her mouth).

My mother's eyes are like two stars in a frosty sky: it's as if she can see the future. She looks through the soul of the doctor sitting on the corner of my bed, and decides to trust him. He talks of third degree, skin grafts, plastic surgery.

The outlook is favourable, he says to my mother. He has a white coat and a stethoscope, and his hair is neatly parted on the left. He looks like a boy she used to know. He puts his lovely long hands over my mother's veined fists.

It's amazing what they can do these days. These new prosthetics are marvellous, he says gently.

My mother nods as if she knows what he's talking about. She feels very weary. But I won't die: that's all that matters to her now.

We just have to be careful about the shock, he continues.

Oh, I'm alright, she says.

He means the shock *I've* had, but he looks at her for a long time and considers the possibility that I'm not the only casualty.

There's not much you can do here, he says finally. Is there someone you can stay with tonight?

I've got five other kids, says my mother.

He looks at her face. She doesn't look old enough, he thinks; she can't be much over thirty.

They're with a neighbour, she starts to say, but then a nurse pulls the curtain back and behind her stands a woman in a raincoat. My mother's new x-ray vision has warned her of this apparition. Next to the woman stands Eva, mouthing something unintelligible. One look from my mother, and Eva joggles Luca lightly back down the ward and through the swing doors.

You'll be the social worker, I expect, my mother says,

turning in her chair and smiling acidly. The woman takes a notebook out of her handbag.

~

They're with a neighbour. Jackson, I think – maybe Johnson. We've only been there a month. Haven't got a clue, love. He's claiming Assistance at the moment. Merchant seaman. No, it's not a Spanish name. Gauci. No, GOW-CHEE. I never left her! Go on then, bloody well file it. I've told you once – you deaf or what? My kids are perfectly safe, Thank You Very Much. They're with a neighbour.

~

They're not.

Celesta has told Mrs Jackson, in her grown-up voice, that they're going for tea with their Aunty Carlotta.

Are you sure? says Arthur Jackson, 'Cos we've got plenty, haven't we, love? He turns to his wife, who holds a dirty potato over the sink; she cuts busily, each twist of peel sending a splash of muddy water into the air.

It's chips, mind, warns Alice Jackson, and pointing the peeler at Celesta, Do you lot eat chips?

Celesta takes Fran's hand and moves to the kitchen door.

No, I don't think we do, Mrs Jackson. But thank you very much for your hospitality. Will you tell my mam we'll be at Carlotta's?

Mr Jackson is afraid he'll forget the name. He takes a folded envelope from his shirt-pocket, pats himself all over in search of a pen.

Just write down the address for us, Sweetheart, he says.

Celesta won't stop moving now, calls out from the step.

Don't worry, my mam knows where it is.

Mr Jackson stands in the kitchen. He's finally found his pen, tucked for safety behind his ear. He licks his lips as he bends over the greasy envelope. Carla? Charlotte? Celina? The names run through his head.

Now. What was the name, Alice?

Celesta, she says firmly.

Oh aye. Celestia.

He writes this down in capitals.

~

We *do* eat chips, Cel. We do! Marina is persistent.

Shut up, says Celesta under her breath. She grips Fran's hand tighter.

I want chips too! yells Rose.

You shut up an' all, Celesta says, feeling their noise scraping away at her thoughts. She tries to remember where Salvatore and Carlotta live. She has to picture it. It's round the corner from their church.

She leads her sisters (but not the dog, who skulks behind them until Rose aims a stone at him) through the Jacksons' yard and into the street. They can't help crossing the road for a look at their house. Celesta peers through the letter box, and the living room looks perfectly ordinary. She presses her face against the thin slit, pushing the sprung flap further open with her thumb, and feels a draught on her eye. Beyond the living room, it's dark; the door that leads into the kitchen looks as if it's been painted black. She gets a sudden smell of wet, of ash: like Bonfire Night.

Round the back, someone has leaned the busted yard door against the frame, where it rocks in the wind. The girls slide around it one by one and stare at the mess.

That's your fault, says Rose, wiggling her finger at Fran.

Shut up, Celesta moans, so quietly, it makes them mute. The chairs and table, the rug and the chest have all been abandoned to the rain. A rough board has been nailed up at the kitchen door: the original lies flat on a patch of grass at the far end of the garden. At the window, the net curtains hang like scorched paper; there's a long curved crack in the glass. Celesta peers into the outhouse: a stash of crockery is

piled in the doorway and, on the toilet seat, someone –
perhaps one of the Jackson boys – has put my mother's recipe
books in a neat pile. Celesta reaches in, lifts one from the top
– *Cooking with Your* New World *Oven!* – and the cover comes
away in her hands. She looks at the illustration on the front, a
smiling woman in a frilly apron and high heels, and thinks it
strange that everything is so burnt and yet so wet.

There's a sound of squeaking: it comes from the blackened
chairs, groaning in the wind. A spill of water on the flags is
streaked with specks of charcoal. The girls in their belted
raincoats stand and watch her.

Come on, Celesta says, sick of it. Let's go.

~ ~ ~

Frankie can't believe what he's just heard. It's ridiculous.
It's so stupid, it makes him laugh out loud. The sound of his
voice in the hallway is eerie; he feels he wants to laugh again,
and does, deliberately this time: it comes out high-pitched
and hollow. Frankie sees Ilya coming up the stairs, clutching
the glass he'd been sent for, and the urge to put out his foot
and kick him full-on, in the belly, is almost too much for my
father. He'd like to watch him plummet to the bottom,
preferably in slow motion. Ilya waits at the turn of the
staircase, says something low as Frankie passes. Frankie doesn't
quite catch it.

You what? he says, turning and looking at the man. Ilya
holds out the empty glass. Frankie puts two fingers over the
rim of the tumbler, tugs at it.

I said, Fly away home, Little Bug, and Ilya laughs then, his
fingers flicking the air as he finally lets go.
Frankie clenches the glass in his fist, ready, but Ilya turns
away, running up the last flight of stairs. Frankie can leave it
for now, he has other things to think about. He swings open
the door at the foot of the stairs. My father hasn't said Yes or

No to Joe's proposition: he needs to talk to someone before he makes up his mind.

The cafe is in semi-darkness, and the man behind the counter is not Salvatore – but Frankie knows him: Martineau is pouring himself a large brandy. Frankie looks at him, and then sees the Tin on the bar, and looks again. Martineau holds out the bottle, gesturing to the tumbler in my father's hand.

You'll need it, he says.

Salvatore appears from the kitchen. He has one arm in his jacket, moving fast for a big man.

Frankie! Ilya tell you? he shouts, sweeping round the counter, Incendio! Your house!

Martineau gulps back the drink, catches Frankie's hot look, holds up his hands.

Not me, my friend, never. Never.

Frankie feels the cafe close in around him. For the first time today he *wants* to think about my mother. He wants to be where she is. He looks at Martineau.

Mary?

She's at the hospital. She's alright, Frankie! he calls to my father's back. But Martineau can't find the words to tell him that I'm not.

Frankie runs from the cafe, out into the street, out into the rain which courses off his glossy head. On the counter in The Moonlight sits his forgotten hat. Salvatore catches it up in his hand as he follows Frankie to the hospital.

~ ~ ~

A slight roughness to the touch; Joe Medora sweeps his palms back and fore across the blotter on his desk, enjoying the sensation. And how smoothly Frankie took his offer! Not a sign in his face: a shame he's not so good at poker, thinks Joe. He's given Frankie a day or so for a decision – the deal is very delicate.

What Joe wants is simple; he wants Marina. After all, he thinks, Marina is my daughter. He thinks, but he can't be sure. He *is* sure: he's seen her, he's seen his blood in her. He stares at the blotter, picturing Mary, and only half-registers Ilya's soft step into the room. But Joe can't ignore the quick snort of his laugh.

You won't believe, says Ilya, his face open with amusement, Frankie's bad luck.

Joe looks up at this.

What now?

Ilya kisses his fingers to his lips, blows them away in a flutter.

A fire, Boss. He's had A Fire. His house is Burnt.

Joe is icy now; sees that Ilya is an utter fool.

My house, says Joe. It's *my* house.

~ ~ ~

Arthur Jackson is ashamed of his vest. He stands in the doorway, forgetting his manners, and looks at my mother. She is lovely in the semi-dark of the street-lamp, her hair in curls round her face and her brown eyes bright and worried. He remembers his manners.

I'm sorry, Missus, do come in out of the rain. Sorry about that! Ah, Mrs Amil, he says, spotting Eva cuddling a sleeping Luca, You'd better come in too, I suppose.

I'm not having that woman in here, says a voice from the living room.

My mother turns her face to Mr Jackson, wonders what she's done wrong. Eva steps in smartly.

It's alright, she means me, love, she says, with an angry laugh.

Eva bends close to my mother, mimicking Alice Jackson's voice – *That woman! Lowering the tone of the neighbourhood!* My mother stares at her in wonder: as if the Jacksons' aren't low enough themselves, she thinks. Eva reads her look.

I'll tell you about it, Mary, she says, If you don't hear it somewhere else first, and then dipping her chin at Luca,

Shall I take the little 'un across to mine for a minute? Number 14, alright?

My mother watches Eva as she crosses the street.

Arthur Jackson shows his teeth to my mother; it's supposed to be a welcoming smile, but he has a funny feeling now that she's standing there and looking straight at him, and he can't quite bring it off.

I've come for my kids, says Mary shortly, as if to remind him, And then we'll get out of your way.

He nods quickly, pulling the envelope out of his trouser pocket.

They've gone here, see? Your daughter said to tell you.

Mary reads the name he's written.

Celestia? Celesta? She turns her head sideways, steadies his hand with hers to stop the letters jumping.

Aye, Mrs – Mary, that's right. They've gone there.

Mary curls her lip.

Celesta is my *daughter*, she says. And suddenly panicking at the thought of the social worker, Who's got them?

No, Mary, that's where they've gone!

Mr Jackson stabs his finger at the name he's written down. Mary snatches the envelope from him and presses it to her mouth. She's thinking. She runs through where they might be: Celesta might have taken them to The Moonlight. Possible. Or maybe out to play. Mary turns her head to the door. It's black outside: too dark. What else would Celesta do? Arthur sneaks a look at her again now, sees her staring into the night. He doesn't know why, but he feels guilty.

Is that door still open?

Another shout from the living room,

'Cos there's a hell of a draught in here!

Mary places the envelope across her heart; she is trying to

calm the juddering in her chest. Mr Jackson sees this gesture, sees her hand drop from her lips to her breast, and it moves him. Alice Jackson appears in the hall. She's wearing slippers, Mary notices, pale blue ones with a band of fluffy wool.

They've gone to their aunty's, says Alice, and seeing Mary's puzzled face, turns to her husband.

What did she call her, Arthur?

He shrugs. He's afraid to repeat what he thinks he remembers. Alice turns her head to one side, pinches her nose. Deep in thought.

Carlotta, she says firmly, That's what your girl said. Gone to their Aunty Carlotta's for tea. Wouldn't eat ours!

She retreats back into the living room. Arthur Jackson watches her go, leans in close to my mother.

Is it far, Mary? Shall I come with you?

No ta, says my mother, It's just a bus ride.

~ ~ ~

Celesta led Rose and Marina and Fran across The Square. She thought, If I don't find Carlotta's house straight off, we can go to The Hospital. I can ask someone the way. Or we can go to The Moonlight; Salvatore's bound to be there.

So she isn't too concerned at first, but when they pass down The Parade, she gets confused. They wait at the corner while Marina runs up the terrace looking for a street name.

What's it say? Celesta shouts.

Dunno, Cel. Uh, hang on. South . . . Church . . . Street. They continue, but the next row is North Church Street, the one after that, Greek Church Street. Intersecting all three is West Church Street. It's like a bad dream. Celesta is furious to discover there is more than one church: she was using her own as a guide.

She decides to take them to The Moonlight. As they turn the corner, they are blinded by the headlights of a big car travelling fast. Celesta pushes her sisters into a doorway as it tears down the street. It's dark and raining hard, and at the wheel, Joe Medora has his mind on other things; he takes no notice of the four little girls pressed flat against the wall.

~ ~ ~

Eva has filled Luca with bread and Chocolate Nesquik, and has put her in one of her mother-in-law's shawls. Now Luca sleeps in the middle of the sofa, caught between Eva's husband Yusuf, and Najma, his mother. Najma says nothing, but she loves having this baby in her house; she watches Eva carefully for maternal clues, tweets soothingly at Luca when she stirs. Luca's mouth is open, her legs are splayed, she has one hand pointing a finger into space and the other curled tightly around the chain she snatched from Eva's throat. She looks very at home.

Aaah, whispers Eva, What a Pet.

Yusuf stretches across the sofa and touches Luca's foot.

Such a beautiful child, Missus, he says, grinning up at my mother in the doorway.

You don't want to disturb her, Mary, says Eva quickly, You can leave her with us for tonight – she's no bother!

Ta very much, love, but she's coming with me, says my mother. She lifts Luca into her arms with a groan. The chain in Luca's fist dangles, slips and falls on to the floor.

Sorry about that, she says, as Eva bends to retrieve it. My mother sighs, pulls the wing of her cardigan around Luca's body.

Suppose I'd better go and have a look at the place first. No point in bringing the kids back if it's not . . . livable-in.

Eva makes a face at Yusuf, and takes Mary's arm.

We'll both go, shall we? See what sort of mess they've made.

~

65

The living room is lit with a faint orange glow from the street-lamp. Eva can see Mary's body quaking in this dimness: she tries the light-switch.

They've turned off the electric!

It's on a meter, says my mother, Under the stairs, in the kitchen. I've not got any change.

And starts to cry. Eva takes Mary's hand and leads her back into the street.

Go and find your kids, she tells her, We'll sort this out for you. Come back in the morning.

Eva takes a ten shilling note from her purse, and presses it into my mother's hand.

Bus fare, love. And get yourself something to eat on the way. You look all in!

~

When the bus finally comes, Eva helps Mary into a seat. She leans over, lifts Luca's fist, and kisses it.

What a Pet! she shouts, stepping back down on to the pavement.

Eva pulls her coat tightly across her chest. She watches my mother's face in the window until the bus moves off.

five

For the second time in our lives, my father stands over me with a clenched fist. It won't be the last, but he remembers the hospital visits as the worst. He's weeping.

Bambina, he chants. Bambina, Bambina, Bambina.

In truth, my name has deserted him; he can't remember what I'm called. All thoughts of Joe Medora, of what he will say to Mary – what he will *do* – are drowned beneath this hymn he sings to me. Salvatore sits next to my bed, now and then passing a hand over the wet hairs on his head. He hears the soft cries of a child at the far end of the ward, and the catch of air in his own throat as he bends to search for his handkerchief. He finds it folded in his trouser pocket and passes it to my father, who uses it to hide the sight of me, holding the square open and drawing it down in a veil from forehead to chin, repeatedly, like a man wiping sweat from his face. He hasn't touched me yet.

A nurse brings two cups of tea; the silence is broken by a rattle of china. My father stares down into his cup, grateful for something to look at, blowing on the surface until a scum forms, then blowing on this until it breaks like muddy ice.

The nurse stands by and fidgets with her clipboard, stuck between these two men in their suits. She takes a sly look at her watch.

Your wife has gone home, she says, her eyes moving quickly from Frankie to Salvatore: they both look so distraught, she can't tell who the father is. She gets no response from this, and tries a sterner tack.

You'd be best coming back in the morning. The child needs her sleep.

She bends across my bed and pulls the light cord.

It's not entirely dark in the ward, but it feels hotter under gauze, a swarm from deep inside me, and with it a noise which comes and goes. At first it's hard to place, it sounds so much like a sigh. It's the wind, swishing the last leaves on the tree outside; but to me it's like the hiss of bubbling varnish. My father reaches over now, wanting to touch me but not knowing how, and the hover of his hand above the ghost of mine is the deepest, blackest heat. The ward fills with a scream like a siren.

~ ~ ~

The bus takes a different route at this time of night; 'the chuck-out run' the conductor calls it. My mother twitches with impatience; she feels the need to count all her children now. After three stops, the bus is full, and my mother and Luca are squashed up against the silvered window by a white-haired man with beer on his breath. He eases himself along the vinyl seat, grips the handrail in front, and launches into song.

A – You're Adorable! B – You're so Beautiful! C – you're a Cutie and a Charm!

pushing his red nose close to Luca, who swerves her head deep into my mother's cardigan.

My mother rests her head on Luca's hair, breathes into it. The 'Alphabet Song', that's it. Funny it should come back to haunt her now. She looks out past her reflection and into the night, beyond the oily rooftops of the city, to a dark hill and a clear dawn.

~

Mary had to walk the two miles from her village to Hirwaun, where Clifford said he would pick her up in his van. She'd planned it well; in her shopping bag she put her purse, her hairbrush, her polkadot dress, her shoes. She clumps along now in her father's old work-boots, the toes stuffed with pages torn from the *Echo*. He'll be mad, she thinks, but he'll be mad anyway, whether I'm there or not. It makes no difference; he's always the same in the morning.

Mary looks at the boots, the tongues flapping up and down as she negotiates the steep path with its slipping stones and frosted gorse. It doesn't bother her that they've got no laces: when she gets to Cardiff, she'll send the buggers back, stuffed toes and all.

She sees her route unfolding like a map; down the curving hillside beside their house, along the back of the Chapel and Coots' Farm, skirting the river-path to the foot of Mynydd Fawr. All she has to do when she gets there is stand at the lip of the mountain and wait. In daylight, the lane is dogged with craters of mud, but at this hour of the morning, before the sun has got to it, the ground rings clear as glass. She stamps along, scuffing at the frozen edges of a puddle, chipping up a lump of ice which she kicks ahead of her. Mary is nineteen, and she's leaving her father and the slate hills behind her and she's going with Clifford to The City.

She wanders up and down the lane. She must be early. Mary looks at the sky falling into blue beyond the ragged fringe of oaks; she'd get a better sighting of Clifford's van if she were higher up. She climbs the shoulder of the mountain, her eyes tracing the curve of the lane as it disappears then comes back to run like a skid mark down into the town. Mary watches the mist unwrap itself from the valley, watches the specks move and come to life, making noises too loud for the size they are down there. Nothing looks like Clifford's van; nothing sounds like it. Ages now, she's waited. Mary puts a hand under her jaw and feels her pulse. She stands so still she might be carved in stone; but she's counting to a beat beneath her fingertips. One hundred, then another hundred, then another, on and on until the sun is directly above her head and she knows he's not going to come. Mary gets down off the mountain and starts to walk.

~

Her father reads the note she's left him. He throws the rip of paper into the fire.

Good riddance, he says, to his empty house.

~

It's supposed to be Spring, but the wind is as stiff as November. Mary hunches into the collar of her coat. Her legs are bare and purple with cold; the side of her face is numb, her hands are raw. But inside she is boiling. Mary sucks in her breath, flinging her words down the valley in a white of air,

You Wastrel, Clifford Taylor! You Bloody Fucking Bastard!

An explosion of birds into the sky, a thick silence. Mary feels her blood pump in her head.

Don't cry, girl, she says quietly, Don't cry now.

She bends down at the side of the road and searches in her bag for her gloves; finds one wrapped around her purse, pictures where the other one is: on the ledge above the fire in the living room. She'd taken them off to write her Da the note. Mary checks in her purse and counts the money she's saved. Every morning, that walk through the weather to Penderyn and The Miners' Welfare, to that stinking yard behind the hut – chiselling at the ice on the water-butt, plunging her hands in and out of the frozen water until the skin on them gave up and cracked like chickens' claws: all winter, standing in the yard, peeling those potatoes. And the nights! The men with their yeasty breath and glazed stares, watching her as she slopped the beer into their mugs, watching her and saying nothing. The heat of their coal-crusted eyes on her.

70

All for you, she says, rubbing her hands together, You Idle Bastard.

Mary swings the shopping bag over her shoulder, decides to go anyway to Cardiff. But she won't waste her wages on bus fare: when she reaches the main road, footsore, welling up inside with rage, she puts out her thumb.

~

Down and down. The sleep my mother thought she'd never have is visiting her now. The bus jerks along The Parade, stop and start, stop and start, and the tinging of the conductor's bell, the hot muddle of drunken chat, seeps into her dreams.

~

Oy! You! Over here!

The man is waving his napkin like a starter's flag, sweeping it high and low across the edge of the booth.

I said two *Lambs* – when you're ready!

Mary would like to snatch the napkin from him and stuff it down his throat. But she smiles apologetically, reloads the unwanted drinks on to her tray, and darts back to the bar. This is only her second night at Luciano's. She doesn't know rum from cow's milk. And they ask for all sorts of things; Gin and Ginger, Pineapple Fizz, Scotch and Threat. She'd like to see how that went down at the Miners' Welfare, where all they ever drank was Mild or Bitter, depending on how they felt.

Mary leans on the counter while the waitress in front of her loads her tray. They're not allowed to pour the drinks here – they have a man especially to do it. Mary studies him; he wears a black suit with the sleeves pulled a bit up the arm, the stiff white cuffs of his shirt turned over so that she takes in his cufflinks, with the pattern of a sunrise etched in gold. The waitress in front is biding her time, flirting with him. He stares over her head, keeping an eye on the evening: he pays her no attention. When it's Mary's turn, he looks at her and speaks.

He give you trouble? he says, motioning with his head towards the man with the napkin. Mary is blank for a second, thinking, he sounds just like Mario Lanza, he even *looks* like Mario Lanza. The blood rushes to her face. To hide it, she inspects the notepad tied to her apron.

He said rum, an' I took him rum, and now he says Lambs!

She shows him the order. He nods, takes two clean glasses from the rail above his head and beckons her into the alcove behind the bar.

Two Lambs, he says, pouring a measure of brown rum into each glass. She moves to put them on her tray, but he stops her, picks up one of the glasses, and turns his back. His jaw moves from side to side, his tongue peeps from between his lips. He spits into the drink.

Don't take no shit from him, he says, wiping the soft white stream from the rim. And smiles his brilliant smile. This is Frankie at his most gallant.

~

I loved him, thinks Mary, stirred from her past by the weight of the man in the next seat. He's given up on the Alphabet and has gone to sleep; his head rests on her shoulder, his mouth popping open and shut like a carp. She heaves him away to free her arm, rubs the racing condensation from the window.

I loved him straight off, she says into Luca's hair, then loudly, Stupid Bloody Fool!

The man jerks awake at this, blinks slowly, starts up again.

A – You're Adorable, B – You're so Beautiful . . .

~

Frankie holds her in his arms. She can't tell if it's the vibration of music from the club below, or Frankie's body, or her body, but they're both trembling now in the little bed.

You're so beautiful – he says, and running his hand along

the curve of her hip, under the tight elastic of her girdle –
Take this off.

~

Two more stops. My mother shifts Luca onto her other
shoulder and bends forward to get past the man, his top half
keeled like a bent flag into the aisle. His eyes swim in his
head as my mother squeezes by. It's been so long since Mary
has thought about the past, it seems like someone else's life.
Frank Gauci and Joe Medora; the two of them so glamorous
and charming – and then she stops herself. She won't think
about Joe – how *that* happened – and she won't let herself
think any more about Frankie; where he was, where he might
be now; what he will do to her when he finds out about the
fire. She concentrates instead on her children.

But Frankie is thinking about *her*. After the hospital, after
our house which he couldn't get near, not with Joe Medora's
car outside it, Frankie goes to Salvatore and Carlotta's home.
He sits in the parlour and waits, mulling things over.

This is the deal.

Frankie gains: the house, enough money to right the
damage caused by the fire; enough money to wipe his slate
with the Syndicate; just that bit extra so that Mary doesn't
have to work all hours to make ends meet. And an offer to
manage The Moonlight when Joe is away.
He loses: Marina.

The terms are generous, he can see that. He also sees, like a
blade twisting a hole in his heart, how long Joe has waited
for this time, for a moment desperate enough to make him
jump. He imagines how Mary has deceived him. He can
hardly bear it. Frankie's thoughts won't stay still; he tries to
follow them but as soon as he glimpses one, it streaks away
before his eyes. Random as fireworks, they crack to life in his

73

head, their bright trails fizzing suddenly to black. His eyes roam Salvatore's parlour in search of something steady to fix on: a carriage clock ticking glumly on the mantelpiece, the cool dome of a plastic snow-scene, an ornate mirror above the fireplace casting its dark reflection. He finds Mary in everything, mistakes his rage for love. He wants her, he hates her, he'll make it up to her, he will tear her into shreds.

It doesn't occur to Frankie that Marina might *not* be Joe's daughter; Frankie sees Joe in the child now, sharp as diamond. He wants her out of his sight – he's happy to be rid of her. He would abandon Mary, too, and all the rest of us if he could. And with just that extra bit of money, over time, with a little luck, perhaps he can: perhaps he can get away.

He pictures his daughters, lining them up in a neat row in his head, and studies each one minutely. Celesta, Rose, Fran, Luca, he checks them off with a nod, convincing himself that they're his. He stops at me: a word forms in his head; he cannot let it free.

~

He has a lot to say. When my mother arrives, the family will be complete again, a full set. Not counting me, that is. It can't last.

interference

I don't remember Marina; I was only a month old when she left, and still in hospital. My mother told me how she went away, listing all the things she packed into Marina's new brown suitcase:

Two pairs of Clarks' Sandals, what with the weather out there being so nice; a new dress with little rosebuds running round the bodice – you know, Dol, like a medieval princess – and three new blouses; a satin nightie; a proper toilet bag from Marks'; a swimsuit in emerald green. Oh, she had everything she wanted! We had to sit on the case to shut it!
My mother would tell me this time and again, her face fixed in a smile.

Years later, standing on the stairs after one of my dreams, the one where I'm smothered by a hot bubble of fat, I hear a voice below, placating and steady, and then the shrill clip of my mother's distress,

You sold her! Don't *touch* me, Frank. You sold her.
Children burnt and children bartered: someone must be to blame.

~

As with all truth, there is another version.

Joe Medora's car slips up to the kerb, the wheel-rims grating on the edge of the pavement. A blonde woman steps out from the passenger side. Standing in his living room chewing on his breakfast, Mr Jackson hears noises on the street. He raises the grey net of curtain at his window, and poking his head round it, looks at the car, admires it and the blonde woman standing beside it, and gazes up to our front bedroom. He sees my mother's hands pressed flat on the pane, her mouth moving silently. He sees my father suddenly appear from our house, gripping Marina's shoulder, helping her onto the back seat, stroking her head as she slides across the leather upholstery. Marina bends forward and waves to our downstairs window, where the faces of my sisters crowd the steamed-up glass like pale balloons. Fran and Celesta wave back; Rose is crying. The blonde woman takes the suitcase, lifts it onto the seat next to Marina, shuts the car door. Joe Medora revs the engine.

My father doesn't look once at Joe Medora, and Joe doesn't turn his face from the view through the windscreen. The road in front of him leads to the high wall with the dead end, which means he will have to turn the car round on the street and drive past the house again. It's not his house any more; but he has Marina, sitting solemnly in the back seat of his car, her little gloved hands folded now over the belt of her raincoat.

My father cuts straight through the house – in through the front door and out through the back – stumbling on to the morning where he stands until the sound of Joe's engine dies to nothing. He takes off his jacket: it's been raining overnight and the smell is sharp, there's a bird singing somewhere which infuriates Frankie, thinking of the songs that Marina will hear, far away in Malta, that he cannot share. He looks at the yard, the washing line empty except for the pegs, and the spiders' webs between them laced with dew. He looks at the old back door lying flat on the ground, like an entrance into Hell.

Then he sets to work; to break the door to pieces, to knock and hammer and make the most terrible screeling noise; he wants to scream, he wants to let out his lungs and howl: anything, to drown out the emptiness that oozes from the house.

He lifts the door from its grave of flattened grass: the hidden side of it is slimy and crawling with woodlice. The saw gibbers through the wood as Frankie devastates the silence. He sings a song without a tune, in a voice that comes from his bones, all day, like breathing.

He hammers until darkness, but not able to leave it alone, he goes out again with the red weals of flesh growing tight on the skin of his palms. Hammers into the black. Something will be Built, he thinks.

It takes him a month to erect the cage. He will fill it with animals. He will buy chickens, perhaps, or rabbits. It is a thing for his daughters.

~

My mother would tell me this story, every time differently, but would always end with the same line:

What he really wanted was to saw *me* to bits, Dol. Like a magician. He couldn't stand it, you see? Jealousy! That's what jealousy does for you, girl.

It didn't occur to her then, or if it did she never let on, that he was doing something about us; about losing everything that winter. He was determined to change his luck.

~

We loved the rabbits. But then they vanished too. My father killed every single one, for food, for sport, for no reason at all. Like a poacher, he used them as a stake; he would take them out of his donkey jacket and throw their soft bodies on the counter of the betting shop. They were currency, and he spent them all: apart from the ones I managed to destroy.

It's an instinctive thing. That's what my mother told me when I showed her, took her down to the bottom of the garden, and *showed* her – those small scraps of flesh, streaks of disgorged skin – all that was left of the babies. I couldn't think what I had done to hurt them; I was *proud* of them. They looked like the sugar mice you buy in sweet shops. My mother said the doe had eaten her young. And that I had done something terribly wrong by touching her babies.

You had to interfere, she said.

I was five; it was the first time I'd heard the word. The way she said it made it sound like murder.

six

Say it then!

Gowchee, I say, spreading my lips over the last syllable. It's not a new word, but I'm humouring my mother.

Now spell it, she says, breaking off a thread of cotton with her teeth. She tacks the needle into the front of her blouse where it twinkles when she moves, folds the mended shirt and places it on the pile of ironing to be done.

G-A-U-C-I, I say slowly.

Well done, Dol. Now do the lot.

I take a deep breath:

Dolores Sebastianne Gauci. Aged Five. Living at Number 2 Hodge's Row, Tiger Bay, Car—

She stops me by flapping her hand in front of my face.

Alright, Dol, you're not going to the bloody moon. Now, you know what to say?

We're sitting round the table, which is heaped with washing, the *South Wales Echo*, my crayoning book, and *True Crime Monthly*, and I have to pass this memory test before my mother will let me go to the corner shop for her. I can feel she's nervous; she never lets me out. I can't play in The Square with my sisters, and I can't go to school. I started there last month, but you wouldn't know it – I've only been twice. Rose says it's because I'm bad luck and I mustn't be seen. She goes on and on until she gets a smack and starts to cry. I think it's because my mother's afraid that if she lets me out of her sight, I might never come back. Marina didn't. No one talks about her – it's not allowed – but sometimes, lying in bed waiting for my mother to come up, I hear her saying her name. And at night, when I'm waiting for the light to start, my mother whispers it in her sleep. It sounds like a sigh.

I should have gone to school today, but I'm off ill: I keep getting what the doctor calls Ghost Pain. Sometimes I'll try to open a door, or pick up my knife, and it's only then I realize I've attempted to use my *left* hand. When my father sees me doing these things, he frowns and gives me a black look: *Sinistra*, he mutters, shaking his head.

Dr Reynolds says it would be normal if I'd ever had my fingers, but he thinks it's strange I should miss something I never knew. It's not so strange to me; I miss Marina, and I never knew her. Sometimes, I dream I'm skipping: I'm holding the handles of the rope with *both* hands, and as it whips faster and faster over my head, someone jumps in. It's Marina, stepping in time with me. It's then I wake up with the pain.

~

My mother pushes back the mound of unpaired socks and reaches for a pen on the mantelpiece. Her eyes search the room; she's looking for something to write on. I shield my crayoning book with my arm – my mother writes notes all the time, she'll put them on anything; a scrap of sugar bag for the milkman (2 gold top, 2 steri), or the back of the Family Allowance Book for my father (Food in pantry, gone to bed). The note she wrote to my teacher at school was scribbled on the inside of an old Christmas card: *Season's Greetings!* Dolores has been Sick all night and will not be in Today.

She flicks through the pages of *True Crime*, looking for a bit of white space to fill with a shopping list, and suddenly, she stops. She holds the magazine close to her face and stares at it for a long time. From my angle, I can only see half the page; the head and shoulders of two grainy gangsters, looking a lot like my father's friends.

Well I never, my mother says quietly.

I'm sitting on the high stool so that I can see out on to the street. The Jacksons have got their front door open as usual, with their dog, Jackson Jackson, perched on the front step, guarding. I knock at the window, and his ears twitch; when he sees me he wags like mad.

Don't do that, Dol, says my mother, not looking up. She puts *True Crime* flat on the table and covers the picture with her hand.

Fetch your coat, then, she says.

When I come back from the hallway, *True Crime* has vanished. My mother helps me on with the raincoat. It's yellow, ex-Luca: ripped pockets and a circular stain on the left lapel which looks like the imprint of a beetle. She gives the shoulder a sharp tug.

If anyone talks to you, run straight home, she says, tying the string on my bobble hat. She turns me round and shouts from the step,

If you get lost, ask a policeman. Tell him where you live. But don't talk to anyone!

I balance on the kerb, trying to remember the advice I've been given. I'm not even at the edge of the street, and my mother's there at my back.

Don't forget this, Dol, she says, pushing the note into my fist. I have to carry it in my hand, these pockets being so useless, with the shopping bag hitched up into the crook of my elbow. I cross the road to say hello to Jackson, and I'm stroking his face and ears when he puts up his muzzle and grabs the piece of paper – he's always on the lookout for something to eat – and I have to wrench it out of his jaws. It's torn and covered in slobber, but I still recognize it; a crumpled corner of blue sky, a fragment of Humpty Dumpty's head, and on the other side, my mother's sloping script. She must have found my crayoning book. I look back at our house and there she is, standing at the window. She's forgotten me: she's studying the picture in *True Crime*.

~

'Do You Recognize This Man?' Eva reads out loud.

My mother moves quickly while I'm safely out of the way; she's summoned Eva from Number 14 to come and have a look.

Eva bends over the table, sweeping her finger across the page.

Which one? she asks.

There – that one! says Mary, exasperated, It's him, Eva, I'm telling you!

They both pore over the photograph. Joe Medora smiles directly at the camera, his arms are folded across his chest; he's puffed out like a pigeon. On his left stands a man with his head tilted to one side. Both are wearing hats: Joe's is pushed up, revealing his brow and an escaped lock of black fringe; the other wears his hat so low the shadow of the brim covers his face. His bony fingers are locked in front of him. Mary doesn't recognize this second man. She's relieved it's not Frankie.

He's involved in all sorts, says Eva, scanning the story, Racketeering, armed robbery – armed robbery! Vice . . . What the hell's that then?

Means he's a Pimp, says Mary, too quickly, They call it 'vice' in America.

So. Will you show Frankie?

Not on your life! says my mother, pressing her lips together, He's a bit more settled these days, Eva. This sort of thing – she gestures to the photograph – It'd send him bonkers.

What about Marina? Eva's voice is low; she hardly dare ask.

Mary can't speak for a minute: she snaps open the lid of the sewing-box and pushes her hand under the cards of wool and glittering pins. She takes out her scissors.

The last I knew, they were in Malta, she says, Now see . . . What does it say? – she snatches *True Crime* out of Eva's hands – 'Recently sighted in Sydney'.

My mother cuts along the page, folds the article in half, then in half again.

He gets about a bit, says Eva, watching as Mary slides the cutting down into the bottom of the sewing-box, He's wanted everywhere!

He certainly is, whispers my mother, working the scissors in her hand.

~

I'm trying to remember what the shopkeeper's name is; my mother calls her Miseryguts behind her back, but is always polite to her face. I open the door, and it comes to me at once – it's Mrs Evans. She's there, hunched over the glass counter with her long face cupped in her hand, talking to Mrs Jackson. They both glance my way, but Mrs Evans carries on her conversation in a whisper. I sneak my bad hand in my pocket while they're talking; I know that any minute now Mrs Jackson will want to inspect it, and then she'll tell me how much better it looks. This is a lie: it always looks the same.

There's a bluebottle flitting about under the glass; it crawls over the tray of bacon, over the mince piled up like worms, then it springs across to the oblong packets of butter. On the far left are scotch eggs, pork pies, and an assortment of cooked meats which the fly has yet to discover. I'd like to get served before it does – my mother wants some Haslet. The meat slicer sits on a slab of marble next to the counter. I've only ever seen Mr Evans use it; his wife stands back while the wheel spins round, as if it might drag her in and carve her to bits.

Don't mind us, Cherub, we're just gassing, Mrs Jackson

says to me. My mother sometimes says that, as well as, I'm Going to put My Head in the Gas Oven, when she can't get any peace.

Now, Dolores, what can I get you?

Mrs Evans leans over the counter. Her brown cardigan hangs over her shoulders and as she bends, it slips a bit: she does a little shiver, crossing her arms over her bosom and hitching her cardigan back into place.

I don't feel the benefit of this heater at all, you know, she says to Mrs Jackson, My legs are blue!

Paraffin, I expect, says Mrs Jackson, peering over the counter to look, They give off more smell than warmth, they do.

Both women turn their heads and sniff. I pass the note up to Mrs Evans. It's in a sorry state by now, and she doesn't seem to be able to read it, because she says to Mrs Jackson,

Just look at this, Alice,

holding the piece of paper above my head. They look at it for ages. I put my chin on the top of the counter and wait.

All on Tick? You're a fool to yourself if you do, Marion, Mrs Jackson says as she takes off her rain-hat and shakes it. Her hair used to be mouse, but now it's shiny and black; the shop fills up with a bitter smell – the same as when Fran changes her sheets in the morning.

That's a lovely shade, Alice, says Mrs Evans, crossing to the window and reaching in for a loaf of bread, Did you get it done at Frenchie's?

Mrs Jackson puts her hand up to her head and pats it.

They've gone, she says, Two days' notice, they got. Bloody council – they don't waste time!

They've sent *us* an order as well, says Mrs Evans, lifting a bottle of milk from the crate next to the counter, They want us out by the end of next month.

Mrs Jackson's mouth falls open,

You're not going? Marion! We won't have a shop left at this rate!

That's what my Graeme says, and then, as if suddenly remembering him, she shouts Graeme! into the back room. She screws up her face,

I haven't told you nothing, she whispers, It'll only start him off again.

There's a noise of rustling newspaper, the flitter of strip-curtain, and Mr Evans, pulling on his pinny. I get a glimpse of the room: an armchair, an upright chair with a television on it, and behind it, shelves, going all the way up to the ceiling; everything looks brown and old. It's a strange sensation, seeing things I'm not supposed to – it makes me want to go in. Mr Evans peers at the note his wife passes to him, wipes his hands down his front, and picks up the roll of Haslet.

Terrible news, Grae, says Mrs Jackson, ignoring Mrs Evans' instructions, Eviction! Terrible!

Eviction my Ar— he goes, then looks at me and smiles.

My Oh My, he sings. He presses the meat against the wheel and the slices fall into his hand, one by one. He slips them carefully on to a sheet of greaseproof paper.

Out by New Year, he says, turning the wheel, If we can find new premises.

Not with what they've offered, says his wife, shooting a narrow look at Mrs Jackson. Mrs Jackson fusses with her rain-hat.

What will you do with all your stock then? she asks lightly, her eyes scouring the shop, Sell it for discount?

Mr Evans silently wraps the meat.

We'll be calling in our debts, that's for certain, he says, taking a packet of Park Drive down off the shelf and sliding it across the counter towards me. Mrs Jackson's neck flushes rose pink.

I suppose the fags are for the children too? she says quickly.

Ah, she's not well, Mrs J, he says. He writes some figures on my mother's note, then some more on the parcel of meat, with two quick lines underneath them. I'm busy with the shopping bag, trying to hook it up my arm, so Mrs Jackson takes the Haslet from him and holds it out to me.

Here you are, Dolores, she says sweetly, Now – Let's have a look at that hand of yours.

~

When I get back, my mother's sitting by the fire. She's got her face turned away from me. I want to ask her everything – about what will happen to the Evanses' shop, and about the picture in *True Crime*, and why did she have to use my crayoning book, and why does Mrs Jackson always want to see my hand – but I can tell from the way she's bent in the chair, with her forehead resting on the corner of the fireplace, that she's been crying. She stuffs her handkerchief up her sleeve, blinking at Mr Evans' additions.

Bloody thieving Bastard, she says screwing up the note and throwing it into the flames.

~ ~ ~

I'm not the only one who isn't at school: Luca and Fran and Rose all left together this morning, but Fran walked in through the front gates, waved Rose and Luca goodbye, and ran straight out again across the caretaker's lawn. She hid behind the wall when Mr Rees came out and rang the bell for Assembly.

At the back of the school is The Arlies – a sooty curve of railway arches bounding into the distance: they cut across our neighbourhood like a serrated edge. On the north side is our school; on the south side, the shops, cafes, and row upon row of terraces running down to the docks. We live at the town end, away from the sea, but the houses on the dockside, near the saltings, are ancient back-to-backs. They have to be knocked down. Each week, another street is crushed to rubble; the grinding of the dumper-trucks gets louder, and overnight, a row of homes where people used to live becomes a stretch of broken brick and tangled wire. The sky gets wider every day.

My father wishes they would knock our house down too; he just can't wait to tell my mother the latest news.

They do Pomeroy Street this morning, Mary. I see them with the tape. Mr Meckis say he get Five Hundred Pounds! We get Compensation, Mary—

My mother would put a warning finger up to his face. They're not demolishing *our* house, her finger says. Because she dreams all the time of a rap on the door, of Marina standing there when she opens it. Marina would be thirteen now, but in my mother's mind, she's still only eight, with that front tooth about to go and the buckle of her raincoat belted a bit too far to the right.

Frankie no longer thinks about Marina. He is fierce about the rest of us though: it keeps him awake at night. The change in the neighbourhood is inexplicable to him. It starts with a few boarded-up houses, a friend waving goodbye from the back of an open-top lorry, and suddenly there are fistfights with contractors, lines of children lying on the ground in front of council trucks, whole families watching as the wrecking-ball swings into their houses. Demolition changes everything: a gypsy encampment mushrooms on the open ground, and gangs of young men stalk the streets, armed with broom-handles and lengths of chain. Frankie has heard them talking in The Bute, of 'defending their women folk', of 'not having it from these Gyppos, these Dagos', and it frightens him.

He notices new things: a dead puppy lying in the gutter outside our house, with its torn grave of sacking slumped against the wall; the Jackson boys staggering home with a fetter of lead between them; a permanent film of orange grit

87

on his shoes. Young women collect on the corner to sell salvage from the derelict homes – a dented lampshade, a grill-pan from an abandoned cooker, cardboard boxes full of clothes. None of it belongs to them, and nobody wants to buy it. They stand there all day, shifting their weight from one leg to another, smoking cigarettes. At night these same girls call out to Frankie in their flat, chilled voices;

Wanna Play, Handsome? See anything you like?

He passes them in a cautious arc – they are known to him. Despite the darkness and the heavy make-up, Frankie recognizes young Ann Jackson and her friend Denise: they were at school with Celesta.

It is this that makes Frankie set his mind on his eldest daughter. He will do what he can for her: the rest of us will have to wait.

~ ~ ~

We Plough the Fields and Scatter, the Good Seed on the Land . . .

Fran hears the voices rise and fall from inside the Main Hall: with the sun glinting on the long windows and the playground empty, it's as though the building itself is singing. She stands near the railings, mouthing under her breath,

For it is Fed and War-aw-tered, By God Awmighty's hand!

She only likes the hymns. When Mr Rees's voice booms out from the high windows of the Hall – You May Quietly Sit! – she turns away. Fran walks along The Arlies, listening to the bright splash of water off brick, to the short and long of her footsteps clapping out beside her. Some of the railway arches are deep as tunnels; others are bricked-in, flush with the bridge itself. Fran counts them, a family of steadily shrinking crescents, with one so small at the end, it might be a dog-kennel: she can see daylight through this. She ducks her head, crawls on her belly through the moist blackness until she's out the other side.

Fran looks as if she's heading for home, but she isn't. She follows the canal path, crossing over the road at Patrick Street to avoid the Evanses' shop; she mustn't be seen. She turns left into Opal Street, over the mound of orange earth and thick cord wire that marks the end of Emerald Place and the beginning of Jet Street – it's due to be brought down tomorrow. She stands on a pile of rubble and looks about. Seagulls pick over the upturned ground: there are no other witnesses.

~ ~ ~

With the plates stacked in the sink and Billie on the gramophone, Salvatore can relax: the breakfast rush is over, and trade will be slow until midday. He picks up his coffee cup, puts it on the polished table, and edges into the booth next to the counter. Salvatore thinks about nothing in particular: about the sunlight slicing in through the far window; about what the weather would be like now in St Paul's Bay; about Carlotta. It would be nice to go on holiday – they could go home for the Summer Festa if he can save enough money.

He tips a spoonful of brown sugar into the cup; it sits on the froth for a second, turns, sinks softly to the bottom. He feels safe these days; Frankie is steady, and The Moonlight is doing well: not many fights, no police, no sign of Joe. It's almost like old times. Salvatore stirs his coffee.

He can't see the door from the dark corner of his booth, but he hears the yawn of the hinge, a flash of street noise, and the slow shush of footsteps on carpet. Salvatore puts his head over the leatherette, stands up when he sees the other man; he's not a regular.

Mr Capanone. How do you do?

Salvatore skirts the low table to shake the outstretched hand.

He doesn't catch the name; the man talks rapidly, his words curling like butter:

Stay, my friend. Stay, he says, waving Salvatore back into the booth,

I'm look for Frank Gauci. He not here? Well, shame! I need a Talk with him!

Salvatore watches as the man turns on his heel, moves around the counter, peers into the kitchen.

Nice place! Good business. Mr Gauci is a Good Business Man.

Salvatore wants to remind this man that *he's* the partner, not Frankie, but the formal sound of Frankie's name and the way this big fellow limps around the cafe makes him nervous. Salvatore sidles past him, cradling the coffee cup against his chest. The man bends down under the counter and hauls up a flagon of soda.

Ah! 'Low's Soda', he reads, and waving the bottle at Salvatore, How much they charge you for this? Salvatore makes to answer, but is drowned out.

'Low's Lemonade', 'Low's Ginger Beer', 'Low's Tonic' . . . My Friend – he carefully places the bottle on the floor at Salvatore's feet – It's all Low's here! But the price, that's not Low,

and laughs loudly at his own joke.

Frankie deals with bar stock, says Salvatore, bending to pick up the bottle, If you have some business – Who shall I say call?

The man stares into the distance. He's thinking of something else.

You know Celesta? The daughter?

Salvatore nods.

She beautiful girl! says the man, Very beautiful.

The man moves around the counter, patting it twice with the flat of his hand.

Ah! I go find him, he says, with a quick smile. He makes

to leave, then turns back, searches in the pocket of his jacket. He produces a small white card which he points at Salvatore:

If you see Frank, tell him call on me. This evening is Convenient,

and places the card with a snap on the counter. He saunters back along the carpet and out through the door. Salvatore stares at the lettering on the card:

P. SEGUNA Esq.
Manufacturer of Finest Family Provisions

Now he knows him: Pippo Seguna, drinks merchant, factory owner, restaurateur – and recently widowed.

~ ~ ~

This is the way. Take this first, and put it like that – no! – Like that, that's right. Now another load on top, uh, there. This one's a bit too . . . not dry enough, y'see? S'gotta be dry. Put this one here, yeah. Now you strike this . . . See! And hold it. S'goin. Easy. Watch it, watchit now. There!

Talking to no one, Fran lights her fires.

~ ~ ~

It must be lunchtime – Pippo Seguna's stomach gurgles as he passes the food shops and cafes that run the length of Bute Street. He pauses at Usman's Delicatessen, tempted by the thick scent of salt beef, and puts his face up to the window. There's a small seating area at the back, but Pippo would have to negotiate the angled tables and the group of young men cluttering the sandwich rail at the front of the shop. This is not Pippo's territory, even though his factory is almost on the dock. He wonders if these men might be his workers. The thought makes him even more reluctant to go inside: they would know *him*, but he wouldn't be able to recognize a single one of them. Pippo removes his watch from his fob and clicks it open: twelve o'clock. He could head back into the city, eat at the Seguna Bay and still have time to look for Frank later. He moves away from the window, thinking about his mother – she's been angry for over a week, ever since he broached the subject of marrying again.

What will people think? she cried, when he first suggested it, With Maria still warm in the grave?
Maria has been dead for just one month.

Mamma, it would be slow, he argues, No wedding until Spring – six months is decent! And it would be good – someone to help you with the house . . .
His Mamma doesn't think so.

Pippo doesn't want to admit to the other thing; that he would like a Real Wife. After all the years of Maria's illness, the bedpans and the constant smell of bleach, and the private nurses with their chewing gum stuck in the corner of their cheeks and their laddered stockings, pressing their indifferent hands against his belly in the dampness of the spare room, Pippo would like – a wife. Someone pretty and young, who could love him and bear him a son. Celesta fits. He's only seen her once, and already he's infatuated with her. That hair coursing down her back like a wash of velvet; her eyes catching his – just a flicker of lashes – and then turning away; her tiny feet in their patent court shoes! Pippo knows his mother disapproves of Frank Gauci, but he doesn't care: he'd be marrying Celesta, not her father.

Pippo moves on in his reverie, unaware of the cut his figure makes along the street. He has a way of walking; leaning forward on the right foot, to the side on the left, so that his body rolls along the pavement like a newly landed sailor. Behind his back, children copy this sloping stroll. Pippo the Hippo! they shout. When he turns round, they face the other way, their shoulders heaving with mirth. Pippo has learned to take no notice.

At Domino's Resto, he decides to call it a day: Frank is not an easy man to find, and Pippo's really hungry now. He sidles into a chair near the door, summoning the waitress by waving the plastic menu. Pippo runs his hand along the centre crease, collecting grit and crumbs and cigarette ash on the tip of his finger. He inspects it closely; he won't be using these at the Seguna Bay – not hygienic. While he waits for his order, he looks around. Len the Bookie, on his way out, catches his eye.

Mr Seguna! says Len with a grin, Checking out the competition, then?
Pippo smiles tightly and looks down at the menu. Then a thought occurs to him:

Lenny, he says, pulling on the man's sleeve as he passes, You seen Mr Gauci?
Len looks blank, shifts his arm away.

You mean Frankie? Frankie Gauci?
Pippo nods, trying not to look at Len's hacked fingers.

Never see him, mate, says Len, feeling that look of repulsion sweep over him, and sending it straight back, We don't do business these days.
He shows his top teeth in a grin, and waves goodbye to Pippo.

This is a good thing, thinks Pippo, worrying about what his mother will say when he tells her he's arranged a meeting; Frank has stopped gambling. She will approve of that.

Len squints into the sunlight, and laughs, and thinks, No, I don't do any business with Frankie these day – and haven't since Joe Coral opened his betting office right next door to The Moonlight. But I won't tell you that, you dupe.

Word is out that Pippo is looking to marry again, and he'll bet his nose that the fat man has his eye on young Celesta. Len studies the form: Odds that she'll have him? Looking at her, and looking at him, any sane person wouldn't give it an outside chance, A Hundred to One. Unless of course, you know Frankie, and then it's Odds-On Favourite. Now, there's an interesting bet, thinks Len.

~ ~ ~

We're making a pie, my mother and me. I'm in charge of the filling, which is blackberry jam with bits of cooking apple cut into slices. I eat one when she's not looking, and the taste is so bitter it shrivels my tongue. She laughs when she sees my face.

That'll teach you, monkey! Wait 'til they're sugared, now. I love this; I love being here in the kitchen with just my mother and no one else. She gives me the bag of sugar, and the first spoonful goes straight into my mouth.

Just think about Roy Jackson's teeth, my mother says. Roy hasn't got any teeth, just a row of brown stubs, like iron filings, top and bottom. My mother swears it's because all he ever eats is sugar butties.

And his eye! I shout, because Roy has only got one eye now. This is important for me. I'm curious about people who used to have two of something and then end up with only one. My mother looks at me darkly:

Don't mention Roy's eye in this house, my girl, she goes.

Why not?

Because it's not nice.

I don't know which eye isn't nice – the one that's there, or the one that's gone – but I can tell by her face that she won't explain. Her mouth goes all tight and her lips disappear. It doesn't last long. My mother prefers to talk about the Jacksons than do stories or nursery rhymes. She uses them as a lesson against everything, as if *we* are the perfect family. Ann, the oldest girl, is Nothing But A Slut, the boys are known as Those Wastrels, and Mrs Jackson was Born Daft, Got Worse. My mother is kind about Mr Jackson, though.

That Arthur! she says, He's A Good Sort Poor Devil Married To That Divvy. Sometimes she talks to me like this for hours, but today she is singing:

Got Myself A Crying Talking Sleeping Walking Living Doll!

which I think is a song about me.

I don't cry! I shout, desperate to join in.

No, you don't, she says, and looks at me as if she's just realized the truth,

No, Dol, you know, you never do.

She wipes a tea-towel over the table to get rid of the crumbs, dusts the surface with flour, and she's just lifting the dough from the bowl when there's a knock on the door.

Get that for us, Dol, she says, scraping the sticky mass from her fingers. I reach up to turn the door-handle, and there's PC Mitchell and Fran standing on the pavement: he's got his hand on the back of her neck; she's twisting like a fish.

Get off, she yells, Get off!

She runs past me and straight into my mother's arms.

Er – Mrs Gauci, he says with a little cough, This is the third time . . .

She was on an errand, says my mother quickly. She tips Fran's face up, wipes away a smear of soot with her thumb, wraps both arms around Fran's head.

We found these on her, he says, holding out a box of England's Glory matches.

How else d'you expect me to light the gas? says my mother, snatching them from him, Will I rub two sticks together?

She looks down at Fran – a hard, knowing look.

Have you got my change, Love? she says, Or has he robbed that too?

PC Mitchell turns away, smiles at the road, looks back at my mother: his eyes are soft now.

It's dangerous on that waste ground, Mary. She could get hurt.

Aye, I know, says my mother, shutting the door, Thanks, Doug.

~

My mother's given up on our pie: she sits Fran on the sofa, pulls up a chair next to her, and carefully places the box of matches on the armrest between them. It is extremely quiet: as if to remind us of what this is all about, the coals hiss in the grate, and a bright flame plays along the bed of slack. I want to sneak off, but I know I won't be allowed to escape this moment: I'm part of it – I'm proof.

What were you doing? asks my mother. Fran picks at the plastic edging on the lip of the armrest. Her hair hangs like a caul over her face.

How many times do I have to tell you? They'll lock you up!

I didn't do it, says Fran at last.

They'll put you away, Fran . . . Didn't *do* what?

I didn't do nothing!

My mother pulls me, jerks me bodily so that I'm inches from my sister: our shoes scuff each other. Fran keeps her eyes fixed on the lip of the armrest: she's still picking, her fingers working busily now at a loose piece of plastic, and she won't look up. We both know what's coming.

Look at Dolores, Fran. Look at Her! See? See what fire can do?

My mother snatches my arm up high: she holds the knot of my fist between us like a dog's bone.

I didn't do it, says Fran, in a burst of weeping, so that my mother bends her head over hers and rocks her, and all I can see is a mess of hair: they've got the same mud-brown hair. I stand between Fran and the hearth like a fireguard.

I know you didn't, love, says my mother, I know.

~ ~ ~

There are two cups on the bar, then three. Salvatore pours the coffee automatically, just for something to do, while Frankie ponders the news: he lifts the fresh cup to his mouth, gulps at the coffee until he's drained it. Frankie is acquainted with Pippo Seguna; he's aware of all the businessmen in his part of town – especially if they're doing good trade. And Pippo Seguna is doing extremely good trade. So what if he didn't get an invitation to Maria Seguna's funeral? He went anyway. He took Mary and Celesta, and sent a large wreath in the shape of a crucifix to the Seguna home. He recalls feeling uncomfortable at the way Pippo stared at the three of them; he recalls also shaking the man's hand – it was soft and damp, like pork fat. But until now he hasn't dreamed that Pippo might have been looking at Celesta all the while. The knowledge gives him heartburn. Frankie puts a hand to his chest as Salvatore talks, asks him to repeat it, asks him what sort of tone Pippo had, how did he look, how long did he stay, until Salvatore has told the story five times and has even begun to invent a few details, he's so bored with the telling. Frankie rubs at the burning itch in his breastbone: it's a jealous pain.

And he say Celesta? he checks again. Salvatore rests his elbows on the counter, covers his eyes with his handkerchief and breathes slowly through his mouth.

He say, 'Celesta is very beautiful' – Frankie, this man, he an old man! You don't want him as your *son*!
Frankie grins at the thought of Pippo as his son-in-law: free lemonade for life.

He's forty-one, Sal. Alright, forty-two maybe – a young man still!

How old are *you*, Frankie? asks Salvatore quietly.
Frankie knows the answer. The fact that he can contemplate giving Celesta to Pippo sits between them on the counter like a stone.

My father gets a hard time from Salvatore, but he knew he would: it's his way of preparing himself for Mary.

~

Not on my life, says my mother. She's frying eggs, so the air is thick with the stench of old fat. The Haslet sits unwrapped, the slices hacked and squashed into a mound, on its paper in the middle of the table – we've already had our tea. Fran and Luca are out playing in the yard; at least they were when I last looked, but from the kitchen window I can only see Luca now, standing with her hands on her hips, shouting at someone through the yard door. It shouldn't be left open, we've got nothing left in our veg patch. My mother blames the gypsies. Luca comes bounding in:

Ma-am, Fran's gone . . .

Not now, says my mother, Your father's eating his tea.
Stiff with rage, Luca turns on her heel and races back down the steps. I look along the windowsill to check on the England's Glory: gone.

My mother puts the loaf of bread next to the Haslet, and my father, trying to please, pulls off a sliver of the meat with his knife and folds it between a thick white slice. When the eggs arrive, he eats them with more bread, chasing them around the plate with his fork. Normally he would have given up by now and gone back to The Moonlight for supper, but he's trying to persuade my mother to consider the suggestion.

Mary, Pippo's a Well-off, he says.

I don't care if he's rich as Croesus, he's not getting his paws on my girl!
My father tries a different tack.

I see that Ann Jackson, he says, nodding into space, It's a bad time for young girls.

Ann Jackson is a Scrubber! Our Celesta knows better. Ask her yourself, she says, looking at the clock on the dresser, She'll be home from work in a minute.

My father doesn't want to do this. He pushes back his chair and edges round my mother. As he passes her, he pats her lightly on the shoulder.

I've said no, Frank, she shouts as he turns the corner of the stairs, So don't you go talking to anyone!

Upstairs, Frankie changes into his best suit. It can't do any harm, he thinks, to hear what Pippo has to offer.

~ ~ ~

It's a clear night. My mother waits at the back door, while I crouch behind her, shielded from the wind coming in by the width of her skirt. I can hear Rose and Luca talking in the living room, and every so often a lull, then Luca's shrieking laugh. It'll be one of Rose's impersonations: she can do all the Jacksons just by changing the expression on her face – a squinty grin for Arthur; Alice, a pout and a sniff; or Roy, one eye shut tight and the other swivelling round in her head. She doesn't spare our family either: she's caught the quick way Fran blows her fringe out of her eyes, and my father's nostrils when he's angry. And me, I'm easy – Rose simply shifts her hand up her sleeve and waves her arm in the air.

I don't know if my mother is expecting Fran or my father: neither of them are anywhere in sight, and it's nearly nine o'clock. Celesta has gone to the Milk Bar and won't be back until later, so I know my mother's not on the lookout for her.

Don't wait up, says Celesta, fishing for change in her purse, I'm on a promise!

Oh yes, Lady, my mother says, And how will you get in then?

Celesta likes to pretend she has a key. She lifts her chin up high:

There are ways, she whispers mysteriously.

What Celesta means is she'll stand in the alley and throw

stones at the window until Rose creeps down to let her in. My father hasn't got a clue about this Carry On, as it's called; but my mother knows all about it.

You'll pay for any glass that's cracked, she always says the following morning, while Celesta feigns interest in her porridge.

What glass? My father will say suddenly, his spoon held in mid-air. My mother changes the subject:

Any more for any more? she says, waving the crusted saucepan over the table. This makes all of us go quiet.

Celesta hasn't heard about Pippo yet. Secretly, my mother wants Celesta to enjoy herself while she can: she knows what's in store.

~

My mother doesn't notice me at first; she's doing her singing thing. She'll hum quietly to herself for a while, but then startle everyone by abruptly breaking into song. At the moment she's making a soft droning noise with her lips, like the sound of the generator on the corner of The Square, and I don't want to interrupt her. From around her body I can see the back wall at the end of the yard, a sky full of stars, a skim of frost on the flags. We're supposed to be getting ready for bed but my mother has put Rose in charge. This is bad; Rose can't be bothered to help me get into my nightie, but Luca will take any opportunity to lord it: she's only just seven, but she acts as if *she's* my mother.

Dolores, she'll say, You've got that vest on back-to-front. Put it right Immediately! And by the time I've hooked it over my head and twisted it round, she'll find another excuse to nag me:

It's inside-out, you Stupid Crip! Do it again!
Luca will catch Rose's eye and they'll both laugh. I may not know back from front, or in from out, but I know when there's spite in the air. I don't want to sit in the living room with them, especially with the back door open and my mother

standing in the draught. She looks like she might just walk out and never come back.

I Had to Run A-Way-ay, And Get Down on my Knees and Pray-ey-ay,

she sings loudly, as if to confirm my fears.

Can you read me a story, Mam? I say quietly, to attract her attention.

She turns to look at me: the night air has smoothed her face, it's pale as she bends down.

Dol! You'll freeze to death. Where are your slippers?

I've forgotten to put them on; they're under the bed. We both look at my toes and then my mother wraps her arms around me and lifts me up on to her hip.

Big girl! she groans, Where's that naughty Fran, eh?

She holds me tight and leans against the lintel. There's movement in next door's yard, then Mr Riley swearing from inside the toilet. Minutes later, he yells.

Della! Where's the bloody *Echo*?

My mother laughs into my neck:

Old Next-Door Riley! she whispers, He's out of paper, Dol. Shall we throw him some over?

Another yell from the outhouse, then Mrs Riley shouting back, followed by a clank of toilet chain. My mother's not smiling now, she's staring out into the distance.

Where's that bugger? she says.

I don't know who she means.

~

Fran has forgotten time. She doesn't think about how late it is, only how bright the fire will be now that night has come. She creeps slowly along the terraced row of Jet Street, looking for signs of life. Even though the families have been evicted, there's still a danger that others have moved in – gangs of gypsies searching for something to sell, or drunks bedding down for the night. Once, Fran peered into the black window of an end house and saw a man and a woman lying in the middle of the floor. Now she presses her hand against the doors until she finds one that swings open. She stands in the hall, listening.

It's even darker with the door shut behind her. Fran waits for her eyes to adjust, but she still has to put out her hands and feel her way along the narrow passage. Instinctively, she turns to the right, into a moon-flooded room. There is a table with a single cup and saucer in the middle, and an airer with a baby's nappy drying in front of a dead fire: the family must have left in a hurry. Paper bags and odd clothes litter the floor. Fran can't quite see them, but she can feel the snagging and rustling around her feet. She moves into the kitchen, hearing her own breath in the silence, and pulls open a drawer. Nothing. Another drawer – nothing. She isn't afraid of all this space and emptiness, nor of the pulsing in her ears: she's searching. She finds a wooden chair in the scullery, and pushes it through the passage, kicking at the struts until they crack.

Fran gathers up the pieces of wood and makes her way into the living room at the front of the house. The street-lamps have been switched off now the road has been con-demned, so there's very little light in here: she must work by touch. Her hands swish across the walls like someone blind; she finds a corner of wallpaper and pulls – it comes away in a loud long strip – then traces with her fingers, finds another join, and rips again. She works quickly, baring the walls until the air is clogged with plaster-dust and the floorboards ripple with paper: enough to build her fire.

~

The Segunas live in Connaught Place, not far from us, but far enough to be a better part of town. Frankie hurries across the black hump of Devil's Bridge, along the empty street leading into the cul-de-sac, slowing his pace as he approaches Pippo's home. The houses on the terrace are all alike; high Victorian buildings, each with iron railings skirting the pavement, and steps leading up to a wide porch. Most of the houses in the Place have been converted into flats, and as Frankie passes them he can't help looking down into the basement rooms for signs of life; he half expects to see himself, craning his head up at the passers-by. It reminds him of when he first washed up in Tiger Bay.

Pippo's house is easy to identify; it's the only one with curtains all the same colour, in a shade of bright orange. Every room is lit up, and above the porch, a coach-lamp casts a cold white glare. The wreath of ivy on the front door is grey in this light. Frankie misunderstands the meaning of the wreath; early for Christmas, he thinks. In fact, it's the Segunas outward show of mourning. Frankie pauses to figure out his strategy with Pippo, placing one foot on the steps before him; they gleam so white beneath his polished shoe, they might be dusted with icing sugar. It's only the frost, as Frankie discovers when he moves: he slips swiftly to the right, almost tumbling down into the basement. Swearing out loud, he rights himself, grasping the handrail as the shock runs through his body.

~

There's a point when the room gets too hot for Fran and she has to move into the corner. She slides down against the wall, watches the shadows on the ceiling in flat then splintered layers, as if they're searching for a way out of the heat. Putting her hands up in front of her, she studies the brightness through them: the bones inside her skin shine like an x-ray. Soon there'll be a moment when she can't control the fire – when it does things she can't predict; sparking all over, melting like syrup across the floor, collapsing in a slump and suddenly flaring again in new gold. A shift of air can make it rage. Fran doesn't understand about risk, but this is what she craves when she makes a blaze – gambling on how hot, how high, on how long she can bear it. She is so like our father.

While Frankie weighs up his chances with Pippo, Fran calculates her own luck: another minute – two – before she has to run. She knows the signs by now; the taste of metal on her tongue, a speckled warmth beneath her skin which courses through her body like an urge to pee. Sometimes she has to, crouching in the hall on her way out, or quickly in the gutter with the fire going Whoof! and the sound of glass cracking like rifle-shot off the houses opposite. Outside, she soars, dipping through the darkened streets with the fizz of heat behind her and the rush of cool air on her face.

On the other side of Jet Street, Roy Jackson leans out of an upstairs window; he's keeping watch while his brother Tommy does a recce of the house. He gets a good view of the docklands to the left, the moonlight slipping along the old tramway like vaseline, smearing itself on the saltings in the distance. Looking right, Roy counts the smoking piles of debris on the razed patch of Emerald Place, eyes the Evanses' shop on the corner: there's a lean-to shed inside the yard which would make for an easy climb. There is no one on the street except for Fran, fleeing from the house opposite like a phantom wrapped in smoke. Roy ducks his head back inside the window and watches her run.

~

Here she comes now, scrabbling over next door's fence and landing silently on our patch of grass. My mother drops me down in the doorway.

Where the hell did *you* get to! she yells, I've been Out of My Wits!
Fran is grinning; her eyes are silver with the thrill of what she's done. She tries to duck past, shielding herself with her arm, but my mother can't help it, she smashes her hand down flat on Fran's head, over and over. Chasing her through the kitchen and up the stairs, she catches her by the leg.

I could kill you! I could kill you!
Her hand beats out against Fran's shin, and then the stair-

tread as Fran escapes, and then her own knees as she bends and sits and weeps.

They'll put you away, she cries.

I sit down next to my mother on the stairs. I try to cuddle her. She's wiping her eyes and muttering to herself,

They'll put her away, you see if they don't. And that'll be another one gone.

~

Frankie raps the knocker twice, and when there's no answer, puts his eye close to the glass. There's a distant pool of light, then a bent figure swimming towards him through the frosted pane, like a deep-sea diver surfacing. The first glimpse of Mrs Seguna gives Frankie a fright; in her black dress and shawl, she is the image of his grandmother. He looks down into her face and smiles. She doesn't smile back: she stares at him in unblinking silence.

Mrs Seguna? says Frankie, I come to see Pippo.

No Pippo here, she says, closing the door again.

Philippo, corrects Frankie hastily through the crack, just as Pippo appears behind her. He reaches above his mother's head, pulling the door open again.

Mamma! This is Frank Gauci – I tell you Frank is coming. Frank, Come and Sit, he says, waving him into the parlour. Mrs Seguna frowns at the two men grinning down at her.

Coffee, Mamma, Pippo says.

The Segunas' parlour is a shrine to mourning; a black mantilla is draped across a framed portrait of Our Blessed Virgin, and on the sideboard beneath, an assortment of keepsakes that Frankie recognizes from when his mother died – the prayer book opened flat with a rosary snaked across the page; two lighted candles guarding a photograph edged with black paper; the bloom of a single white lily, crisping brown at the edges. Frankie hopes it is this, and not Pippo, causing the strange smell.

Pippo stands too close to him. He thinks Frankie is paying his respects to the dead, and approves of this by gently nodding his head. Frankie catches on; he bends his chin to his chest, ostentatiously making the sign of the cross in the air in front of his body.

Scusate, says Mrs Seguna sharply, nudging through the door with a tray held in front of her. She places it on the bureau next to Frankie, bends low to pull out a kidney-shaped table from the side of the chair and bangs the tray down on it, muttering all the while. She slams the door behind her as she leaves.

Sit, my friend, Sit! says Pippo, his loud voice cheery, Drink some coffee with me.

The thought of more coffee makes the bile rise in Frankie's throat. He fingers the handkerchief in the breast pocket of his jacket, but doesn't pull it free. Instead Frankie covers his mouth with his hand, belching quietly into the curve of his fist. The burning in his chest is mighty. Pippo sits opposite; he's taken a good look at Frank Gauci – the thin smear of sweat on his forehead, his trembling hands – and he's heard the dialect unearthed in Frankie's nervous talk: this is a Sliema man, a country boy. Pippo decides to play it cool.

Ah! Business! he begins, Me and You, Frank, We are Business Men.

Frankie closes his eyes with a slight smile, a slight incline of the head.

And we are Men, continues Pippo.

Frankie holds his smile in place. He opens his eyes to see that Pippo is not looking at him at all, but at a point fixed approximately two feet above his head: Pippo appears to be addressing the curtain-rail.

You see, Frank, he continues, You see, it's hard, A Business Man with No Wife.

Frankie nods, resisting the urge to turn around and find what it is exactly that Pippo is staring at.

You follow me? After Maria – Pippo gestures to the mantelpiece and another photograph of his late wife – After Maria, I not think to marry again.

Another nod from Frankie. Come On, he thinks, Get on with it.

But . . . I have no children, Frank—

No son! says Frankie, blundering into the pause. Pippo raises his voice; he hasn't finished:

—So if I do, *If* I do marry – I pick and choose *Who* I Want.

Silence. Frankie's not sure if he's allowed to speak yet. Pippo sighs, unhooks the top button of his shirt and scratches his throat. His eyes finally meet Frankie's.

But Celesta! She a very beautiful girl, Pippo says on the out breath, A beautiful daughter, Frank.

Frankie looks at Pippo squashed into his armchair, taking in the shiny curls of hair peeping out over his collar, the fabric of his shirt stretched across his midriff, down to the naked ankles bulging over his brown leather slippers – until Frankie can look no more. He takes a sip of his coffee; the milk is off. He thinks of Celesta, her slim hands held tight by this sausage-fingered man, and imagines Pippo easing the straps of his braces off his shoulders. Frankie doesn't want to think like this. His eyes flit to the far side of the room, to the grandfather clock and the mahogany cabinet full of chinking glass and silver. A big room; carpeted, warm, with pictures of Saints he can't identify and of Jesus, who he can, with a ray of sunshine booming from his chest. Jesus is holding out his arms to Frankie as if to say, What's the problem, Frank? It's a Good Match!

He's so – *ugly*, Jesus, argues Frankie to himself. But . . . he's rich. And not *so* old. Frankie looks from Jesus to Pippo and back again. Jesus is still smiling. Frankie nods at the picture. Alright, he says in his head, Give me a sign then.

Pippo notices the downward turn of Frankie's mouth, and

the fist held tight against his chest; notes too that Frankie has hardly touched his coffee. Perhaps he thinks his daughter is too young.

So, Celesta. How old she is? asks Pippo casually, bending over to pour more coffee.

Seventeen, says Frankie, covering his cup with his hand.

She have boyfriends? She a beautiful girl, Frank, she have boyfriends?

Pippo, still bent close to Frankie, grins, rubs his thick fore-fingers together.

No, says Frankie, insulted by the gesture, She's a good girl.

Pippo laughs out loud, slapping Frankie's knee. The coffee cups jump on the tray.

Go talk with her, Frank. I'm a kind man, tell her. Then we'll see, ah?

~

Outside, Frankie grips the railings that border the Segunas' house. He glances up at the scrubbed white steps, the heavy black door with its shiny brass knocker and its ghoulish wreath, the warm light in the window. He should feel pleased – it *would* be a good match – but there's a heaving in his chest and a clamping sensation at his jaw. Frankie's mouth fills with liquid, bitter, slippery as egg-white: he leans on the railings, sweating, with the dark square of basement pulsing below. He heaves up the sour milk and burnt coffee in one raw burst.

~ ~ ~

Bending her head so that her chin rests on my shoulder, Fran's face against mine is cool as marble. I can smell bonfires in her hair. She gives me a squeeze, and from the way her cheek moves I can tell she's smiling. I've come up to ask her to try to be good and not upset our mother, but anyway she's here now; I don't want to spoil it. We're sitting like this on

Rose's bed, staring out beyond the garden wall and the alley, down the hill past the street-lamps to the blacked-out rows of condemned houses. The rooftops are blue in this light. We're waiting for something to happen.

Just you see, Dol, they'll be here in a minute!
The excitement washes through her: her heart flashes madly at my back. I can just make out my mother's hand-print on her leg, but Fran's forgotten all about it, she's so happy.

There's a drum of footsteps up the stairs, and the sound of a familiar song:

And So it Begin-za,
Rose's voice gets louder, the door opens,
Needles and Pin-za!
She's caught the tune from my mother. Rose stands in the doorway and switches on the light. In the window, two reflections leap out of the black: Fran's face is ghostly, mine looks like the moon.

What *you* doing in here? says Rose, What's wrong with your own room?

Ssh! Turn that light off, Fran waves an arm at her, We're listening!
Rose kneels on the bed and prods Fran's shoulder.

Why do you need the light off to listen?

Because there's a fire!
As soon as Fran says this, the sound of a siren cuts the air: it comes in waves, it makes me shudder. My bones start to twitch and my head goes all hot down one side, like boiling water on my scalp. Rose bounces back over the bed and flicks the switch off, and suddenly there's a great flash, a roar in the distant street, and the night is full of sparks.

~

Crossing Devil's Bridge on his way back home, Frankie catches this shower of falling lights out of the corner of his eye, brilliant orange, a sunburst in a midnight sky. It looks to him like a sign from God.

seven

I hear their voices before I open my eyes; it's Saturday – the only time my mother and father are both at home all morning – so there's usually a row.

No, Frank, says my mother.

Yes, Mary, says my father. This one is serious. My mother is shouting too.

We've already lost one daughter!

I haven't, he says.

My mother's voice goes soft: I imagine her moving through the house, picking up the heap of folded washing from the living room and carrying it into the kitchen, bumping my father's chair as she goes past. Him sitting at the table with the *Sporting Life*, a Joe Coral pencil stuck in his mouth, staring at the forecast.

She's only seventeen, Frank, she pleads.

It's enough, is all my father says.

He means old enough. My mother won't argue like this for long – my father has a method for getting his own way. It goes very quiet downstairs. I lift my head off the pillow and see that Luca's side of the bed is empty. Over in the far corner, in her own bed, Fran is hidden under a mound of blankets. Luca races back in through the door, puts a finger to her lips when she sees me.

They're at it again, she whispers, Celesta's going to be married!

Is she down there? I say.

Luca curls her lip,

Don't be Stupid — she's at work.

Although Celesta's only been working at the Co-op for six months, she's already in charge of the meat counter. My mother says it's because she's got her father's way with business, but Celesta knows better: Markus the Manager's in love with her, he likes to have her on display.

Meat is his Thing, she says proudly, as if everybody has to have a Thing or their life's not worth living. She comes home with Bowyers' Pork Sausages and thick grey parcels of bacon, which my father has taken to eating raw. Anything but Haslet.

Worms! warns my mother, when she sees him stretching the rasher between fist and mouth, You'll have a tapeworm inside you six foot long!

I don't know what a tapeworm looks like. I picture the coiled spool of measuring tape in my mother's sewing-box, slithering over the faces of the men from *True Crime*; imagine it inching up my father's throat like a creamy yellow snake. Maybe it's this that gives him heartburn.

There's a wet hiss of frying, a stink of sausages, a knock on the front door. My parents don't hear it, but Luca does; she's over the other side of the bedroom in a leap, sliding the net curtain over her head. She angles her face against the corner of the sash.

It's the police! Come and see!

Fran pokes her head out of the cocoon of bedding; her hair's all on end and her cheeks are flushed. She lets out a high-pitched cry as she ducks back under the blankets.

At the window I see the top of the policeman's helmet, and one shoulder with a number on it. There's a woman standing next to him. She's not wearing a hat. They both bend down and look through the letter box, then shout through it. I try to get a better view of them, but Luca's breath has steamed up the glass. She wipes at it with the net, so they're haloed in sketchy fog. The front door opens below us.

Mrs Gauci? says the woman, Would you mind if we came in and had a chat?

Luca turns and pokes me.

You go and listen, she says.

No – you go.

You! I'll stand guard.

Standing Guard is a swizz; it means Luca's out of danger. She'll just wait for me to report back or get caught on the stairs. I can't get caught on the stairs. Luca knows what this means for me, but she doesn't care; she puts her face so close to mine that only her bared teeth are in focus.

Go on! she hisses.

~

The door at the turn of the stairs is slightly open. I put my head round and have a peep. Through the blue of smoke I see my mother standing at the sink, clutching a plate to her breast. My father sits at the table, with the woman just next to him, her notebook open on the cloth. The policeman's facing away from me, so I can only see the back of his head and the dent in his hair where his helmet has pinched: it sits like a giant tea-cosy on the table. They're still as a painting. I don't know *her*, but I can tell he's PC Mitchell by the way he coughs before he speaks.

Erm – it's a very serious offence, Mrs Gauci, he says, Mr and Mrs Evans could have been killed!

As it is, they've lost everything, says the woman.

Are they hurt? Maybe – my mother starts to ask, but my father bangs both his hands down flat on the spread pages of the *Sporting Life*.

Bring her! He shouts, Bring her Now!

From behind me is a sound light as silk: it's Fran, brushing past in her nightie. She creeps down to the bottom step.

My father leaps forward at the sight of her; she jerks like a puppet off his fist. He holds his arm raised high – he'll club her again if she moves, but Fran knows the best way to behave in these moments. We all do. She stays absolutely motionless, taking small sips of air through her mouth. PC Mitchell steps forward, but my mother gets there first. She cracks my father against the pantry door.

What proof have you got! she cries, not to the police but to Frankie, Prove she did wrong! Go on!

They stare at each other, panting. My mother has her hands by her sides now, but she holds them open. She's ready to tear.

Roy and Tommy Jackson, says PC Mitchell quietly, Erm – they've made a statement, Mary.

He moves her back to the table and gently presses her down into his seat,

They saw her in the Evanses' shop last night. Lighting a fire, they said.

Below me, Fran sips air.

~ ~ ~

It's been a whole week since the Evanses' shop burnt down. I keep getting pictures: of the back room in flames, with the shelves collapsing down on each other and the brownness of it all colouring to a hot rich red; Mr Evans' pinny going up like the title sequence of *Bonanza*; Mrs Evans flapping out into the street with a thick rim of smoke round her mouth and her cardigan hanging off her shoulders. Tins of exploding peas, butter bleeding, blocks of cheese sighing into a sweaty pool. What I *don't* see are the Jackson boys, flashing their endless cigarettes around – Park Drive, Sovereign, Players, Craven A – when all they ever used to smoke were butt-ends off the street. Nor Mr Evans, holding the torched remains of his accounts book between finger and thumb. He won't be calling in any debts now. And no one in the neighbourhood blames our Fran.

~

We've been sent up to our room again because the social worker's back. The door to the stairs has been locked, but if we wanted to listen we could, by pressing up against the wood. We know all about the things she made Fran do, drawing pictures, choosing colours from a book, and about the statements and the reports and recommendations. Eva told my mother that the whole street thinks the Jackson boys are liars, but that isn't news; and that the Evanses' will use their insurance money to buy a new shop in Llanrumney. We've heard it all; we're bored with listening now. It's been decided: Fran is going to The Priory. The social worker makes it sound like a holiday home, but Rose is better informed; she says you can tell a Homes kid a mile away.

They hit you first and ask questions later. You'll have more of them, I reckon, she says, nodding at the bruise above Fran's eyebrow. In the last few days it's changed from blue to rusty orange. Fran wears my father's handiwork with pride, but there will be more to show before she goes away. She prods the edge with her finger.

Hope it don't fade 'til I get there, she says, I'll look hard.

You'll *want* to, warns Rose in agreement, Those Homes kids are Rock Hard!

What *you* need is . . . a tattoo, suggests Luca softly. She's at her usual place near the window, clutching the balding head of her Sindy doll. She dangles it by a thin strand of hair, moves it in a bouncing motion across the sill.

A tattoo would really scare 'em.
Luca has been saving the transfers from her comic, and as she says this, she casually hitches up the sleeve of her pullover: a small blue Spiderman is scaling her arm. Rose snorts with

laughter, but I can see that Fran is keen; she catches hold of Luca's wrist and inspects the shiny surface, the deep blocks of blue and linear red web on her skin. Sindy's head twirls in Luca's grip.

~

The social worker's name is Elizabeth Preece – Just call me Lizzie, she says to my mother, who ignores this invitation and doesn't call her anything – and she's fat like Carlotta. She probably buys her clothes from the same shop: green tweed coat, thick wool dress, sludge-brown stockings. Lizzie gets upset when she finds Eva's always at our house, feeding my mother cigarettes and teacups of rum. She doesn't approve of smoking or drinking. She doesn't approve of my father either; she's made a note in her file about him. History of violence, it says. She likes me though – she calls me Cariad.

Lizzie does all the talking, spreading her papers across the kitchen table as she lists out loud the forms that need signing.

Alright now, Mary, she says, This one here's just to say you've understood the Conditions of Care Agreement, and this one's for stuff that Francesca might be taking with her – bits and bobs – that she'll want to help her settle in.
Mary jerks her head away as if she's been slapped.

It's not for ever, you know, says Lizzie, holding out her pen, You said yourself you can't cope with her. Think about the others, love.

She'd cope better without the likes of you, says Eva, lifting the lid off the teapot and frowning into the rising steam. The charms on her bracelet jangle as she rattles a spoon inside the pot. Lizzie ignores this, glancing over her notes at my mother. Mary has a glazed, clean look which troubles her; it's not the expression of someone about to sign away their child. Lizzie has also made a note in her case files about my mother: Mental Instability, Bouts of Depression; second child fostered to extended family in Malta.

She thinks she knows our history because she's written it down; and she has seen that Fran is in danger.

We need to make sure we're shipshape, Mary, she says gently, Dotting the i's, et cetera.

After all, it's not every day you take someone's kid away, mutters Eva, overfilling the cup so that the tea slops into the saucer, Or maybe it is? All in a day's work, then?

Mrs Alan, says Lizzie.

Amil, Eva snaps.

This is a family matter. I'm sure Mary can see what's best, can't you, Mary?

I don't know, says my mother.

Mary really *doesn't* know. She doesn't know anything. She feels a dangerous shifting in her skull, as if it's full of shards; she has to keep her head still to stop them sliding. When she tries to sort things out, she gets a bright, jabbing pain at the corner of her eye. And the voice that comes – so close and tight against her ear it causes her to flinch – doesn't leave her any room to think. *Your mother's blood! Your mother's blood!* It's the voice of her father.

Mary looks at the social worker, at her smile, her apple-cheeks, at the papers stealing across the table towards her. And the pen held out like an answer. She's expected to say something. She tries to, working her jaw and opening her mouth. Nothing comes out. Mary gets up from the table and walks away. They don't stop her. No one stops her. In the street, two women shelter from the rain in the Post Office doorway. They remark on the way she staggers along the pavement, and the fact that she's got no coat on – then they forget her. Mary passes the betting shop just as Martineau swings the door open. He would see her immediately, but he holds his newspaper in a shield over his head to stop the rain from driving in his face. He doesn't notice. Mary turns off the road, almost at a run now, and scales the greasy embankment which leads to the railway line. She climbs up, clawing at the blackened grass and sliding shale. There's the glinting track, the old timber pond with its skin of algae, the swelling River Taff in the distance. But Mary doesn't think of these: she just thinks that the Gas Oven is not an option, not with those people sitting in her kitchen.

~

It's Arthur Jackson, picking along the edges of the track for booty, who catches a glimpse of something tumbling down the side of the cutting. He mistakes her for a heap of rags. Arthur scans the horizon for tippers – probably gypsies, he thinks, but never mind, sometimes there's something of value to be had. He gets close enough to make out the arms and legs and the brown hair, and he's afraid. He thinks of murder and of Henry Fonda in *The Wrong Man*. He edges closer, looking for witnesses, then he sees her face.

Mary! Fuckin 'ell, Mary!

The shout makes her start. All she sees are Arthur's boots, moving towards her, caked with mud and much too close. It's my Da, she thinks, in a panic. Hand and foot she crawls away, but Arthur holds her, his voice going Shh, shh, as he sits her upright and hooks his coat around her shoulders. Her knees are green-stained and bloody. He takes the hem of her skirt and arranges it gently over them.

Mary! What *have* they done to you, girl?

~ ~ ~

We're not allowed to see our mother: she's in the Box Room and the door is kept shut. We should all be in bed but the doctor's due, so we are on display, to show him everything's alright. Except everything is not alright.

~

My mother had a visitor earlier. It wasn't Mr Jackson, checking to see how she was, but it was definitely a man. She came upstairs and stood me at the window.

Give us a shout if you see him, she said, meaning my father. Her face was very white and her eyes wouldn't keep still; they jerked around the room as if she was following a fly. She switched off the bedroom light.

So he don't see you first, she said, and laughed. It made me feel scared – not the dark, I'm used to that – but the way she laughed. Close, like a secret. My mother's had a funny look all day. When Mr Jackson brought her back, she got straight in the bath. There was no hot water but she climbed in anyway and sat there, filling up the jug from the cold tap and pouring it over her head. Then she signed the papers Lizzie Preece had left her. Then the man came, and I had to keep watch. But it was so rainy outside, and I was so tired. By the time I saw my father it was too late. I tried to warn her.

~

My father shoots his eyes at me – terrible, warning looks that make me want to hide away – as if he's guessed what I'm thinking about. He's nervous about the doctor coming; he thinks he'll be found out. I won't tell – none of us will, not even Fran. I could go with her to the Home; we could have a nice time together, without him giving us those looks.

We're watching telly with the sound down when Dr Reynolds arrives. He's brisk and dark and leaves a trace of winter in his wake. My father says nothing, takes him straight upstairs. The whole house is hushed, as if there's been a death. We listen hard at the ceiling. The lightbulb in the centre of the room is bare, with a crack running across the plaster like a vein under skin. The doctor's feet find a loose floorboard outside my father's room; a door opens, then closes; bed-springs creak.

Luca sits at Rose's feet, her mouth shut in a tight line and her eyes fixed on the telly. There's nothing on, just dots and mess. I can't watch it. Rose plays with an elastic band, yawning it open and shut in her fingers; she was weaving plaits in Luca's hair but they've both lost interest now. Luca looks unfinished – one side of her head is tamed into a straight red braid, the other is a mass of frizz which Rose strokes slowly, repeatedly. I hunch up next to Fran. Normally she would cuddle me, but she's put her arms inside her sweater so that her sleeves hang empty on either side. Her hair falls all over her face. We don't know what to do.

When the doctor comes downstairs again he stands in the middle of the room and looks at us for a long time. Takes us all in. He leans over and strokes the bruise above Fran's eyebrow.

Smashing colour, he says, Any more to look at?

Fran's eyes jerk to the floor; she gives a tiny shake of her head. Dr Reynolds turns his attention to me, runs the back of his hand down the scar on my cheek. His touch is massive, cool.

This is well on the mend, Dolores.

I'm so proud, I almost forget what he's here for. *He* doesn't. He raises his eyes and gives us a look.

Now then, girls, your mother's very ill. And she'll need your help to get better. Lots of peace and quiet. And *no* trouble.

He glances pointedly at my father, who is waiting to see him out.

When does Francesca go? Dr Reynolds asks.

Social worker come tomorrow, says my father. He doesn't look at Fran.

I'd better give you something for Mary then, he sighs, unclipping the locks on his briefcase. He takes out a small brown bottle of pills and holds them out to my father.

But, you know, Mr Gauci – keep them out of the way, won't you?

~ ~ ~

Fran is well-dressed today. My father shines her shoes, sitting on the bottom step of the stairs with his tin of Cherry Blossom and his pile of rags. He makes neat matt circles across the toes, jamming the pattern of daisy holes with polish. Then he takes the brush and scrubs hard; short, brutal swipes at the leather. These are Fran's best shoes, bought for the Corpus Christi parade. Now she will wear them to the Home. The leather smells of richness to him, but at the top of the stairs, watching his shadow flit back and forth on the wall, it comes to me like fear. He polishes his belt this way too.

Celesta is downstairs with him. She has got up early to press Fran's pinafore. They don't speak to each other and they don't speak to Fran. Celesta spits on the iron, watches the balls of saliva leap and growl as they fry on the plate. She has no spit left by the time Lizzie Preece arrives.

Fran removes her treasures from under her bed; she selects one white cigarette stub, the marble with the twisted turquoise eye, the priceless lump of emerald, and slips them into her pocket. She leaves her dolls and her comics, and for the first time ever she forgets to strip her bed. She doesn't come back upstairs to say goodbye.

The Box Room door stays locked.

~ ~ ~

The Priory sits at the bottom of Leckwith Hill, with tall iron railings running around the perimeter and bushy evergreens lining the road. No one can see in for the trees, but sometimes there are sounds, like the noise of playtime in the schoolyard. In summer the drive is so thick with cow parsley you could easily miss the main gate with its mottled brass plaque:

TALGARTH PRIORY CHILDREN'S HOME

It's all died back for the Winter, so Fran gets a good view of the field to her left, and the low outbuildings, and the large grey house which fills the windscreen of Lizzie Preece's Mini.

There are cows in that field come summer, says Lizzie,
And the Reverend Mother's got a little dog, you know!
Penny, I think it's called. Or is it Pepe?

Fran pays no attention; pain is everywhere. Her skin feels
paper thin – and so tight, she's afraid it might split, spilling
her blood all over Lizzie Preece's car. Fran holds herself rigid,
feels her own infliction throbbing under the white cotton of
her sleeve. It's hot when she puts her hand there, stiff when
she twists her wrist. This is hers; it belongs to no one else.
She hopes it hasn't made a mess.

~ ~ ~

Frankie stands in the garden. It's a beautiful blue morning. He
sees a long graze of frost in the shadow of the wall, and a
dew-soaked patch of flattened grass, glittering like evidence.
He rubs his fingers together. They feel greasy. There is a stain
of black on his fingertips where the polish has leaked. He
thinks about Marina, and Fran, and the house at his back with
its mass of children filling every space. Mary in the Box
Room. He wants open air, sunlight, quiet. This place is too
cold for Frankie.

~

We lie in bed until we think it's safe to get up. The usual
odour fills the room, but instead of Fran, silently folding
her sheets in the half-light, there is no one. We change the
bedding for her. Luca wrinkles her nose as she pulls back
the blankets. There's the wet patch in the centre of the sheet,
cold to the touch. Then we see. The pillowcase is flecked
with round brown stains. Beneath it, stars of scarlet streak
across the bed in criss-cross lines. Luca touches one thickening
splash, inspects the smear on her finger, wipes it across a clean
part of the sheet. She is impressed:

Must be *some* tattoo!

eight

Celesta wears a two-piece of shocking crimplene pink, a turtle-neck blouse, and a pair of white patent lace-up boots which don't quite reach the knee. American Tan tights. A look of cool defiance on her face. She makes her entrance as my mother stirs the gravy on the gas ring. Tonight, Celesta has a date with Markus the Manager from the Co-op, and she is not remotely hungry. She is also in disgrace. She stares from a safe distance at the bubbling gravy.

Here she is, says Eva, What a Bobby Dazzler!

The kitchen is full of us; my mother at the cooker, me and Luca and Rose at the table, Celesta in the doorway, and Eva at the sink. She's invited herself round to help my mother, who seems to have forgotten how to do ordinary things like comb her hair or cook our tea. But any attempt at assistance sends her into a fury, so Eva just stands about and smokes. She lights up another cigarette from the stub of her old one, dropping the butt into the bowl of potato peelings.

A real Bobby Dazzler, she persists, trawling the silence.

Rose makes snake-eyes at Celesta, who leans against the pantry door. Celesta stares down at her boots, shifting her handbag up into the crook of her elbow. She looks ready to bolt.

You are going to eat something, aren't you, love, says Eva, pulling out a chair for Celesta.

Last Supper, murmurs my mother darkly. Her displeasure is expressed in code, but we know why she's vexed. Celesta's supposed to be meeting Pippo Seguna tonight; she agreed to it when my father was here. But now he's gone out, and she's got other plans.

You're the image of Cilla in that hair-do, Eva continues, broaching the subject of Hair. A deafening clatter of gravy-pan on stove.

Celesta has been to Panache! in the Castle Arcade, and she's had nearly all her hair cut off. What is left is high and black, and glossy as spun sugar. She reaches up with her fingers to poke at its springiness. A pair of new-moon curls lie sharp along her cheekbones, as if she's been licked by the Devil; deadly spikes fringe her eyes. She is already affecting the habitual jerk of the head which will so infuriate my father. I notice for the first time that Celesta has the makings of a double chin – and tiny ears.

Two photographs, framed in gilt, sit on the mantelpiece in the living room: both of them are of Celesta. Here she is as a very small child, a monochrome bridesmaid standing on a table, a pair of Champagne glasses at her feet, a towering wedding cake on her left. She looks as if she could be a gift – a wonderful doll from a foreign land. My father loves this picture.

In the second photograph, Celesta is clutching a Communion Book. She gazes beatifically into the space beyond the lens, seemingly unaware of the storm around her head. She is backlit and sidelit and glowing like a nebula. So much hair, Mrs Richards from the salon down the street asked for a copy to put in the window. Celesta's face sat there for a year, so that every time my mother went by, she would stop and look, pointing it out to passing strangers.

That's my girl, you know,

as if her daughter lived in the window, behind a skin of yellow foil, and not at home. It didn't seem to matter that Celesta had never entered a salon in her life. Until today, that is: it's her final act of defiance against the prospect of Pippo. Naturally, my mother is raging.

Look at the state of you! she says, waving the spoon, You're in for it, my girl. Celesta sits gingerly on the edge of her chair and puts her handbag on her knees. She stares at the tablecloth. It's my favourite, Exotic Birds of The World, protected under vinyl.

Eva's smile is a conspiracy; she winks at us through the screen of smoke.

It's all The Go now, Mary, she says to my mother's back, Wouldn't mind that style myself.

Suddenly, I'm aware of everyone's heads. Eva's hair is platinum, except for a nicotine-streak of amber running up the left side. She ties it into what she calls a Pleat, with an arrangement of primped tendrils over her brow. I can't see my mother's hair – she's wearing her cap from the bakery; she won't start back until next week, but she wears it all the time. I know what it's like underneath; thin and streaked with grey. Her scalp shines through.

Rose and Luca have the wildest hair, like barbed wire. Mad Locks, my mother calls them, when she's trying to tame them for school. Everyone blames the shock of the fire for my lack of hair. Sometimes, my mother licks the palm of her hand and runs it across the brittle furze on the crown of my head. My hair will be yellow when it grows.

My mother moves round the table, slamming down plates and cutlery and plastic beakers spilling Seguna's orangeade. She lays a place for Fran, forgetting, then snatches the knife and fork away and throws them with a wail into the sink: it's been a month since Fran got taken away.

Just wait until your father sees you, she says, And Christ knows what Pippo will think!

Celesta opens the clasp of her handbag with a soft click, drawing out an assortment of devices; powder compact, lipstick, eyebrow pencil, Mary Quant Matte Make-up. She lines them up in front of her like instruments of torture.

I won't have him, Mam.

You will if your father says, he's gone to a lot of trouble. The trouble he *will* go to − is what my mother means − to make sure Celesta doesn't end up like Ann Jackson.

Celesta opens the tablet of mascara and spits on it, dashing the little wand along the cake until it's muddy. Holding the brush to each eye, she blinks hard, her mouth widening as she sweeps. When Celesta's finished, her lashes are weighed down with the effort. Tiny grits of blackness gather at the corners of her eyes; she picks them out with a pastel fingertip.

No, I tell a lie, it's Dusty, Eva says, pointing her cigarette end at Celesta. Eva inhales and exhales all at once, sucking on the filter as two jets stream from her nostrils. The ash grows long and grey, it bends, it falls, just as she raises the cigarette again to her lips.

Well, it's supposed to be Cathy McGowan, says Celesta, pouting into her compact.

But she's got long hair! cries Rose.

I *know*, Celesta shoots her a look, I meant the *fringe*, stupid! She smooths the powder-puff along the line of her chin; creamy dots sprinkle onto the table. I am awed by this process of beautifying.

Look at this, Dol, she whispers, drawing the powder-puff across my cheek, Close your eyes now.

She draws it once, twice, down the side of my face. There is a faint scent of lilies. She holds up her compact mirror for me to see: my scar is almost invisible. I hold out my bad hand for mending.

~ ~ ~

There are three Pippos reflected in the dressing-table mirror – left-side, right-side, full-on – and as he leans forward to adjust one of the wings, his image bounces into infinite regress. Pippo studies the crown of his head, checks the lick of hair that won't stay flat, pouring more oil from the bottle into his already soaked right hand. He slicks, bends his chin into his neck, takes up his comb and rakes it carefully across his scalp. Pippo casts about for something to wipe his hands on, and finding nothing, grips the ornate handles with his fingertips and drags the top drawer open. It's still full of Maria's underwear, tangled flesh-toned stockings and thick crêpe bandages, bloomers and petticoat slips and a mysterious length of white rubber hosing. He takes up one of the bandages from the pile and holds it to his face; Maria comes back to him in Wintergreen and roses.

Downstairs, Pippo can hear his mother running water in the kitchen, the deep metal thunder of a bucket being filled and the shunk of the pipes as the tap is turned off. He could clean his hands properly, really get rid of the oil – except he doesn't want his Mamma to see him in his good suit and his polished shoes. She'll be scrubbing the steps again, probably – it's a job best done in anger. He hears the front door open and feels the change of air it brings into the room. He'll go out the back way. He tiptoes down, shoes in hand, cringes as the stair-treads creak mutinously under his weight.

Philippo, Ey! cries his mother, swinging the door wide open. She's on all fours in the porch, holding out the scrubbing brush with a rough red hand.

You're not going? she asks.

Pippo sits at the bottom of the stairs and pulls on his shoes.

Yes, Mamma, he says, bent double over his laces. They slip under his greasy fingers, he can't get a loop.

Eh? she says, waving the dripping brush at him.

Yes, Mamma. I'm going.

Pippo softly touches her shoulder as he edges past. Mrs Seguna plunges the brush into the bucket of suds and slaps it down on the front doorstep.

Philippo! Your laces! she cries, as he takes the steps two at a time, almost running into the street.

Pippo doesn't look down, or back, but as the rasp of scrubbing dies away, he can hear the tips of his laces clicking freely against the shiny leather of his shoes.

~ ~ ~

I find out what happened to Celesta on that first date via Luca. She gives up her version grudgingly, sometimes casting her eyes to heaven as if deciding whether I am worthy of being told.

Well. She met Markus in the Milk Bar, she says confidently. And stops. She stops for ages. This is my first brush with suspense.

And then what? I say, jiggling my legs over the side of the bed.

Let me see, she pauses, finger on chin, eyes to ceiling. It's so quiet, I can hear ringing in my ears, the soft whining of Jackson Jackson, and his chain as it grates against the door of Number 1. He's been put out in the rain again. I jump off the bed and go to the window where I can see his soaked back end protruding from the open door, his tail wagging hopelessly from side to side.

What's it worth? Luca muses. Nasty. I think of all the things I've got that Luca might want. It amounts to every-thing, except my impetigo, which no one on earth would want. I make an offer.

Fuzzy Felts?

Her lip curls. Nah, she says.

Of course not.

How about . . . She stops, shakes her head, thinks, continues, How about your Bunty collection?

I'll give you two, I start to say, but as soon as she realizes that I'm trying to bargain, she draws her finger and thumb across her sealed lips with a sharp Zipp! I'm so desperate to know what happened to Celesta, I give in. Luca sidles up to the window, spits on her hand and holds it out to me: I do likewise, and we shake.

Luca says after they went to the Milk Bar, Markus took Celesta to his Mansion, where they had a whole pig for dinner (from the Co-op meat counter), served with Barley Wine, and Knickerbocker Glories for pudding. I'm suspicious of the Barley Wine detail. Luca has been fixated with it ever since she found a bottle in the cupboard under the stairs and drank half of it in situ. But I let it pass. After this, they went to see Gene Pitney at The Capitol. That's when Celesta fainted and had to be lifted over the barriers they use to protect big stars like Gene. When she woke up, someone had stolen her boots.

This is not true. Celesta's boots are on the floor of the pantry. They're not white any more, they're a dingy grey; the laces are treacle brown, and some of the eyeholes have closed up as if they've been in a fight. On the right leg, the plastic has swum down in slow waves. Burning does that. The left boot suffered only minor meltdown, which suggests that Celesta was sitting with the bar-fire on her right when It happened. I'm not sure about what It is, but it must be shocking if it makes your boots melt. My mother says she should have known better. This is true: Fire and the Gaucis are a deadly combination.

No one, not even Rose, knows exactly how Pippo got involved. We question her thoroughly. Her answer is always the same:

I hear a stone at the window, I look out, and there's our Cel and Mr Seguna, standing there looking up. I go downstairs and he's gone. I swear on Mam's life!
and she makes the sign of the cross on her throat.

Celesta says nothing. She hides in her room for most of the day, playing 'All or Nothing' as if her life depends on it. By teatime my mother loses patience.

Will you come down and eat your tea! she shouts from the door of the stairs, And don't mind your father!

We had forgotten about *him*. He hasn't seen Celesta since yesterday morning, and he's keen to find out how her meeting with Pippo went. He doesn't know about Markus or the boots; he doesn't know about Gene Pitney. And my mother has neglected to tell him about Celesta's hair.

My father sits at the table with a claw of garlic in one fist, a rasher of raw bacon in the other. He eats like a dog, with his head down, quickly. He doesn't touch my mother's cooking; he'd rather scavenge.

What's the matter with her? he says, looking up at my mother. She coughs nervously.

Last night, she see Pippo? he says, She see him, Mary?

Not exactly, she says, Now, Frank, before you start . . .

Celesta turns the stairs. She sits down at the edge of the table. Her hair is a fright; the left side is battered flat where she's been lying on it all day, but the right side has compensated for this — it's a cliff.

My father puts the garlic down on the table in front of him, slowly. He studies it for a minute. There's nothing to see, apart from a few flakes of tissued skin and the wound where he's torn out a clove. He flicks at it with his fingernail, making it spin on the plate. He looks at my mother. He looks at Celesta. Mother. Celesta. Mother.

Don't look at *me*, says my mother, It's her hair, she can do what she likes with it!

My father leans across the table and puts his face very close to Celesta. She's staring down at the pattern on her plate: she can smell his breath on her. Celesta shuts her eyes, waiting, and when the blow comes it whips round the room like gunshot. The birds on the tablecloth rock in front of my eyes. My mother jumps at my father and holds his second punch by the wrist; she won't lose Celesta this way.

That's enough, she cries, I've had e-bloody-nough! It's done, Frank!

I concentrate on the trembling magpies and kingfishers until I hear the chair scrape back, footsteps, and finally Celesta above us, sobbing through the ceiling.

What he say now, says my father, breathless with rage, What Pippo say about her!

~ ~ ~

Pippo would say he loves her, even though she stood him up. He would say Fate brought them together. He would say her hair, like her love, will grow.

Pippo waited for Celesta. He stood outside the Seguna Bay with his watch sweating in his palm and felt the seconds, and the minutes, and the hours drip away. He thought about how Celesta might at any moment turn the corner; he would look towards the far end of St Mary's Street and then look back, his face ready to light up when she appeared. He practised it on strangers. Guests arriving at the restaurant thought him overly proprietorial, opening the door for them as they went inside. They couldn't know that Pippo was imagining how he would welcome Celesta this way, smile, shake her hand, ease her coat from her shoulders and pass it nonchalantly to one of the waiters. He would lead her to the table he'd prepared in a private corner of the restaurant, and Massimo would serenade them over Champagne. Pippo warned his staff to be on their best behaviour, but as he stood there in the soft night drizzle, he could sense their eyes staring at his back through the plate-glass window, feel them grinning to each other as they flicked at the tables with their napkins.

While Pippo waited and worried and imagined, Celesta sat

in the glow of Markus's bar-fire, her knees pressed tightly together as his hand fed itself along the hem of her skirt. She pushed it away: it crawled back. Away and back. All the while, his tongue trying to wedge itself between her clenched teeth, and Celesta slipping sideways along the couch. The bristles of the fabric pressing into her shoulder; her boots sweating in the fire's heat; Markus's fingers zippering against her American Tan tights. The way his face looms close to hers – unfocused, but the heat so familiar, she cannot stand it. At last, out of breath with her lipstick smeared all over her face, Celesta opens her mouth to him. Bites hard on his bottom lip. A taste of blood. She flees.

~

Ten o'clock: Pippo decides there must be something wrong. Perhaps Celesta's had an accident; perhaps her mother is sick again. It doesn't occur to him – because Frank Gauci has given his word – that Celesta might just not turn up. Making his way towards our house, Pippo catches sight of a young woman clinging to the ironworks at the town end of Devil's Bridge; he switches over to the opposite side of the road, but when he recognizes Celesta he crosses back again. She's crying. She jumps when she first sees him, then her shoulders sink and she turns her back. He can't think of anything to say. He looks down at the puddle of rainwater near her feet.

Celesta, he whispers, thrilling at the sound of her name on his lips, It's me, Pippo.

I know, she says, dismissive, We met at your wife's funeral. Remember?

Celesta blows heavily into her handkerchief. She doesn't want to look at him; after what Markus tried to do, she'd be happy not to look at another man in her whole life. But staring at her boots simply reminds her. The tears come again. Pippo waits quietly at her side.

We should have met *tonight*, he says, when she's composed herself, But perhaps your mother is unwell?

Celesta looks at him properly. He's offering her an excuse.

She's much better now, thank you.

Pippo smiles shyly at her, his face cast down so that Celesta sees his long eyelashes beneath his thick brows, and the wild sprig of hair standing proud of his head, the broad shoulders of his rain-soaked suit glittering under the streetlight. He looks harmless. Celesta makes a decision.

Would you like to walk me home? she says, holding out her elbow to be taken.

~ ~ ~

Markus tries hard to make it up to her; he realizes raw meat is not the way to win Celesta's heart, let alone any other part of her body. Over the next month there follows a whole Christmas of gifts: a round tin with a cake inside; a small black velvet box—

An engagement ring? asks my shocked mother.

A locket with his hair in it, says a miserable Celesta.

—followed by a Monopoly-sized box of chocolates, some with silver wrappers on; a pair of Dior stockings; and, finally, a wreath.

Is he off his top? my mother cries. She has spent the last five minutes trying to convince Errol, our exhausted postman, that there hasn't been a death in the family. Celesta studies the wreath, flipping the card with an air of indifference.

'From Your One and Only Markus', my mother reads, over Celesta's shoulder.

You'd better tell him about Pippo, my girl.

~

Pippo is also keen. He's been Walking Out with Celesta, as Eva puts it, every night for two weeks now, always bringing her back to our door, where he bows and kisses her hand but never imposes on her face. Sometimes he drives her into town to see a show, or out to the Valleys for supper. He's even doing his own deliveries. Seguna's Soft Drinks

Wagon now calls every weekday; Pippo parks right outside our door.

You must get through a lot of pop, says Alice Jackson archly.

Just be grateful you don't have to walk so far for yours, snaps my mother, Or will I ask him to shift up the road again? She waits until the other women have bought their drinks before she gets her order. These days, we get it all at a discount. We call him Pip the Pop, but not to his face, and never in front of Celesta – not now she's had time to think it through. In her dreams, Celesta would go to London, become a model, marry a rock star. Mick Jagger would be nice, but she'd settle for Peter Noon. Celesta knows these are not real choices. She can have Markus with his creepy hands and his greasy parcels of bacon; or she can have big soft Pippo and all the fizz she can drink. It helps that Pippo has lots of money and a nice house. It helps that he's kind. But more than anything, it is my father who helps Celesta choose. She thinks about the thick sting of his rage, his hands on her, his breath hot on her hair. It happens as quickly as blinking: she will have Pippo. Suddenly, Celesta is fiercely protective. Loyal as a wife.

Aw, Mam, look, she says, holding up the curtain at the front window, Look what he's gone and done!

Pippo has discovered that Celesta likes Dandelion and Burdock best of all, so he's had the side of the wagon repainted; a huge dripping heart with a motto inside: *All Because Selesta Loves D&B!*

He's nothing if not original, says my mother.

Aye, says Eva, deadpan, He isn't, is he?

He's spelt it wrong! shouts Rose.

Aw, Love'im! says Celesta, determined to be smitten.

nine

We're supposed to be bridesmaids. Eva's made our costumes
– she's very handy with a Singer – but there's something
wrong with the fit: you could put another one of me inside
my dress, but Luca has to be jemmied into hers. Every time
she moves, her bodice creaks with the strain. The wedding's
tomorrow. Not much time to sort things out.

Have you put on weight, love? Eva says, frowning at
Luca.

I don't think she has, Ee, says my mother, turning Luca
round and yanking at the seams, Let's measure again, shall
we? Fetch us the sewing-box, Dol.
I put my lolly in my mouth so that I can lift the sewing-box
off the sideboard. It's been pushed to the back, it's a bit of a
stretch and before I can grasp it, the box slides off and upends
itself on the mat. Everything spills out. A troupe of buttons
roll away like a *Come Dancing* formation team; the measuring
tape yawns across the lino; a stack of pins sits on the folded
cutting from *True Crime*. I don't want my mother to see it;
she's been much better since Celesta agreed to marry Pippo.
She's started cooking our dinner again and not burning it, and
she hardly ever stands on the back doorstep at night, singing
that humming song. Rose says it's because my father stays at
home, so she doesn't get the chance. I think she means the

chance to run away, but when I say this, Rose just gives me a look.

You are one stupid Crip, she says, She's waiting for that Joe Medora to come back.

If my mother sees his picture, it might set her off again. I'm reaching over to hide it when she shouts at me,

Quick, Dol, find those buttons!

And hearing Luca creak, she yells:

Stay where you are, You! Don't Bend!

I crawl under the table and inspect the floor. Balls of dust roll like tumbleweed in the draught of my breath. My mother lifts the *True Crime* article by the edges and slips the stack of pins back into the sewing-box. She opens the page, folds it again, puts it away.

Any news? asks Eva, her eyes darting at the box. My mother shakes her head.

Not a thing, she sighs.

I can feel Luca listening in the silence. I will her not to ask anything, not to make a sound; it'll only stop them.

You'd think they'd send a picture – or something! _

How long is it now? asks Eva.

It was – when? My mother takes a deep breath in – December, 1960. Some Christmas that was!

Five years, says Eva, her eyebrows high on her forehead

An' five months, give or take. And nothing. Nothing! She could be dead.

There's deep silence, except for the sound in Eva's throat. Her lips pop open and shut.

You've seen *him*, though, she says, He's been round here. My mother looks at her.

Has he? she says, so it sounds like a challenge, and then slyly, How d'you know that?

Eva waves a hand in the air.

Take no notice of me, Mary. It's your business. Anyway,

135

she says at last, Your Marina's probably leading the life of Riley!

Like Next-Door Riley? asks Luca.

Never you mind, snaps my mother — then suddenly noticing me — Dolores! What are you doing with that lolly? You'll be ruined!

She'll be just fine, says Eva soothingly. She stretches the measuring tape along the length of Luca's body, You'll see, Mary, it'll all be just fine!

~ ~ ~

Salvatore watches Frankie intently. Frankie the Manager is just like Frankie the Partner — bossy, extravagant, full of deals and schemes — except, these days, Frankie doesn't worry about profit.

It's Joe's Business, he laughs, when The Moonlight is empty and takings are low, Not *my* Business, habib!

Salvatore doesn't join in at these times: it's half *his* business, too. But he gave in when Frankie suggested they hold the Men's Party at The Moonlight. After all, they are old friends. As long as Joe didn't find out; as long as Frankie paid for the drinks. But Frankie *never* wants to pay. He rinses out the empty Seguna's drinks bottles and lines them up on the counter.

Pippo gonna know, you know, Salvatore says.

Frankie takes the funnel and up-ends it into the neck of the first bottle.

Pass it, he says, nodding at the flagon of Low's Soda, He won't. It taste all the same, this.

Frankie fills each bottle in turn with the cheaper substitute, wiping them down with his tea-towel before wrapping it around his hand and screwing the caps up tight. When he finishes the Soda, he starts on the Lemonade. He'll do the same with the Pale Ale too. Frankie has to pay for the party tonight, and the wedding reception at the Seguna Bay tomorrow. So much for having a tycoon in the family. Since the marriage has been agreed, discount has gradually stopped; now Pippo charges business rates for everything. Frankie shouldn't care – he has a steady income – but he's also got a plan. Once a week, he follows Salvatore up the wooden stairs to the top room where he is paid his wage. The amount Frankie gets hasn't altered in five years, but it isn't this that hurts him. Following Salvatore up the stairs! And then waiting outside until he's called, as if he's casual labour, a nobody. He doesn't understand what Salvatore, in his simplicity, does: that Frankie should be grateful to have this job at all. Frankie sees only the mean way Salvatore has of bending at the safe, his arm crooked around the metal door like a child hiding a drawing. Over time, Salvatore relaxes his regime, and Frankie is able to notice other things: the sound of the top drawer opening before Salvatore calls him in; the chime of a key; the way the wedge of bank notes inside the safe grows and vanishes; grows again, and vanishes. He makes a careful study of this cycle. This week, the safe is full of money. Everything is in order. He looks at his friend Salvatore, and almost starts to feel sorry. But Salvatore, enjoying the sight of Frankie at work, shifts on to his other elbow, and starts again:

I can tell, me, Salvatore boasts, If *I* can tell . . .

He lets his words hang in the air, shaking his head in mock warning. Frankie flashes him a hot look. Shut up, it says.

You finished making the food for tonight? asks Frankie, knowing this change of subject will give Salvatore something else to lament.

When Salvatore heard that the wedding was definite, he made a special trip to the Seguna Bay, declared to Pippo that he would be honoured to prepare the wedding lunch. Pippo refused him.

You are not family, Salvatore, he admonished when

pressed, Frank may bring a dish to the restaurant if he would like. But my *chef* will cook the wedding lunch.

Salvatore's cheeks burned scarlet.

Not family! he cursed under his breath, *Your* chef – he's not family!

But Pippo simply smiled as he showed him to the door.

~

Now Salvatore is fired again by the insult.

It's tradition, Frankie, he cries, You should have insist! The family of the bride make the food!

The Segunas make the profit, says Frankie slyly, lighting a cigarette. The smoke rises, then buckles as he waves his hand in the air. He leans across the row of sticky bottles. Confidential.

Habib, this man is not like us. He's city Maltese – a 'Business Man', says Frankie, mocking Pippo's clipped tone, He want us to *pay*.

And how you pay? asks Salvatore. With a despairing sweep of arm, he takes in the bruised velvet of the booths, the dark stains of hair oil on the walls above, the carpets shiny with wear,

Where you find the money?

Frankie looks directly into Salvatore's sad brown eyes. I know where to find it my friend, he almost says, But I won't touch it. *I* won't touch it.

No worries, Sal! He says finally, It's a sure thing. This is *my* problem, he smiles, Not your problem!

Frankie takes up the tea-towel and sweeps it across the spills and circles on the counter. Balls it up and throws it into the sink.

I must go and make a dish! he says, winking at Salvatore. He rubs his hands together. Sticky.

~

In the yard at the rear of The Moonlight, Salvatore pauses. Something is nagging at him. Something Frankie said. He goes over the conversation in his head as he unhooks the hasp on the outhouse door. Salvatore has stored the food in here, away from Frankie's hungry gaze, his quick fingers. The odours rise up in flashes of colour; pink meat, brown pastry crust, salt beef, and the slippery green damp of brick − a palace of smells. So absorbed is Salvatore that he almost doesn't see the rat. It sits upright on his mound of meat pies − the muslin lifted daintily back from the corner of the rack − nibbling on an edge of crust. Salvatore snatches the spade propped against the cobwebbed window and smashes it down on the escaping rat, and the rest of the pies, and the hock of ham which flies at him like a severed limb before bouncing on to the flagstones. Salvatore's skin prickles with sweat and fear. He forgets what it was that was bothering him. Leaning heavily on the shank of the spade, he surveys the floor beneath the trestle. All he can see are blobs of aspic, twinkling like diamonds against the dusty stone.

~ ~ ~

In the six months since Celesta met Pippo on Devil's Bridge, not a hair on her head has been cut. Now she sits in the window of Panache!, swivelling from side to side in the plastic chair.

Well, says Veronica, drawing in the air with her comb, I could do a sorta posy.

A what?

Like this, see? she says, lifting the mass of curls and scooping them on top of Celesta's head.

I could fix it like tha', see?

A bun, mutters Celesta, I'm not having a bun.
Veronica stares gloomily at Celesta through the mirror. She lets the hair fall.

An' you can't cut it? You sure?

Positive.

Celesta studies her reflection as the hair softens around her head. She hasn't slept, what with the dress fandango and Meek's not being able to match up her shoes and gloves, and as she looks into the mirror her eyes glint back like two slivers of jet. I look like a bear, she thinks, a Grizzly. Veronica scratches her own head with the pointed end of her comb.

I dunno then, she says, leaning behind the mirror to look through the window into the arcade, Maybe something with Spring flowers?

Like a May Queen? asks Celesta, inspired.

Something like that, yeah, says Veronica, waving and smiling at someone through the glass, A May Thing.

~ ~ ~

We're waiting in the long hallway for Fran. The top half of the wall is painted cream, the bottom half chocolate-coloured gloss, with wavy scratches running all the way along. The windows remind me of school; too high up to see out of but big enough to show you what you're missing – to let you see the sky. It goes from blue-white to soft grey as we wait. This place smells like school as well.

Peugh, says my mother, Carbolic.

She's so nervous, she keeps swapping her handbag from arm to arm. She strokes the side of her face with her knuckles, fiddles with my clothes.

Sit up straight, Dol, she'll be here in a minute, she says, twitching the collar of my coat. She dances a finger lightly across the scab on my knee.

Don't pick it, she warns, even though I wasn't going to.

Luca runs up and skids to a fantastic halt on the lino, like an ice-skater.

Where's our Fran? she moans, swishing her feet from side to side, watching as the pleats on her skirt fan out, It's *boring* here!

She'll be along soon, says my mother, Come and sit down.

Luca runs to the end of the corridor and slides around the

corner. We watch her go, then appear again holding the hand of a tall woman in a costume.

Aw God, whispers my mother, Sister Anthony.

The nun smiles at us as she hands Luca back.

We found Lucia running up the corridor! she says brightly.

I wasn't! shouts Luca, I was sliding!

It's *Luca*, says my mother tartly.

Sister Anthony beams down at Luca, her hands pressed together like an angel.

A boy's name! she exclaims, How uncommon!

Not so uncommon, Sister *Anthony*, says my mother, clipped.

Sister Anthony passes by, opens a door – filling the corridor with the cries of children – and shuts it again. Quiet. The next time she appears, she's got hold of Fran, who's carrying a little grey suitcase.

Here we are, Mrs *Gorsy*, says Sister Anthony, See you soon, Francesca. Be a good girl!

She is, says my mother.

I know, says the nun, smiling again.

It's awkward for a minute. My mother isn't standing up or going anywhere, she's sitting with her palms turned out, as if she's testing for rain. Luca studies the scuff-marks she's just made on the lino and I watch her do it. It's like we've forgotten where to put our eyes.

You fit? says my mother to Fran, which means, is she ready to go. Fran nods. My mother takes the suitcase.

What sort of size is this supposed to be? she says, holding it at arm's length and frowning.

It's called a vanity case, says Fran shyly.

Ah. That's good. They teach you lots here then, says my mother.

She pushes open the big door and we duck under her arm, out into the fresh air. My mother walks in front with Fran; they don't touch but they bump against each other as they make their way up the drive. Fran's only just eleven but she's nearly as tall as my mother. And thin. She's wearing the Home's uniform; brown blazer, brown skirt, tan stockings. The hem on the skirt has come down, and Fran stops now and then to scratch the back of her leg where the thread is tickling. Her hair is in two plaits.

She looks like the Four Marys, whispers Luca to me.

What, all of them? I ask.

Luca pushes me so hard I lose my balance and fall on to the gravel. Now my other knee will be scabbed.

No, stupid! Luca exhales loudly, Mary Cotter – the ugly one!

All the way home, on the bus and down the road to our street, I worry about what Rose and Celesta will say. It's true, Fran doesn't look like one of us any more. She looks strange. Even my mother talks to her politely, as if she's a neighbour's child. I think it's because she's still angry with Fran over the fire and all the trouble, but when we reach the front door my mother lifts her off the pavement and squashes her tight against her chest.

Lovely to have you home, she says, My Little Angel!

~

From the brow of the hill, Frankie sees the bus pull into the kerb. He shifts the box under his other arm, feels the tipping weight inside and the scuffling against his chest. He watches as the four figures make their way towards Hodge's Row; that unmistakeable gesture Mary has – stopping dead in the road while she waves the children across – and then he sees us, he sees Fran, and he starts to run for home.

~ ~ ~

Salvatore's top lip glistens with sweat. His hands are moist as he carries the racks of food from the outhouse, along the narrow passage, then sideways through the back door into The Moonlight. He uncovers the pies and slides them on to a silver tray, holding the rack down at his side as he arranges and rearranges them into a neat pile, nudging them into position with the tip of his finger. Then back out into the night air for the salvaged hock of ham. It looks fine, coated again in fresh breadcrumbs. Salvatore picks off some imaginary sawdust, eyeing the spread of food on the long counter: cuts of meat in various shades of pink, spicy sausages, cool slips of cucumber in a bowl of vinegar, blistering chillies on a plate. Frankie said, Why bother with all of this, just make a few sandwiches – but Salvatore is proud. Salvatore is angry. He wants to show Pippo how well he can cook. This is Men's food. There are no sweet things here, nothing dainty, apart from the little almond biscotti he made to go with the Vin Santo. They're Mary's favourite. He looks at them now, fanned out golden against the white lace doyley. He'll save some for her. Salvatore fetches a linen napkin and counts out one, two – five – biscotti for Mary, placing them carefully in the palm of his hand before transferring them on to the cloth. He casts about for somewhere secure to put them. Not back in the outhouse – he's been on guard all day, he can't stand there all night as well. He has an inspired thought: he'll put them in the safe in Joe Medora's office! No rats in there.

~ ~ ~

Celesta won't come down, says Rose as she opens the front door, She says the wedding's off and her hair's a mess. Fran! she yells suddenly, pushing past my mother to get a better look.

What now, groans my mother. She moves to the foot of the stairs and shouts.

Celesta – your sister's here! Frank? Frank!

He's gone to the market, says Rose, hands on hips. Fran wanders over to the mantelpiece, picks up the Communion photograph of Celesta.

What's wrong with her hair?

Pippo don't want her to cut it, says Rose, So she went to Panache! to have it — she searches for the word — Twiddled.

Oh, says Fran, running her hand over the brass bell.

Where's Bambi? she says, looking around the room for the glazed fawn.

Don't ask, says Rose, then tells her, Dadda broke it.

Ah, says Fran. Rose grins at her.

What's in your case then? she says, clicking the locks. Fran opens the lid. Inside there are two pairs of knickers, a vest, a balled-up pair of white socks, a Gideon's Bible, a cream card with a prayer on it in tiny writing, and a rosary.

What's this, says Luca, putting it over her head, A necklace?

It's called a rosary, says Fran, digging in the little pocket sewn into the lid.

Look, Rose, says Luca, a Rosie!

It's for praying with, says Fran, Don't let Dadda see it. Luca tucks the rosary down the neck of her sweater just as my father appears in the doorway. He puts the big box down on the floor and stands there, looking at Fran. His arms open for her, but she's welded to the lino. We've all stopped breathing.

A cough from my mother. She's standing in the kitchen doorway.

You going to give your Dad a hug? she asks. Fran steps around the box and presents herself. She turns her head when he bends to kiss her; her eyes are dead as stones.

Have you brought Fran a present? Luca says, staring at the box. She twists her fingers, dying to open it. My mother gives my father a look. He looks back, shrugs.

No, this is for tomorrow, my mother says, trying to get past Rose so that she can take the box away. She bends to lift it, pauses at the sound of scratching.

Aw, Frank, not alive! she says.

He shrugs again, and before he can stop her Luca pulls up

the flap and peers inside. I know what's in there with the darkness. I wish it wasn't that; Please let it be a Something Else, God, I say quietly. Luca bends back the other flap; a small black and white head pokes out.

Look, Fran! Dadda's bought you a rabbit! she cries.

~ ~ ~

The car is rented, anonymous. The driver wears a suit of grey flannel with thick white stripes woven through it; showy, fashionable, slightly cheap. He slows down as he passes the shopfronts of the old town and the Seamen's Mission. Only the bars are open at this time.

Nice to be back? he asks.

Joe Medora doesn't reply to this.

Surprise him, he says, Tell him I will do business.

Paolo swings the car past The Moonlight and parks around the first corner.

Not coming in for the party?

Joe holds out his hand for the keys. Either Paolo is very stupid or he's playing games with him.

This is business, says Joe emphatically, I'm doing business. With Frankie.

Paolo slips out from behind the wheel, walks with a bright clip towards the end of the street. He can feel Joe's eyes watching him through the windscreen.

No, no, Boss, he says under his breath, *I'm* doing business with Frankie.

~ ~ ~

Sitting with her skirt up over her knees, Fran warms her legs in front of the fire. She's taken off her stockings for my mother to mend, so I can see the bare flesh of her shins, laced with a sheen of long thin stripes. Fran cradles the rabbit in her lap, stroking the soft white belly and the woolly pads of its feet. It lies there with its head turned to one side, eyes closed, perfectly still. She's never had her own rabbit before, not one that was really *hers*: the others – the ones that used to live in the hutch in the garden – they don't count. She doesn't like to think of them, so instead Fran goes through all the things she could feed it. She could go to the Evanses' shop and ask them to save all their old veg. Then she remembers that the shop is burnt down, and that she will have to go back to The Priory. Reverend Mother won't let her have the rabbit there; maybe even the big boys would be cruel to it like they were with that cat one time. She will have to leave it here.

He's enjoying that, says Eva, her mouth riddled with hairpins. She's prodding the side of Celesta's head, tilting it sideways, but her eyes are on Fran.

What you gonna call him, then?

Joey, says Fran, curling her fingers round the paws. Celesta lets out a loud yelp as Eva, jolted, digs a hairpin into her scalp.

Sorry, love, she says. She clears her throat, What about Fluffy? she offers, Or Flopsy?

Joey Joey Joey! cries Luca, bouncing on the chair, so that my mother comes and stands in the doorway. My father appears behind her.

Shut that racket Now! she shouts at Luca, and pointing at Fran, Take that thing outside, you.
My father is wearing his best suit. He is not smiling. His hand goes up, curves itself round the back of my mother's neck – under the nape where the hair is fine and soft – and brings it to rest on her collar. His knuckles are white with pressure. I can feel the air being squeezed from her, but I can't look any more: I can't look at the rabbit, or my mother, or my father, or Fran. Soon there will be nowhere safe to put my eyes.

There! Eva says to Celesta, Now you *are* a Picture!
Celesta gets up from the chair in the middle of the room and stretches her arms out. She peers in the mirror above the

fireplace, side on, head down, chin up. Then she turns round, holds up her compact mirror so that she can view the back.

That's lovely, Eva, she says, You've saved the day.

We'll have to do it again tomorrow, mind! It won't sit like that all night.

Eva has managed, with Kirbygrips and satin buds, to do what the whole workforce of Panache! couldn't. Celesta looks like Cinderella in my *Book of Wondrous Tales*. A princess. Pippo will faint when he sees her.

With her mouth slightly open and her eyes hard, Celesta turns to face my father and mother.

What d'you think? she asks.

My father nods quickly; short, dismissive.

Just like your mother, he says.

It doesn't sound like a compliment. My mother eases herself from his grip.

Go on, Lady, she says to Fran, Put him back now.

Fran slips her bare feet into her sandals and sidles past my father. His head turns to watch her. He picks up his hat from the table and jams it on his head.

Frank, says my mother, nodding at the rabbit, Remember what I said.

Sure thing, he says, Sure Thing.

~ ~ ~

Salvatore stands in the darkening outhouse, one hand on the broom, the other gripping the door. He's searched all over; he still hasn't found the rat. He imagines it escaped, cowering under the bar, or beneath one of the booths, ready to spring out just when Pippo makes his speech to the men. He opens the door wide, but the light has gone now; he can hardly see the flagstones under his feet, let alone the rat. Salvatore is relieved; he tells himself he would kill it if he did. Sure thing, he whispers, trying out his courage. Sure Thing, he says again, suddenly remembering Frankie. That was what he said. Just like last time. As if it were yesterday, Salvatore sees the slow curve of Frankie's last coin on the polished counter, and a house on fire, and a hospital ward with a screaming child. Salvatore realizes that Frankie has formulated A Plan. He rests the broom against the spade; they grate together, sliding down the wall and smashing on the stone floor. In the top room of The Moonlight, the window-blind shifts once and is still. The birds screech in the tree next door. A car backfires on the street.

~ ~ ~

I walk the plank. It's slippery in the darkness, I can't keep my balance. I fall off twice into the squelching mud, but no one notices or cares because we're all concentrating on Fran and the rabbit hooked up against her chest. She moves slowly in front of me. The rabbit's eyes glow red over her shoulder. After the plank, there are housebricks for stepping stones, difficult to see now that we're at the far end of the garden. The old hutch squats against the wall. I don't play at this end, not since Rose and Luca locked me in. There's straw and paper in there, and sometimes there are babies. I must not interfere with anything.

Stand back, says Rose, I can't see! She bends down to open the little square door, fumbling with the catch. Luca pulls me out of the way so that the light from the kitchen window shines down the path. Looking back towards the house, we seem too far away. I can see my mother in the window, moving about in the square of light like an actress on television. It's the end of May but it's cold out here. It's often cold out here.

Fran eases the rabbit inside the hutch, lifting the back legs gently over the wooden shelf; it scrabbles against this new home, bucking in her arms. Once in, Rose slams the door.

Got a scratch? asks Luca, watching Fran inspect her wrist.

It's nothing, says Fran, rubbing. She holds up her arm in

the faint light, to show us the two red score marks rising on her skin. She's yet to show us her tattoo.

Bang!

We all turn to face the house. I'm thinking of gas ovens exploding, of *True Crime* and murderous men in hats, but I can hear my mother's sudden laugh, and Eva shouting Cheers, Cel! against the dull clunk of mugs being knocked. Eva's tall frame fills the doorway.

C'mon, kids, she shouts, We're drinking a toast to your sister!

Forgetting the rabbit and the plank, we run through the slippery mud into the house.

~ ~ ~

The Moonlight is thick with men in suits: Bonni Ferrugia, big in timber; Mario Cordona, tipped as favourite for the next Lord Mayor; the O'Connell twins, head and shoulders above the rest. They're really smart, they wear silk cravats instead of ties. Only Lou Peruzzi, known all over Cardiff as Mr Metal, is casually dressed. Salvatore knows Cordona by his picture in the *Western Mail*, but he doesn't recognize Peruzzi. When he sees him saunter up to the bar and help himself to two glasses of Champagne, he intervenes, gripping the little man's arm above the frayed cuff of his shirt and levering it back down on the counter. He removes the glass from his hand, puts it back on the tray.

One is enough, eh? says Salvatore smartly. He searches the room for Frankie – he'll throw this bum out as soon as he gets the nod. Peruzzi stares at him, astonished.

This is Lou Peruzzi you talk to! he says, pointing a thumb at his own chest. Salvatore looks down at the man; his collar's askew and the middle button is missing off his shirt. His vest pokes off-white through the gap.

Ah, Lou, says Frankie, suddenly appearing at his side, Take another Champagne! My friend Salvatore – we need a talk!

He smiles politely as he moves among the guests, but Salvatore feels a rage rising like steam off Frankie's back. He follows him through the kitchen and out into the yard. Frankie slams the door.

You crazy! he shouts, Peruzzi is important man!

A slob! shouts Salvatore back, outraged at the thought of Peruzzi's grimy fingers on his food, See how much he drink!

Who cares? Me – I don't care! Let him drink!

But the money, Frank. Champagne—

Frankie turns his head away as if to spit, then puts both his hands up close to Salvatore's face. He speaks very slowly, as if he's addressing a child.

Just – give them – the drinks, he says quietly, For me, Salvatore. Just serve!

Frankie turns away, shrugging inside his suit as he closes the door.

Salvatore gazes up at the mess of stars. They look like punch-holes in the night. The way Frankie speaks to him! He stands at the back door, letting the anger ripple through him until he is breathing normally again. At the kitchen window, he sees the crowd part as Pippo ambles through the gap. Frankie greets his future son-in-law in a swift embrace. Salvatore thinks it is a sacrifice for Frankie, to give his beautiful daughter to this man. It's important, he thinks, softening, An important time – for all the family.

~ ~ ~

Rose drinks the water down in one long draught then uses her petticoat to dry the glass. She upends it on to the floor just beside the bed.

What you doing? asks Luca, tunnelling her nose with her finger.

We're going to have a seance, says Fran, We do it all the time in the Home.

No we're not, says Rose, bending down low, We're going to listen!

We all listen. You don't really need any equipment to hear Eva — Foghorn, my mother calls her — but the other voices are a muddle, indistinct. Rose makes a noise like Dr Reynolds does when he listens to my chest.

Ah, she goes, Ah, Uhh.

Let me hear! cries Luca, bouncing off the bed. She crouches down and puts her ear to the glass, her eyes staring up at us. The blood rushes to her face. She raises her eyebrows.

What they saying? I whisper.

Shh!

Let me!

I want to listen too, but Luca puts the glass behind her back.

They said — she stops to think, her eyes going sideways now to get it right — Eva said, 'Cel, you have to do a sexy with Pippo!'

Luca lets out a raucous scream, falling back on the bed; Rose slaps her thigh with mirth. This is obviously a funny thing. Only Fran is unimpressed.

You have to have *sex*, she says quietly, That's what she'd have said.

I s'pose you do that in The Home as well? sneers Rose.

Some of them do, yeah. I do other stuff.

Like tattoos? asks Luca innocently.

Yeah, says Fran, taking the bait.

~ ~ ~

Salvatore leans on the counter and sips his Advocaat. The room is densely crowded now with lots of people he doesn't know. Beautiful, fresh-faced girls with their hair piled up high and their coral-coloured mouths, hanging on to a man or to each other. Sometimes he pours drinks for them, smiling shyly with his tongue stuck in his head, or he passes round a plate of food, moving his way slowly among the pastel scents and cigar smoke. Pippo Seguna is wedged in the corner, his head cocked at an angle as he tries to read the label on a gramophone record. Frankie leans against the booth, talking; his hands make circles and close, emphatic chops in the space in front of him. He is having a conversation with someone Salvatore doesn't recognize. Salvatore is struck by the other man; the way he listens to Frankie, nodding, a slight smile now and then. His face is full of concentration, but his look is sidelong, fixed on the door marked Private. He wears a suit with stripes in it which glint every time he moves. This man cannot stay still; he repeatedly touches his hair, a nervous, agitated swipe across his head. Pippo, standing just behind the man, mirrors this gesture. Salvatore realizes that they are brothers.

Salvatore! cries Frankie, noticing him, Come meet Paolo. Salvatore shakes the man's hand. It is damp. He doesn't like him at all.

~ ~ ~

Fran uncovers her left arm first. From the crease of her elbow to an inch above her wrist runs a long thick scar, a blue-white strike against the sallow brown of her skin. Intersecting the wound is a shorter slash, trailing down at one side: the two lines form a pale blue crucifix. The wound is puckered like a burn from repeated scraping. Fran lets Luca run her finger along it before she hooks up the other sleeve. This time the tattoo is inky; bits of blue leak out from the lettering. FRAN, it says.

Bernard did that for me, with India-Ink.

He your boyfriend? asks Rose, her eyes fixed on the letters.

Yeah, says Fran, But don't tell Mamma.

Why not? I say.

Fran pulls her sleeves down and folds her arms,
She wouldn't like it, she says, He's a Half-Caste.

~ ~ ~

Frankie drags the girl through the crowd, gripping her hand tight as she bumps and trips behind him, right up to the counter and Salvatore.

Sal, he shouts, Say hello to Rita!

Salvatore looks at her. She is plump and dark with a fine down of hair covering her bare arms. A gold locket at her throat.

Gina, she says, hurt, I'm *Gina*.

Give her a drink, says Frankie, ignoring her.

Salvatore smiles kindly as she holds out her glass to him. They are always Rita, or Sophia, or Gina. The girls change but the names don't.

I'd like some champagne, she says.

Salvatore bends down behind the bar and fetches up another bottle, so he doesn't see Paolo moving quickly across the room. Salvatore unwraps the foil, twists off the wire, eases out the cork, and pours. The foam shoots up the glass. He loves the effect this has on the girls, the tiny shiver of panic on their faces as the bubbles flash to the rim, the way they close their eyes for that first sip. Salvatore is watching this. He isn't watching the door marked Private as it opens and shuts.

It takes a minute for Paolo to find the key to the safe. Another minute, his pockets full of money and his mouth full of biscotti, and he is back at Frankie's side. Frankie is laughing now, his eyes on Salvatore as all four raise their glasses in a toast. He doesn't need to look at Paolo to know: now, he can do business with Joe.

~ ~ ~

I lie awake waiting for my mother to come up. I can't sleep until I've asked her about half-caste. Because that's what *we* are: that's what they call us at school. I can't see why my mother wouldn't like Fran's boyfriend if he's just the same as us. I try to concentrate on Half and Whole, but through the bedroom wall I can hear Rose talking to Celesta. She must be telling her about Fran's tattoos and her boyfriend, because every now and then Celesta goes, Oh my God! and, Wait 'til Mam finds out! Then it's quiet, just Luca grunting in her sleep and a strange mumbling sound from Fran. I know this noise – it's like Carlotta, telling her rosary. It makes me very tired to hear it.

amulet

The kitchen doesn't get the light in the evenings. I'd forgotten. My way downstairs seems shorter too, a few quick steps, a right turn, the final three steps with the last one wider than the rest. You could sit here, on the bottom step. I try it now. It feels awkward, cold; there's a draught blowing down from upstairs. I haven't checked the other bedrooms properly. Perhaps there's a window open, or a pane smashed. It feels wrong to sit on this step, my back exposed to the chill. Nothing to lean against. The door shutting off the upstairs has been removed. That's what the difference is: you used to be able to rest your back on the closed door. The hinges have gone, leaving two shallow depressions top and bottom of the frame. I put my hand on the one nearest me. It's been painted over. Beneath my fingers, the solid drips of gloss feel like a message in Braille. I wonder if my mother painted it. The idea of shutting off the stairs, hiding up from down, it appeals to me now.

I want to run away. I want my warm flat, my warm yellow kitchen again. This room looks so empty. In my head, it's full of people, steamy with smoke and cooking smells and talk. Perhaps my mother had a home help; or maybe the social services have been here and cleared up. I should go through the drawers before the others arrive, sort things out: if there's something to be found, I want to find it.

I'm sure it used to be sunny in this room: it *was* lighter in the mornings. I try to recall it, with the chill coming down and the darkness coming down – what it was like, the day of the wedding.

Something wakes me and I can't place it; a sound perhaps, a cry. It's early yet, but I'm excited: I've never been a bridesmaid before. My mother is still asleep and as I slide away from her, she turns herself round towards Luca. I creep downstairs. The air tells me that the back door is open, but there's an odd smell drifting up, like iron: a hot tangy heat. Such a wet smell.

The kitchen is full of sunshine, the back door slightly open; it's like the outside has come in. The taps dazzle over the sink, and the sound is rushing water, spilling from the cold tap, trapping threads of sunlight in its stream. I can hear birdsong and feel a warm breeze, and everything is Right and Summer, except for that smell.

From the last step of the stairs, I see it all: my father with his hand inside the rabbit. He's pulling hard on the split fur, tearing the length of the body. The skin slides back on itself. Underneath, the flesh is purple and shining like rubies.

When he sees it's only me, he smiles.

Come and look, he says, as if he's going to do a party trick, produce a coin from my ear, or a rabbit from this bloody skin,

See, the heart.

He glides his hand over the naked head, stops just below the neck. The chest throbs once, twice. The sun sparks on this wetness.

Look, he says, Fresh! I cook a special dish for the marriage! He peels the fur. It squeaks over the thighs, the hind legs. My father takes up his knife and hacks at the feet. He puts the rabbit's foot aside, turning it with a slick thumb.

For Good luck, he says, For Celesta.

ten

You've got to eat *something*, Dol. There'll be no food, mind, until after the church! My mother strokes my hair, but the feel of her hand sliding down my head makes me want to be sick. The rabbit, naked, slippery. It looked like a new-born.

Excitement, I expec', says Eva, Best not to force her. Hasn't put *you* off though, has it, Petal? she says, watching Rose scoop up a forkful of food from Celesta's plate.

It'll only go to waste, says Rose, spraying blobs of scrambled egg as she speaks.

Yeah, your waist, says Celesta. She scrapes her chair back with disgust, but that look could be nausea: her face echoes mine with its green, damp tinge. I wonder if it's because she can smell the dead rabbit smell. I haven't told anyone what I saw this morning, not even my mother. She knows though – when Fran gets up from the table to go and feed the rabbit, my mother stops her.

Come here, You, she says, holding her by the wrist, Let's try this frock, shall we?

Fran's grown so tall in the past six months, her old clothes don't fit her any more. We've tried her with Rose's, but they're no good; they hang from Fran's narrow shoulders like sacking. Eva has donated a frilly yellow summer dress;

puff-sleeves, full skirt, layers of petticoats underneath. I think it's fabulous. Fran is having none of it.

I'll look like a banana, she says, pulling away.

I'll give you banana, my girl, Now stand still!

My mother jerks her round, starts undoing Fran's shirt.

I can go in my uniform! she cries as my mother lifts it, half-unbuttoned, up Fran's body.

You bloody can't!

Fran's cuffs are still done up. My mother pulls the shirt over Fran's head; her hair stands high with static, clings to the sides of her face. My mother is pulling now on the sleeves and all I see is the rabbit with its skin folding back on itself. I'm sick again, quickly. It comes out like it hasn't got anything to do with me; a river, a rainbow, a blackness. The lino on my cheek is blue and very cool.

~ ~ ~

In his big draughty bathroom, Pippo is singing a medley.

I eat Antipasta twice just because she is so nice, Celesta Gauci!

slapping at the suds floating like islands on the surface of the water,

Buonasera, Signorina, Buonasera! It's time to say good-night to Napoli!

He scrubs his chest, rosy from the hot water, as he goes through his repertoire. Salvatore may not be the best cook in the world, thinks Pippo – not enough salt for *his* liking – but he has a very fine collection of gramophone records. He dips the flannel between his thighs, swirls it in the foam, slaps it up over his neck. The steam smokes off his body.

He ponders the business of the drinks, remembering the stickiness of the bottle, the gummy feel of the label as he poured himself a soda. Shame, he thinks. As if he, Pippo Seguna, wouldn't notice the difference! Two-bit crooks!

Pippo frowns into his bathwater, recalling the embarrassment of Frank Gauci kissing all the guests.

Peasant! says Pippo, so loudly that his mother, spooning another egg onto Paolo's plate, looks up in surprise. Then Pippo's clipped English gives way entirely,

Ti Amo, Celesta! he shouts, Mia Regina!
Paolo pauses, looks enquiringly at his mother.

A queen, eh? he whispers across the table.
She throws her head back in a silent laugh.

~ ~ ~

Rose and Luca are congratulating me. This is unheard of. They're sitting on either side of the bed, taking turns to wipe my face with the cloth. It smells of Domestos. They talk like spies on a mission.

Well done, Dol, says Rose, Good tactic!

First rate! shouts Luca into my ear, The commander would be proud of you!
Apparently, I fainted, which prevented my mother from seeing Fran's tattoos. This is a good thing, or as Rose says in her strangled voice,

Top Hole, DSG! Sterling work!
I don't want to faint again, if that's what she means. It was like being turned inside out – which I must not think about. I do what my mother does when she wants to avoid things: I start to hum. Eva appears in the bedroom doorway with Fran behind her. She takes her hand and pulls her into view. Fran is wearing Eva's yellow dress with a white cardigan over the top. It's one of Celesta's, silky, with a pattern of tiny roses round the neck.

We know everything, Eva says, looking at all of us, Don't we, Fran?
Fran nods, glum.

And we're not going to say a word to *anyone* until afterwards. Especially not your mother. Right?

We all nod. I'm feeling much better now I think that Fran knows about the rabbit, and Eva about the tattoos. Soon there will be no more secrets.

~ ~ ~

Pippo stands at the altar. He turns his head left and right, raises his hand half-heartedly when he spots a familiar face. A bee knocks against the swathe of flowers before him; he sees a sharpness of gold; a prism of stained glass purling across the marble floor. Behind him, people cough and whisper. Someone blows into their handkerchief. Pippo looks round again, catches Salvatore wiping his face. Paolo closes one eye and grins.

Your hat, whispers Pippo from the corner of his mouth. Paolo snatches his hat off and runs a bony hand across his thinning hair, tilting his head a little to the right.

Mary takes her place just in time to see this gesture. For a moment, she thinks she recognizes him. She forgets to genuflect, looking across at Pippo's side of the church to see if anyone has noticed. Mrs Seguna smiles grimly at her from under her black mantilla.

Fuck it, says Mary under her breath, almost sliding out of the pew and starting all over again. But the organ staggers like a bagpipe, searching the air for a tune, and Celesta wanders ghostly up the aisle.

PHOTOGRAPH 1

Bride and Groom. Pippo with his cow's lick of hair on end, Celesta with a flower tipping gently out of hers, so that her hands are caught in mid-air, trying to fix it. Eva calls this picture 'I surrender'.

PHOTOGRAPH 2

Immediate Family. Mary and Frankie, Celesta and Pippo, Mrs Seguna and Paolo in a straight line. Salvatore is just behind them, edging his broad face into the frame. They are all squinting. The grass at Celesta's feet holds the shadow of the photographer; it falls long and thin and black.

PHOTOGRAPH 3

Bridesmaids. Luca has one hand clawed at the neck of her dress – it's the only way she can breathe – and the other one pinching my arm, so I'm not smiling. My mouth looks like a hole's been jabbed through the picture. Fran stands, arms folded, with Rose bent double in front of her: she's doing her impersonation of Quasimodo. You can't hear the bells in this picture, but they're ringing.

PHOTOGRAPH 4

The Best Man Kisses the Bride. Paolo with his hat back on, the brim tipped forward to keep the sun out of his eyes. Behind him, in a far corner of the churchyard, another man is handing something to Frankie. They're frozen in laughter, arms out cuffing each other like a boxing still.

PHOTOGRAPH 5

The Rings. Mary doesn't see this one until it's too late. Frankie stands between Celesta and Pippo, holding their hands together in the cup of his palm. Celesta's ring is heavy and yellow; Pippo's is plain, a thin hoop belonging to his father. He knows the feel of it. And Frankie's ring – a noose of gold with its ruby knot at the centre – is back on the little finger of his left hand.

~ ~ ~

Salvatore sits at the far end of the table with Carlotta to his right, Rose to his left. Then there's Luca and Fran, and opposite them, two boys I don't know. I'm at the other end between Eva and Martineau. It's all wrong, this formation, and Carlotta gets more and more furious as Eva rearranges the place settings.

I promised Mary I'd help Dol cut the meat, Eva shouts down the table, You can't expect her to manage on her lonesome!

She pushes me back down into the seat opposite Salvatore. He gurns at me, smiles widely, puts his thumbs up in the air and waggles them. Carlotta thumps him on the shoulder.

Basta! she cries, so loudly that the two strange boys stop kicking each other and look at her. They spend most of the time lifting the thick white tablecloth and peering underneath. You'd think they'd never sat at a table before.

Salvatore has a gesture for everything. The first course arrives – a pink fan of king prawns covered in orange cream – and Salvatore picks one up, dangles it over his plate, frowns and shakes his head. He holds a conversation with it, bending his ear so that it's nearly touching the prawn's big black eye.

Pardon? he says, What you say?

I can't touch the prawns: you have to break the skin off and I won't, I won't remove the skin from anything ever again. Eva waits until Martineau's finished his and then offers up mine for him to eat. She cracks open the casing on each one, holding them out to him as if she's feeding a dog. I think she's glad Mr Amil wasn't invited.

There's a shout from the kitchen and my father appears, carrying a big metal pot. I know what this is. My heart starts to bang. He leans over my shoulder, spooning some of the stew into my bowl; globs of oil float like blisters on the surface; chunks of dark flesh cling to the stems of yellow bone. I shoot a warning look at Fran, but she's already tearing the meat, holding it dripping to her mouth as her eyes meet mine. I touch the shiny head of a half-submerged potato with the tip of my fork. It slides away from me, sinking beneath the dark red sauce, and I sink after it.

~

You missed the sweet, Dol, says Celesta. There are two of her; she sharpens into focus, falls together. I'm lying on a sofa behind a big curtain. I don't know where I am. My mother's holding my hand.

Did you save her some, Cel? she asks.

Yeah, no worries! God it's hot, she says, fanning her fingers in front of her eyes, No wonder she's out for the count!

She leans over me, rustling like a crisp bag. Celesta is completely transformed. Her white wedding dress is covered in a scatter of green and brown squares. She looks like a chrysalis; the wing of veil around her head, her red face sweating. As if she's squeezing herself through an old, cracked membrane.

What's them? I say, lifting my head from my mother's lap.

Money! says Celesta, her eyes going wide.

I look closely; the squares are ten shilling notes, one pound notes, five pound notes, pinned to the fabric of her dress. My mother removes a sheaf of them with expert plucking.

Mam! What you doing?

Got to make room for more, she says happily, rolling the notes up tight in her fist, Go on and have a dance, love. I'm taking Dol out by the river – get some fresh air inside her.

You can take this an' all then, says Celesta, her mouth going into a moue. She holds up a bandaged lump of fur, unties it from a drawstring around her waist. It's the rabbit's foot. My mother inspects it.

What d'you reckon, Cel, she says, twirling it in front of her, Old, New, Borrowed or Blue?

Smelly, I'd say.

An' dead, counters my mother.

They cackle like a pair of witches.

Aye, alright then, says my mother, I don't expect you'll need it. But don't let on to your father, mind!

I won't tell Paw, says Celesta, sending them both into shrieks of laughter.

My mother undoes the clasp on her handbag and slips the

rabbit's foot inside. I can sense it sitting in the dark at the bottom of her bag, its soft fur flattening as it nestles against her lipstick, her powder compact, her comb. Rubbing its smell all over.

~

Salvatore is not a drinking man – Advocaat, sometimes, when the sadness comes, or a small glass of beer on holidays – but the food was so salty, and the Champagne so light, he's soon quite drunk. He sits on the edge of the stage and watches as the bride and groom do another circuit of the hall, shaking hands and kissing guests. A small boy in a suit races up to Celesta; she bends down for him to pin the money to her veil. Salvatore looks about for Carlotta – they should give something, and she has the purse – then he catches sight of her through the crowd of dancers. She's watching Eva demonstrating the Twist. Eva leans her body forward at an angle, and Salvatore admires the way her waist is nipped in tight, the swing of her golden sandals in her hand, her red toes inching across the wooden floor. Eva's so neat, she could dance in a shoebox, but every part of Carlotta is fluid, like water in a bubble: she goes all to jelly when she Twists. Salvatore likes this too.

~

We stand on Park Place Bridge, next to a low wall covered with moss. I want to touch it, because I know the feel, spongy then wet underneath, but I daren't do this because I'm still wearing my new white gloves. I've had mittens before, but never gloves. My mother has padded out the fingers of the left one with pipe cleaners wrapped with wool. It's wonderful; I can bend them into any shape I like. My hand looks normal, nearly.

Deep breaths, Dol, my mother says, Get some air in those lungs.

She turns her head at the sound of a car. She looks very

beautiful with her new Auburn rinse in her hair and the creamy pearl earrings she borrowed from Eva. Her outfit is a thick brocade of blue with shiny stripes running through it, her handbag is white and hooked over her arm. After a while, she rests it on the wall. Below is the river.

Mam, I say, You know Fran's rabbit?

Yeah, she goes, cautious.

Did Dadda cook it?

She doesn't answer my question. She's looking at the river; she's thinking.

I saw him kill it, I say, staring straight up at her face.

Don't be silly, Dol.

Where is it then, Mam? Where's it gone?

I'm beginning to whine. My mother won't take her eyes off the water.

It escaped last night, she says, turning her head from me so her words are lost to the wind,

. . . Daft sister forgot to put the catch on.

This is a lie. My mother is a liar. I *saw* Rose lock the cage door, and I *saw* my father with his hand inside the rabbit. I saw it with my own eyes. I can't believe anything now.

~

Martineau swings Eva under his arm and spins her, spins her, makes to set her free and then imprisons her again. Her mouth is wide, she laughs and breathes him in; close up, a scent of leather, the gold flecks in his eyes; flung back, the room, all twirling lights and colour. Dizzy, Eva folds her fingers round the edge of his lapel, puts a hand flat on his chest. Where the heat is.

Steady, Tino, you'll have me over! she cries.

Martineau looks down at her and smiles, then glances over her head to the far end of the hall. She watches him as he watches something else. His smile fades and falls. Eva feels his heart jump under his shirt. She turns to follow his gaze, sees two men cutting swiftly through the couples on the dance-floor. The first is Paolo, the best man, but now she knows him from another place – the picture in *True Crime*.

Pippo's brother? she asks, only half a question. Martineau puts his hand over hers and presses it against his chest.

I've not seen him before, he says, his eyes still fixed on the men, But the one behind him is Joe Medora.

Eva looks about for Mary, tries to pull away but Martineau holds her fast.

I've got to find Mary, she says, She'll want to see him.

Too late, says Martineau, directing Eva with a slight nod. They both watch as Frankie joins the men, his hat held low at his side and his coat slung over his arm. All three disappear into the crowd.

~

Mary rummages in her handbag, holding it at an angle to catch the fading light. She pulls out a slim bottle of clear liquid, unscrews the cap and takes a long drink from the neck. The sky falls into grey. The street-lamps go new red, then orange. She takes another swig, coughs against the lip of the bottle. The cars swing under the bridge, headlights slip across brick, sweep over her, move on. Mary pulls a stray lock of hair from the corner of her mouth, curls it around her ear. She pictures the best man. She speaks very low.

Paolo.

Paolo, with the shadow falling in a slice across his brow. She sees the black and white of *True Crime* fill with colour. Do You Recognize This Man?

Oh yes, she says, I Recognize That Man.

~

The men walk in single file to the rear of the hall. Paolo carries his overcoat hooked on his shoulder, his finger bent like a beckoning below his ear. Joe follows with head down until he reaches the little side door that leads into the alley. He holds it open for Frankie, who pauses halfway, feeling the cool air of escape on his face. He looks back into the crowded room. Rose is chasing Fran around the edge of the stage, she catches the back of her dress so they both fall giggling into a couple on the dance-floor. Frankie sees Celesta in the distance, talking to someone he hopes is Mary. He would like a last look at her. He stands on tiptoe, his eyes squinting past the lights and the bodies and the thickening cigar smoke, but the woman with Celesta is obscured by Pippo's back.

Frank, says Joe quietly, Let's go.
Frankie squeezes through the door, follows the two men into the alley.

~

Dol, you stay right here, okay? Don't move! Promise?
Mary sees them on the street; Frankie, Joe Medora, Paolo, moving quickly. She turns, clacks under the bridge towards them. They pause at a car parked at the kerb, open the doors and duck inside.

Joe! – shouts Mary – Frankie! Joe!
She is running. The bottle in her hand sends a spray of liquid into the air, once, twice, a crystal shower in the headlights of a car at her back. A noise comes out of her as if she's falling down a well,

Joe!
echoing off the roof of the bridge,

Marina! My girl!
Up ahead, Joe Medora's car pulls away.

Frankie peers through the little rear window, sees Mary with her hair blowing around her head and her blue dress shining as she runs, the bottle in her hand curving in an arc as she throws it into the night. Even though he knows she can't possibly see him, Frankie raises his hand – to say goodbye, to say he's going, to say his ship came in – raises his left hand, the one with the ring on it.

missing

I could have waited for ever. She didn't come back. Some five-year-olds would fear the worst; that she had been hit by a car, abducted by aliens, spirited away by ghosts. But I knew my mother – I *knew* – just like my father, she too had run away. When it began to rain, I moved under a tree. I stood so quiet in the darkness that Eva nearly missed me. She saw my mother's handbag, abandoned on the flat edge of the bridge, the narrow gap in the wall just big enough for a body to slip through, the skidder of mud running in a tramline down the bank. Eva as I'd never known her, dashing backwards and forwards along the low wall, shouting our names over the black water,

Mary! Dolores!

Cupping her hands over her eyes like a sailor looking for land,

Oh Christ! Mary!

I can't stand under a tree now without the memory of it; the circle of earth with the roots proud and deadly as trip-wire; raindrops in a softness all around me; car headlights skinning the bridge, and Eva tracing her body against the mossy stone. When she finally saw me, she stopped shouting and leaned a hand on the wall. She took a deep breath, tried to smile.

Hello, Petal, she said quietly, her eyes taking me in, All this muck – Slippy!
and began to scrape the point of her stiletto heel against the stone. Then, casually,
Where's that mam of yours gone, eh, Dol?
so that everything would seem ordinary. So that I wouldn't be afraid.

~

When I imagine what Eva looks like now, I get a picture of Linda Harris – she's taken over the reference section while I'm having what the library calls Compassionate Leave. Linda's tall and acid blonde. She must be near retirement age. Her boyfriend's called Mehmet – I like 'em dark, she says, as if I'm genetically programmed to understand. Perhaps it's her taste in men that reminds me of Eva. Perhaps it's simply the charm bracelet she always wears.

I need to put Eva and Martineau on my list. It's in my holdall – upstairs still with the bag of presents I've bought for my sisters. What do you buy for strangers? Not perfume or scarves or jewellery. I got chocolates, a basket of candied fruit, an African violet wrapped in a cellophane sleeve. They look like stuff you see on a petrol station forecourt.

I try the switch at the bottom of the stairs, hoping for a light to come on at the top of the landing; of course, it doesn't work. The kitchen has a naked bulb in the centre of the ceiling which is much too bright. It emphasizes all the things this kitchen should not be. Empty. Silent. Uninhabited. The living room is in darkness, but even with the curtains drawn, there's a feeble grange glow in the room from the street-lamp just outside our house. I can see the dim outline of a single bed under the window. My mother must have had it brought down towards the end. It looks like my father's bed, from the Box Room. It's still made up. There is a dent in the pillow where my mother's head had rested, and a wider flattened circle near the foot of the bed where Mrs Riley sat and fidgeted the tea-towel in her hands. At the time I didn't want to touch it, but I cross the darkened room now to inspect it: pure white, with its red boast of 'Irish Linen' running round the outside. Folded up tight into a long sausage shape. A sensation riddles through me; a feeling that everything is in the wrong place. Someone who didn't know this home has been through it, putting objects where they think they go. Either that, or my mother simply forgot where things belonged.

The Toby Jug sits precariously on the front ring of the cooker, and the painted plate with a view of Tenby has been put in the middle of the kitchen table. A circle of patterned Vymura marks the space on the wall where it used to hang. The ornamental brass bell which should be on the fireplace with the photographs of Celesta is now on the dresser. It isn't brass, I realize: it's lacquered tin. I hold it up and shake, but the bell makes no sound – someone has removed the clapper. I used to get it down off the mantelpiece and clang it. You'll drive me mad, my mother would say, snatching it from me and putting it out of reach. The bell seemed huge then, but now I realize that it's small and light, there's nothing to it. And nothing is out of reach any more.

I find a biro in the Toby Jug. I try to write 'Eva' on my arm, but it doesn't work: I get a scrape of white and then a dusty blob of red ink smears itself across my skin. It reminds me of Fran, and painfully, of Luca. I think instead about Salvatore; whether I remembered to put him on my list of the missing.

eleven

A crowd has gathered on the street: not just the wedding guests, but young men on their way to the Carib Club, and red-faced drinkers hoping for a lock-in at The Bute. The night girls edge out of their doorways to get a look at the bride. Celesta has changed into her going-away outfit, but no one can see her new cream two-piece; Pippo insists on cloaking her with a startling knitted cape – his mother's gift.

It's red and bloody yellow, Pip! she whispers angrily in his ear, Bloody stripes! I look like Speedy Gonzalez!

Pippo smiles as he wraps her up. Celesta nudges him aside and yanks open the taxi door.

Where's Mam? she shouts into the crowd. Rose shrugs. She drags Celesta's suitcase across the pavement until Salvatore bends down and takes it from her. He carries the case a little way, then he too drags it until he reaches the back of the waiting car. He lets the driver struggle it into the boot.

Typical! Where's Dad? cries Celesta, peering into the mass of smiling faces. Pippo slides in beside her on the back seat. His mother leans in at the window. In the darkness of the cab, Celesta can only see the whiskers, lines and open space of the old woman's mouth as she puts her head through the gap to kiss Pippo. Fierce sucking kisses. Fierce whispering,

Ciao, Philippo, figlio mio, sangue mio! Mio . . . Mio . . .

To Celesta it sounds like a prayer.

What's she going on about? she says. But Pippo ignores her. He winds up the window as the taxi pulls off. Martineau steps through the crush of waving arms and the stinging shower of rice, to touch Salvatore on the shoulder.

~

Two streets away, at the Salvation Army Hostel, another crowd has gathered. Mary sits on the pavement with her back against the wall. She can't remember what she's done with her handbag; she's lost a shoe.

What's your name, love? asks a voice above her. She looks up at the faces: all men, all old men.

Mary Bernadette Jessop, she says, in a voice from child-hood. But she knows that isn't right. She thinks her name might be in her handbag, written on a slip of paper in case she got lost, or in blue biro on the silky inside pocket. She can see the name in her head but her lips can't say it. Mary closes her eyes. She would like to weep, but she doesn't, and when a young girl in a bonnet comes down the steps and tries to talk to her, Mary feels a silence wrapping itself around her like a shroud. The girl knows her; Mary brings her children here on Sundays when there's no food at home. She takes her hand and leads her up the steps. Mary will go with anyone now. She doesn't care who.

Inside, the hostel is busy. A line of men sit on a long red bench, smoking, aiming soup at their mouths, sleeping upright; an elderly woman walks around the edges of the room, talking to a dog under her coat. Two drunks hold a tug of war over the ownership of a blanket. Mary's teeth chatter. She sits on the far end of the bench with the young girl on her right, feeling the smoothness of the girl's palm shiny on hers. The light is so bright, it hurts to look up. Everyone has the same blue-white tinge to their skin. Mary stares at the walls, where the Sunday School Children have an exhibition.

Our Day Out to Leckwith Fields

is written in large loops on an orange banner; below is a series of drawings – trees with thick brown branches and tiny green buds; one with an autumn theme, the leaves tipping gently from the sky into a pile at the bottom of the picture. Mary concentrates on the fallen leaves. I want to be under that, she thinks, dreaming of lying down in the earth, the joy of just melting away. I want to *be* that.

~ ~ ~

The Moonlight, says Salvatore, They'll be there for sure. Martineau shakes his head, but turns the car round anyway. He knows that Joe won't hang about – especially now he's shown his face at the wedding – he'll be out of town again as soon as he's finished his business.

What's he up to? he muses aloud.

Salvatore's round eyes shimmer in the darkness. He shrugs.

Search me, Tino. But it look bad, this. Bad for Mary, eh? Martineau is silent, thinking not of Mary, but of Eva – clutching his sleeve to steady herself as she hooked up the straps of her sandals, her diamanté earring rocking gently against her neck. Him itching to put out a finger and touch it.

If you see Mary, tell her I'm looking for her, she shouted, her face suddenly grim.

As usual, thinks Martineau, the Gaucis ruin everything.

The Moonlight is in darkness. Salvatore doesn't bother with the lights, heading straight through the door marked Private and up the wooden stairs. Martineau wanders round the empty cafe and sniffs the scent of Joe Medora on the air. He lights a cigarette to while away the time, to disguise the smell – like bitter aloes working its way through his gut – of something going badly wrong.

Check the safe, he shouts, with a shiver of foresight, Check the safe, Sal!

~

In Joe Medora's office, everything is still. Salvatore closes the door behind him, moves past the low sofa and around the long desk to the safe, wedged discreetly underneath. He draws out his key and crouches, balancing on the balls of his feet. And he stares into the dark inner, at the shelf compartments with the papers on the top half and the space underneath where the money used to be. Five thousand pounds yesterday morning – half to go to Joe Medora, sure – but half of it is his. *Was* his. Salvatore smooths his hand around inside, as if his eyes might not be seeing, feeling the coolness of metal on his palm. And then he finds the napkin, pushed to the back, with one remaining biscotti inside. It is this more than anything that makes Salvatore rage.

~

Eva searches for the doorkey in my mother's handbag. She pulls out the length of fabric with the rabbit's foot hanging from it.

Christ–Shit! she says, throwing it back in, Where's the bloody key!

Rose pushes her hand through the letter box and pulls up a grimy tangle of string with the doorkey attached. Eva snatches it from her, waggles it in the lock.

You have to pull it towards you, says Rose from behind, You *obviously* haven't got the knack.

It hasn't taken Rose very long to claim superiority. Celesta's not even out of the country, and she already thinks she's boss. She's angry with Eva for not telling her where our mother is. I know she'll torture me later to get the details. Luca and Fran bolt in ahead of us, shouting up the stairs,

Mam? Mamma?

Eva puts my mother's handbag on the sideboard, then her own, takes off her gloves and flings them on top.

C'mon, girls, get those coats off. Rose, why don't you make us all some tea?

You're not my mother, says Rose sharply.

Be glad I'm not, young lady, says Eva, Waiting on you hand foot and finger! Now do you want some tea – or not? No one else is talking. We watch Eva kneel down by the fire. She lifts the fireguard off the hearth.

Get this going, she says, rattling the poker among the grey coals. As soon as they are turned on their backs, they give off a disgruntled glow. She waits for a minute, places a few shiny lumps on top, covers the whole lot with a sheet of newspaper. The flames jump to life behind the print.

Where's our Mam? asks Luca for the tenth time.

Run off with the gypsies, says Rose, nastily, And she's *never* coming back!

Eva drags the spread of newspaper away from the chimney; a bowl of smoke rises over the mantelpiece. Luca starts to wail.

Look what you've done now! cries Eva, For God's sake, Rose!

She turns to comfort Luca, who wrenches herself away.

She's just gone out for a bit, Lu. I'll ask Mr Amil to look for her, will I?

Run away with the gyp-sees, whispers Rose, her mouth split in a grin. Luca howls again.

That's it, shouts Eva, In bed! All of you. Now!

No one asks where our father is.

~

The car turns off the main road, down a pitted track off Tyndall Street and on to the broad concrete wasteland of the East Dock. Joe and Paolo sit silently in the front. In the back seat, Frankie twists the ring on his finger in silent agitation; there aren't many street-lights in this part of town. No people, no one to see them. He feels vulnerable now that he's thrown in his lot with Paolo. Five thousand pounds buys him a ruby ring; a passage on the *Athene*; Paolo's silence. There is a balance of power between them: Pippo won't get to hear of his brother's links with Joe. And Joe won't be told where Frankie's got his money from. It delighted Frankie at first, this plan; to buy his father's ring back with Joe's own cash. It seemed – correct. But Paolo is relishing his secret. Now and then he winks at Frankie in the rear-view mirror, makes sly references to The Moonlight.

Must bring in a lot of profit for you, that club, Paolo says.

Some, says Joe, not wishing to be drawn.

What would you say – a clear hundred a week?

Maybe, Joe shrugs, A good week.

More, even – with a sideline. Hey, Frankie, you'll know! Does Salvatore, uh, diversify? Card school maybe? Girls? *Passage* papers?

Frankie stares at the back of Paolo's long neck; avoids the dark eyes flashing in the mirror. He says nothing.

Ah Salvatore, muses Paolo, Poor Salvatore!

Joe pays no attention. He's got the money from Frankie; now he just wants him out of his car and on that ship. Business completed.

~

Mr Amil is downstairs shouting with Eva, there's a lot of door banging, then only the sound of the telly. Fran creeps down to find out what's happened. Eva and her husband have gone, and they've left Mr Amil's mother in charge: she's sitting on the couch eating peanuts and watching *Double Your Money*.

Fran flops back down on her divan. She's got my mother's vanity mirror off the dresser and she's frowning into it, combing her fringe with her fingers. In the other corner of the room, Rose and Luca are holding a conference. They pass whispers behind their hands, shoot me calculating looks. This is designed to frighten me.

You'd better tell, says Rose, One last chance, Crip.

I've already told them all I know. I consider making something up, but then Luca sidles round to my side of the bed, slowly, like a cat stalking a sparrow.

You know where we'll put you, she says.

Leave her alone, says Fran sharply.

Alright then, says Rose, pausing, Cradle!

She snatches up one of the folded sheets at the bottom of Fran's bed and flings it over me. Everything goes soft and ghostly, but their voices fizz with excitement.

Not a word! says Luca, close to my ear, Or you're a goner!

There's no point in fighting them. Rose rolls me across the bed, wrapping me tight inside the damp sheet.

I can't breathe, I say, my mouth hot and blocked, I can't breathe!

Rose pinches up the fabric in a pocket around my face.

That'll do, she says, and then I'm lifted through the air, swinging, bumping my head on something sharp, falling. I hear them laugh, Rose's ecstatic shriek as she heaves my legs up, Luca barking a chorus of hard yowls through the space around me. They drag me across the floor, rolling me over, over. The smell in my nose is biting.

~

The Junction Dry Dock is drained and empty; its lock gates creak against the spread of black water pressing in from the East Basin. Behind the dock, the hot flare of the Union foundry roars and is quiet; sparks up the night, and dies again into darkness.

Martineau parks the car on the slip road between the Engine House and the West Dock offices. All the way, Salvatore has kept up a storm of shouting; now as Martineau switches off the headlamps, he falls silent. Salvatore talks to the sailors in The Moonlight; he knows when a ship is set to leave port. The *Athene*'s due out on the dawn tide, bound for Cyprus. A Maltese crew. Salvatore suspects there will be one extra deckhand by the morning. He's no betting man, but he'd put money on it.

On the east side, sharp as cut-outs against the floodlit grain store, three men are walking. Frankie leads, drawn by the ship in the distance. It's a long time since he's been to sea; he doesn't think of the rope-burns and the stiffness and the mad-making boredom of the nights. To him, the ship ahead is a romance; a future. The men approach the far side of the dry dock, filing along its edge like a troop of rats. At the start of the wooden footbridge running over the lock gates, Joe and Paolo stop. They won't cross.

Salvatore has been listening to their footsteps echoing over the empty drop of the dock – Frankie's clicking gait up front. He sees the space between Frankie and the twinkling lights of the *Athene*, and this time, he won't let Frankie escape. Before Martineau can stop him, Salvatore jumps out of the car.

~

They've knotted one end of the sheet to the banister, the other around the pipe that runs up the wall and disappears into the loft. I'm suspended over the stairs. It doesn't feel safe; I can hear the handrail creaking as I sway. My feet are higher than my head, I'm getting a bloodrush.

POW Dolores Gauci, says Rose in her flight-commander voice, Spill the beans!

She went for a walk, I say, but my voice feels tiny, a thousand miles away.

Liar, says Luca, somewhere above me.

Liar, shouts Rose, poking the sheet so that I swing in space. They begin to chant.

Liar! Liar! Crip's on fire!

~

Frankie moves along the bridge, his arms out like a scarecrow. He places his feet carefully on the wooden boards. On his right is a sheer drop into the dry dock, with paint-cradles suspended at intervals along the walls. They squeak greasily in the wind. It's so far down, the concrete floor is invisible. On his left, the black water of the basin makes its sucking-licking noise. The soft rain which has fallen at intervals all day begins again now, scattering the fairy-lights reflected on the water, making the distant gangplank of the *Athene* shine like a strip of silver. Frankie turns his head, sees Joe and Paolo in the distance. As they fold into the darkness, Paolo raises his hand in a farewell salute. They don't see Salvatore striding up to the edge of the dry dock.

He knows, thinks Frankie, catching sight of Salvatore rumbling towards him. Frankie steps off the bridge, puts his hands on Salvatore's shoulders to try to keep him quiet. To reason with him. To beg.

~

Help me, I say, then louder, Help me!

I don't care if old Mrs Amil hears me now; the sheet is wet and stuck to my face, my legs have gone to sleep. I'm scared to move in case the rocking tips me over and tumbles me down the stairs. And I know my mother won't be back to save me.

Help!

There's a warm grip of arms around my body, a low grunt, and I'm lifted into space, feet first, flying or falling, I can't tell which.

Sssh, says Fran, unwrapping the sheet from my sweating head, Ssh now, they'll hear us!

~

Salvatore holds his fists tight into his chest, throws them out above his head.

Fottuto Bastardo! You do this to me? Why, Frankie, Why?

Frankie calculates the distance, whether the sound will carry, whether Joe is still in earshot. There's no calming Salvatore now.

Habib, he says, with half a smile, the Frankie grin, Habib . . .

He tries to hug his friend, to stop the noise coming out of him. Anything to stop him.

And the biscotti, Frankie! cries Salvatore, almost pleading. He takes one step back, then another.

In the brief flare of the Union foundry, Frankie sees Salvatore as he flies, falls, slips away into the concrete pit of the dry dock. There is no more shouting. Frankie looks down into the darkness, then across to where Joe and Paolo were standing. They've gone. Frankie hears a car engine in the distance. He is alone, he thinks.

twelve

Luca holds my arm out like a flagpole over the kitchen sink. She's placed her body between me and my sacrificial limb, but she still tells me to close my eyes, as if I might see through her. I lean against the table; behind Luca I can see the long enamel bath we used to share, daily converted by its wooden lid into a place for Domestos, Jeyes disinfectant, and things for washing up. I'm looking out for hazards just in case I fall. Luca's going to give me a tattoo; she's using my arm as a test-bed for her own.

It won't hurt if you concentrate on something else, she says.

I try to think about the water dripping into the sink, but it's slow and thick and sounds like blood. She holds the knife up for inspection like she's Dr Kildare, turning it this way and that, and there's a moment of stillness except for where sunlight jumps off the taps and the sharp edge in the air between us.

I didn't see her choose the knife. I didn't see her heave open the cutlery drawer and chink about, draw out the yellow horn of the handle of my father's best blade. It is curved like a grin, worn down by the constant scrape of the Steel. My father used this knife to skin the rabbit.

~

Luca caught me off-guard. A fiercely bright morning, I'm scrawling out the numbers on my hopscotch grid with a nub of coal:

10

ten fingers ten toes and pinch me

9–8

my mother's lucky number, and the days since Salvatore and my father disappeared with all that money

7

Luca's age

6–5

the number of girls we are, and my age

4

days since the social services found my mother.

~

I'm pondering loss and gain: Marina, the rabbit, my father; almost my mother. Celesta's gone on honeymoon so she doesn't count. Fran doesn't count either; they say if she behaves herself, she might come back one day. Gain is harder. Can't think of a single thing. I'm wondering about 3–2 and 1, and what they might mean, but suddenly my sky is darkened by Luca. She's standing over me.

You've got the six back to front, you Crip! she goes, snatching the coal from my hand. She scrubs at the backwards six with her shoe until it's faint, then draws it in again.

I'll go first, she says. She throws the coal out in front of her, skips and jumps.

One fuck, two three, four shite five, she yells. She bends over to pick up the marker, legs twisted at the knees.

This is a Crip's game! Pupsy!
and throws the lump of coal into the long grass.

I'm going to play a *hard* game, she says ominously, Come on!

And she turns back into the house. There's this feeling twizzling away in the back of my head, which I get when Luca's up to something. It's bound to be unpleasant. But it's almost midday; Carlotta will be here soon. I'll be safe then.

~

Carlotta sits in her parlour with her hands tucked between her knees; she's sobbing. Above her, the footsteps of the men cross the room. Tearing sounds, the scrape and crash of furniture overturned, then the brittle snap of shellac as they work their way through Salvatore's record collection. Opposite her, in Salvatore's armchair, Ilya the Pole keeps up a steady monologue.

Awful, eh, this business, Mrs Capanone. I'm very sorry for it. But Joe is crazy, you understand. He's mad. If he finds Salvatore – he's a Dead Man.

Salvatore would not do this, she says, To steal from his own business!

Ilya closes his eyes, nodding.

I know it – we know! But where did he *go*?

Carlotta pulls her handkerchief from her sleeve and crumples it over her nose.

To The Moonlight. Of course. I tell the police this! They don't believe!

On Seguna's *wedding* day?

Even to Ilya, it sounds preposterous.

To fetch the biscotti for Mary, Carlotta says, sick of explaining, He *tell* me this.

Ilya doesn't really care for the conversation. He's just being polite. Keeping her out of the way. He searches in his pocket for his cigarette case, raises his eyebrows at her,

Do you mind?

Carlotta gets up to fetch the ashtray from her cabinet. It's made of onyx, a large yellow agate with a rough edge. She stands behind him, holding the cold chunk to her breast.

Where is he? she says to herself. Fifteen years married and not a single day without him. Carlotta isn't fooled by Ilya's smile. He knows how it is: the men leave the wedding and they go to a bar. And they drink, and they play poker. And they come home. But he didn't come home. Salvatore *always* came home. But he didn't come home.

She could smash the ashtray there, right in the middle of the shiny pond of Ilya's head. Carlotta takes a breath, places it carefully on the floor near his feet.

Nothing, Boss, says a young man, pushing the door open, We'll check the back, alright?

Carlotta follows them into the kitchen. This room is hers. The two men turn out the cupboards and drawers with expert skill, rattling tins, popping open her jars of pickle and pre-served fruit. One of them hooks a lump of jam into his mouth and sucks it off his finger.

Cut it out, Roy, says Ilya, Get on with it.

Here – this only, says Carlotta, taking the tea-caddy off the shelf and banging it on the table, My savings.
Inside the tin are a few rolled-up notes, some Green Shield Stamps, a dusty collection of sixpences.

Come on, Ilya says, Let's go.
The two men stop immediately. They wipe their hands in unison, as if everything they touched was dirty. Ilya pauses at the door,

Don't forget that, he says to Roy, nodding at the tin on the table.
Carlotta sits still in the kitchen, with the cupboard doors gaping and the mess of pots and sticky lids all around her. She presses her hand against her heart. No, she thinks, No Salvatore, you are not a dead man. I would feel it.

~

Luca takes up my father's rabbity knife, licks her finger and runs it on the edge; she's about to skin me.

Not that one! I shout, as she positions the point. Luca lets out an exaggerated breath. She steals my mother's voice.

184

Do you want to be hard or not? she says, flicking the blade at my face, You know what Fran said about the Homes, Dol! I nod, miserable; not at the prospect of going into the Homes, but because I want to be hard and I don't think I'll manage it. Fran says I'm too little; I'll get beaten up.

Well then, Luca says. She starts to cut. I don't feel a thing. This is easy, I'm thinking, and then she stops. When I look there's no blood, just a faint scoring of white on pink. Luca leans over and pulls a pen out of the Toby Jug on the table. Toby is laughing at me, both his eyes are closed in mirth, or maybe fear.

I'll need to draw it on first, so I know where I'm going, says Luca. With her tongue in the side of her face, she writes a big D: then she pauses. Luca is crackling with power.

Do you want Dol, or Dolores? she asks. Her voice is high and slight. Outside the window the birds aren't singing. Perhaps there's a cat in the yard.

How about DG? I venture. There's a flip of disgust on her face, so I rush on, Or maybe DSG?

Luca takes up the knife, draws the edge across my arm. The first cut is ragged, I can feel the resistance of skin. I lean across her just in time to watch my blood bobble out in a long line. She goes in again, tracing the arc of the D with my father's best cutter, and the snagging races up my arm and into my head. I start to hum, with a noise like pain escaping through my nose. Luca suddenly stops to look at me.

I said close your eyes.

The sun is behind her, falling against her head and the taps which waste my blood, and Luca's face is black and flecked with barbs. I'm seeing neon rip across the air.

Keep still, will you, she says. The tension in her voice tells me she's scared too. I want to cry.

Let me have a look, I say, casual going up into a wail.

Luca has scratched a crooked D into the flesh, raised and open like the gills of a fish. I pretend to examine it, but my arm is jolting up and down, or the sunlight is flickering, or I am. She lets go then, the thick white imprint of her grasp remaining on my skin.

Just D will do, I say, before the walls skid into floor.

~ ~ ~

Eva's got me by the hand; she's wearing her gloves again but I haven't got mine any more. I don't know where they are. None of us knows where anything is any more.

Carlotta comes in the mornings to clean the house and cook for us, dripping her tears into the big aluminium pan which she uses for stews, soups, frying bacon. But she hasn't got a clue where to put things. The airing cupboard is a mess of fighting stockings and slumped towers of underwear. At least when my mother was here, we knew where to find our clothes – on the chair in the living room.

My mother is in Whitchurch Hospital. She's not coming out, so I'm going with Eva to visit her. Eva takes me everywhere with her these days.

You're my little lucky charm, she says, jangling her bracelet and smiling, you could come and live with me, Pet, but Mr Amil – her voice goes down to a whisper – He's funny about it, Dol. Old-fashioned.

What she really means is that he's superstitious about my bad hand; I heard her tell Martineau. He comes round at night to help her look after us. He uses the back door, just like my father did. Martineau swears he knows nothing about my father, or Salvatore, or why The Moonlight has got boards up at the window and a For Sale sign above it.

Silent as the grave, says Eva, when she tells me these things, But I like 'em silent, Dol. Can't stand a nattering man. Mr Amil, you know – and she pulls a face just like him – Yak-Yak-Yak all day long! Gives me such a head!

We've all seen The Moonlight, so I know that bit's true. Me and Rose and Luca stood outside while Eva went into the grocer's next door to the betting shop and bought us all an ice-cream. We'd just said goodbye to Fran. I licked my Whippy and the cream ran down my hand. I should have been thinking about how Fran would've liked an ice-cream, especially with a Flake, but all I could think of was how my one hand suddenly looked like the other, with the fingers hidden behind the cone and the thick drips running down. Rose had finished hers. She had her face pressed right up against the window of The Moonlight, cupping her hands over her eyes.

D'you think they've left any pop? she said.
Eva had finished her lolly and was wiping her hands with a handkerchief. She bent over and smeared it across my mouth, once, twice.

There you go, Dol – Clean as a Whistle! Come on, Rose! she shouted, grabbing Luca by the hood of her raincoat. I licked all around my mouth. It tasted of vanilla and Eva's scent.

~

Whitchurch Hospital has big gardens, and a long winding road running up to the front door. We go through the reception and into a summerhouse at the back. My mother is sitting in a deckchair behind the palm plants. Her hair's gone grey.

Look who I've brought to see you! Eva says. I try to edge on to my mother's lap, but I can tell she doesn't want it. She lets me sit there for a second and then she eases me off again.

Her legs are a bit sore, Dol, says Eva, watching my face.
I look down to my mother's legs; they're like two huge sausages sticking out from under her skirt. One of them is wrapped up in a thick bandage.

What have you done? I say, Who did it?
No one did it, Dol – Eva's talking for my mother – Your mam's still a bit poorly.

My mother smiles and at this, and for a second, her face looks normal. Then it closes itself up.

Pretty little girl you've got, she says to Eva, Whatever happened to her hand?

~ ~ ~

There's an outing. Lizzie Preece escorts me and Luca and Rose into town to buy new shoes and dresses. It's nobody's birthday, it's not Christmas, and it's not Corpus Christi.

What's all this in aid of? asks Eva on our return. She makes us stand in a line while she inspects us. We're a bit ashamed – we didn't get much say in what we could have; Lizzie Preece said we could only go to a shop that took Council vouchers. So we're all in brown.

What she playing at? Eva says.

She soon finds out. Our next trip is to the photographer's shop in Queen Street Arcade. Eva comes with us this time. She grabs my hand as usual, so Lizzie Preece crosses behind me to take the other one. Then she remembers and her face goes puce.

You'd be better off keepin' an eye on *that* one, says Eva with a nod to Luca, She's a terror in the traffic, she is.

They walk ahead of us. Luca swings off Lizzie Preece's wrist like an ape off a branch. Eva laughs and puts her mouth close to my ear,

Old Prissy'll soon get tired of that!

~

The photographer's called Mr Lovell. He takes us through a black curtain into the back room.

Now, girls, this is the Ste-u-dee-o, he says, as if we're incapable of understanding plain English. He positions us on a long leather bench. It squeaks when we move. Rose does farting noises by lifting her fat legs and slapping them down on the leather.

Don't touch that! he shouts as Luca grabs the tripod.

Ex-term-in-ate! she yells, waving the legs in the air.

Mrs Preece, please try to control them! he says.

We're so amazed, we all stop fidgeting and look at her. She's supposed to be in charge of us? Eva takes a step back, red-faced.

What do you want these photos for? she asks, suspicious.

For their mother, says Lizzie Preece quickly, It'll help her recovery.

Eva stands in the corner, her arms folded and her foot tapping. My mother used to do that too, when she was angry.

Mr Lovell takes my photograph first. He tilts my head slightly to the left, then moves my shoulders the same way.

Look at me, he goes, from somewhere behind the lights, and I turn back to look at him. He steps out again and repositions me.

Just move your eyes, he says tiredly, *Not* your head.

Tricky. But I get the hang of it, and it's all over with a ssshunk. Rose and Luca's take a lot longer; they won't sit still, they pose and then pull faces when the shutter goes. By the end, Mr Lovell is sweating.

Terrible, he says to Eva and Lizzie, Don't build your hopes up − Sow's ears and all that.

Back after two then, says Lizzie, ignoring his insults.

~

We are taken − For a Treat, says Lizzie Preece gaily − to Pippo's Sarsaparilla Bar. Eva and Lizzie fight over who's going to pay; they both wave their pound notes about and push each other out of the way, going, No No Let Me, until finally Eva gives up and slides next to us on the high stools. She shrugs,

Let her pay then, she says, The fat cow.

Lizzie Preece wedges herself in between the round table and the window. I can tell by the way she shifts her body towards Eva, she wants an adult conversation. Rose does tricks with her straws, blowing bubbles into her limeade, shooting a stream of green liquid at Luca, pretending to make a straw disappear up her nose.

Do you think *they'll* look after them? Lizzie Preece asks Eva. She means Pippo and Celesta.

You must be joking! says Eva. She stirs the scum on her coffee, takes a hot sip.

But he's not – he's quite mature, isn't he? They're a ready-made family, argues Lizzie.

He won't take them, says Eva, finally, They're not even back off their honeymoon.

They know then? asks Lizzie, shocked.

Oh aye, says Eva, casually, You can see how much *they* care. And Celesta – she won't want a whole load of kids in her posh house, will she?

Lizzie Preece looks at us and I try not to catch her eye,

Not *this* load, she says.

~

The photographs are ready. Mr Lovell hands them to Lizzie Preece in an assortment of brown cardboard frames.

I've done you a set of duplicates, he says, For the mother. Lizzie glances at Eva, then sighs and opens her purse. She pays this time and no one argues.

The image of me is nervous, shifty, scowling over my shoulder like a fugitive on the run. Any second now, the sniffer dogs will leap up behind me and tear me to ribbons. The pictures of the others are even worse. Rose holds her chin high, her nostrils flared like a hippo emerging from the swamp; Luca has her eyes crossed like one of the Keystone Cops. Our group photograph makes Eva laugh out loud.

The Bash Street Kids and no mistake, she says, bending double in the middle of the pavement. Lizzie Preece doesn't think it's funny.

The Agency won't use these, she says, We'll never place them!

The Agency, goes Eva, Now would that be the Adoption Agency?

Not in front of the girls, Mrs Amil, whispers Lizzie Preece. But that's the point; they are in front of us. We can hear every word.

~ ~ ~

Martineau thinks he can avoid it. He doesn't have to go back. What he saw was a scuffle, that's all. But Salvatore has been haunting him all week.

Is not all, my friend, he admonishes, deep in Martineau's dreams. Determined not to sleep, Martineau visits Eva, sitting up with her in the early hours, drinking coffee. When she tells him to go home and get some rest, he leaves her. Goes to Domino's Resto, where the talk is of Frankie and Sal and what they might be doing with all that money. The clientele from The Moonlight rub shoulders with Domino's regulars, favourite seats are argued over, the girls fight over their patch, until a night or two passes and things begin to calm down. Len the Bookie, his audience doubled, holds court.

What price on Malta? he shouts, licking the nib of his pencil. His little notebook is open on his lap, filled with numbers and coded initials. The men around him shake their heads and laugh.

Ten-to-One, he tries again, It's a fair price, boys, a likely venue.

It bloody isn't, yells Domino from behind the bar, What if Joe don't find them?

What if he does? shouts the man next to Len, What odds have you got on a concrete overcoat?

And they laugh again. Len stands on his chair, crouching slightly to avoid the low lamp swinging above his head. He looks across the heads below him, shiny as beetles from Vitalis and Lacquer.

Now, Ladies and Gentlemen, a bit of hush! You at the back there, get sat down.

Len licks his pencil again as he waits for the laughter to subside.

Next bet, Ladies and Gentlemen – The Moonlight! No arson, no Acts of God. Barring that, any odds?

A woman at the table below hands him up his whisky and soda. He raises it to the crowd.

What about a new restaurant? he says, his eyes wide in mock innocence. Domino jabs his finger in the air,

Or a betting shop, he shouts, getting his own back on Len. The crowd roars again with laughter.

Put a sock in it, you. Come on now, fellas, he'll need a front. What'll it be – Massage parlour, sex shop? Something nice and respectable!

Martineau cannot bear it. Two more whiskies, and he's on the road and heading for the docks. Drowning the voice in his head with the radio on loud.

You make me feel so young, you make me feel so spring has sprung!

And there's Salvatore, skating his duster across the counter as he polishes, peering at his own reflection in the brass. Smiling into it.

And every time I see you grin, I'm such a happy individual! Dancing the tray of empties back up to the counter.

Martineau flings open the car door and runs. He passes the loading bays, their mechanical arms like giant beaks against the sky; the grain store with its carpet of white powder and its musted smell of rats. He stops short at the dry dock. Martineau edges towards it as if he's drawn on a string. He disappears against the black silhouette of the prow, rests briefly on the mooring before he finds the courage to look down. Blackness, a harness, a cradle laden with tins of paint. No Salvatore rising out of the caked mud. Nothing.

~

Mr and Mrs O'Brien want me, but they don't want Rose or Luca; Mr and Mrs Edwards are happy to foster Rose and Luca, they'll even consider Fran if she ever gets let out – but they won't have me. They'd rather have a pyromaniac in the family than be seen with a damaged child.

We do want to keep you all together, says Lizzie Preece, But in the short term, girls, you'll be split up. Just 'til your mum gets better. I'm sorry about it.

Can't we stay here? asks Luca.

Luca loves it; no school, no one to tell her off when she jumps all over the furniture. The Test Card's on all day, and when Eva looks after us, we have chips from the Chip Shop. She's not like Carlotta – she never forces us to have a bath. Or pray.

Cleanliness is Next to Godliness, is it? Who'd *want* to be next to God! she says, dipping the flannel in the washing-up bowl, Give me the dirty old Devil any day!

But when Carlotta comes and Eva has to leave us, she always says GodBless before she kisses us goodbye.

Carlotta spends the nights here, lying in the Box Room with the door open, just like my father used to. Sometimes I can hear her talking to herself; it's like she's having a conversation. I'm awake a lot too; it's hard to get to sleep. Luca and me roll together into the dip in the bed, then she kicks or punches me and I have to cling on to the edge to stop myself from drifting off and rolling in again. I don't really mind if we get split up. I just miss my mother. And Fran. And I'll miss Eva too.

~ ~ ~

You're looking so much better, Mary, says Lizzie Preece to my mother, You remember Dolores, don't you?

My mother gives her a look. Of course I do, it says, What do you take me for? But she doesn't speak, she just puts her arms round me and squeezes me until my ribs hurt. It's nice.

You'll want a bit of time together, says Lizzie, I'll leave you be.

Can I take her for a walk? asks my mother. Her face is bright and shiny, and she smells different, but she's definitely my mother. So why ask Lizzie Preece?

Lizzie considers. She takes a little breath in, then says,

Yes, I don't see how it could hurt. Just round the gardens, mind?

And my mother takes me by the hand and leads me out of sight.

~ ~ ~

Carlotta has stripped all the beds, the sheets have been put through the mangle and are blowing on the line, and now she's scrubbing the front doorstep. Della Riley leans against the wall, a look of disbelief on her face. No one scrubs the doorsteps round here any more.

Dowlais'll ruin that in a flash, she says, clicking her fingers with grim satisfaction.

Alice Jackson crosses the road to have a word.

Terrible, Della!

is the first thing she says. Carlotta sits back on her haunches and looks up at them.

Those poor kiddies, Alice continues, What have they done with them – in care, is it?

Families will have them, says Carlotta, leaning a red hand on the wall and hauling herself up off the mat, Families all over.

She makes a waving motion.

Can't you see to them? Della raises her eyebrows, Only, you're bound to do a better job than that mother, aren't you?

I'm not allowed, says Carlotta, repeating the words that she's heard over and over, I am a woman on her own.

She raises the bucket and tips it so that the grey water dashes all over the pavement. Alice Jackson has to jump clear. The women fall silent, Della and Alice smiling at each other over Carlotta's bent back. She takes up the broom and sweeps the suds into the gutter.

Will they sell this place? asks Alice.

Carlotta shrugs, watches the bubbles fizz along the cracks in the pavement.

They keep it for Mary, she says, For when she is better. She lifts the bucket and turns to go inside.

Excuse now, she says, I finished here.

The two women cover their mouths with their hands.

Gonna scrub your step then, Alice? asks Della.

Oh aye, says Alice Jackson sardonically, I does it every morning, don't I?

~ ~ ~

We're walking along the railway line, my mother and me. I'm wearing my new brown clothes underneath my new brown Mackintosh. I'm going to the O'Briens' this afternoon.

It's starting to rain, Dol, my mother says, holding her hands out to the sky, But we don't mind, do we?

We trudge along the gravel in single file. It rains harder, the water runs in a curve around the rim of my plastic hood and splashes on and off my collar. My mother is silent, bent in front of me. I don't know where we're going and something about the way she is walking won't let me ask her. I try to match my gravel steps with hers. We crunch like this for a long while, so long that the rain becomes more important than it was, and it's leaking in at the neck where my hood is fastened. I've turned my ankle twice on rough stones. The railway lines twist in the distance.

Look, she says at last, bending down. She lifts a piece of stone from the ground and turns it in her hand.

Flint, she says, excited, You can start a fire with flint.

Why? I ask. As soon as the word is out, I know I've asked the wrong question. It should have been 'how', which would let her tell me practical things. But my question is, for what reason, why would we want to start a fire? She holds out the flint for me to look at, swivelling it so it shines and then doesn't. Her nails are all chipped.

Broken, she says, Broken in two.

She bends again, crouching, and I can see beyond her, to the rain in sheets and the blackberry bushes shuddering in the wind. She lays her head down sideways on the track. People choose to die this way, but I don't know this yet, at five years old. I know about dinosaurs and pop music and harvest festival, and about the Virgin Mary and how Christ suffered for us, but I don't know about suicide or what the weight of a passenger train can do to the bones in the skull. She smiles up at me from the track, and her hair slicks across her cheek like pond grass. She rises, flays the water from her face with her hand.

No trains coming, she says.

~

We run across the track towards a blackberry bush. My mother surveys it with her eyes, up and down, and lifts the bottom branches with a stick. Underneath, the berries are rich and black, they peel off from the stem in liquid blobs, dissolving to the touch. She holds them out to me in her stained palm: they taste of water.

This is our last day.

part two

waiting 2

The house is still here, and the bedroom we shared is just as it was: two sash windows facing out on to the street; a built-in corner cupboard; a glass-topped dresser with its triptych mirror. There's a black run across the floorboards where feet have walked from door to window and back again. The wallpaper must have come later; its repeating pattern of stylized blooms look like onions sliced in half or, in a certain light, like the pale bud of my fist. I perch on the end of the big double bed – an ordinary size now – and feel the cold iron of the frame bite through my jeans, my skin, my bones. Under the window sits the chest. I wait for my eyes to adjust, for the outline of the wood to separate from wall and shadow and become itself; long, low, oblong. It belonged to my father, and now it will be mine: I'm claiming it back. I will take what I can. Darkness has come down. While the waiting happens, I go through it all again.

I was put in this chest, when I was newborn.

~ ~ ~

I set off at Wednesday lunchtime with the letter from the social services telling me my mother had died. I put a change of clothes in my holdall, and two pages torn from the library's phonebook listing all the Gaucis in Cardiff. The funeral was arranged for Friday morning. I knew nothing and I wanted time. In my head I lined up my sisters in front of me, ageing them, dealing them families, playing out their lives. Celesta, Marina, Rose, Fran, Luca – slippery as a set of new cards. We never kept in touch: I don't know whose idea it was. By the time I started at my new school, I had become an only child. My friends had brothers and sisters; I had dreams – Luca and Rose tormenting me; Celesta, cool and distant, whose face I could never quite see. I would wake up feeling bandaged, hot, smothered. Gradually, the nightmares crept away, leaving only Fran as I remembered her, standing in the dawn light with her shoulders hunched, folding her blankets in silence.

The others in the pack were distant too – my father, Salvatore, Joe Medora. Knave, Joker and King. I last saw my father on the night of Celesta's wedding. I could only be certain of one thing: I would never see my mother again.

~

Cardiff glowed beneath a painful light. A bank of clouds boiled up orange in the lowering sun, and there was the saturated clarity of air after rain. I was unprepared for such colour. It used to be a place of grey; a dull pearl sheen, leaden buildings, the stink of the Dowlais like charcoal on the wind. There were pin-sharp moments – trips to the pierhead to watch a ship come in, once to the circus, too often to the hospital – and tingling tram rides in the night to Carlotta's house, sitting in a stunned row and watching my mother argue over the fares. There were people my mother had to avoid, the hiding places in arcades and alleyways where she would look down at me with her finger pressed to her lips. Still and close, we waited until the threat had passed. All the rest was under the gauze of time.

But now the city was busy, set and full of purpose. At the front of the taxi queue, a woman pushed me out of the way.

I stood on the pavement, waiting for some recognition of what she'd done to me, as if my grown-up self had come unstuck and fled back to Nottingham and safety.

Never get a cab if you stands there! Come yer, love!

A mini-cab driver, poaching for business, shouted at me from across the road. He wore a tartan cap and a white vest two sizes too small, a motif of a cowboy boot emblazoned across the front. Under the thin cotton, a mass of curly chest-hair lay flattened like the stuffing from an old sofa. Frowning and smiling at the same time, he sat me in the back of the car.

Where you takin' me? he joked.

I told him where I wanted to go.

Are you sure? It's all been brought down, that bit.

My mother still lives there, I said.

He consulted on his radio.

We'll get as close as we can, he said.

We stop-started through the traffic, edging the length of St Mary's Street. Spying a gap, he turned a half-circle into an empty stretch of wide new road. From the window I could see fresh black tar, vivid white markings, a ribbon of traffic cones wending into the distance. Saplings had been planted on the embankment, shivering in the evening light. The driver pointed out the sights through his window,

The Retail Park's over there on the right, look . . . in a minute you'll see the Bute Dock? It's brilliant what they've done. Exchange Building there – really smart now!

I wound my window down as far as it would go, let in a smell of ash, and then a drift of something else – salt. A scent I'd forgotten I knew: the smell of the foreshore, of a lover's licked skin. A mechanical digger in the distance juddered like a wind-up toy, bright yellow against the glint of the mudflats. Minute gulls rose and fell like shreds of blown paper: something was being unearthed.

We left the roadworks to enter a dense block of streets, then another and another until the tang of salt had vanished and there was only the pressure of brick bearing down. The sky between the rooftops fell heavy here. The cab slowed to a crawl.

All this yer's condemned, he said.

I scanned the houses for people. Two young girls stood side by side on the corner with their hands tucked up their sleeves; a pale child, naked apart from a red pullover, ran out of the black hole of his front door, chased by the cry of another inside. The driver pulled into the kerb.

Can't get you no closer – unless we go all round the 'ouses.

This'll be fine, I said. But it wasn't fine; I was thinking of who might still be here after all this time: Eva, the Next-Door Rileys, the Jacksons. Perhaps the taxi driver was right and everything would be rubble and dust. He took one strap of my bag and swung it up off the floor of the car. He held out a card – Carl's Cabs – and smiled.

Give us a bell when you're wanting out, he said.

It started to drizzle, a dirty, familiar mist, greasing the pavement.

On the corner I tried to get my bearings. What was once the Evanses' shop had become a squat block of maisonettes in mustard-yellow brick. Behind them, the crisp outline of a new hotel complex, a half-built car park, a girder swinging from a crane. Most of the streets looked dead, windows smashed, doors boarded up. The sign for Loudoun Place had been spray-painted with stripes of red and gold and green. At the far end used to be The Square, but I could only see a line of dented garage doors, a lamp-post with its wires hanging out like a disembowelling, and a horse, grazing on a patch of stubbled grass. Holding my hand out in friendship, I walked towards it. We got eye to eye before it veered suddenly away, lumbering off as far as its rope would stretch. From an upstairs window at the end of the terrace, a voice shouted down at me.

Oy! You! Leave it!

It was a child's voice. The boy leaned out of the window; he looked about eight years old.

It's alright, I said.

Ho-er! he shouted, breaking the word into two, Fuck off, Trollop!

I didn't want to run. Round the corner, down the alley into Hodge's Row. The door of Number 2 – my mother's home, and mine – was coated with a film of dirt. Rain darkened it. The living room curtains didn't meet in the middle. There was no one there.

At the dead end, the high wall was still standing. A car was parked on the pavement, the bonnet forced up against the door of the last house. Eva lived halfway down. I knocked, waited, then crouched and pushed open the letterbox. It was murky inside, bare apart from a faint glow from a room at the far end of the hall. A sheet of green tarpaulin hung from the doorway like a dying flag. I could see a pair of knees jutting out below it. I put my mouth to the letterbox and called out,

Eva? Mr Amil?

The legs shifted suddenly out of view. I shouted,

It's Mrs Gauci's daughter! I need a key!

There were no slow footsteps, no grate of a chain. When I bent to look again, the knees were back in the doorway, just as before.

In the front window of the Jacksons' house was a sign, tilted to one side, showing a picture of a German Shepherd dog with its tongue lolling out. I Live Here! it said. The bell made no sound when I pressed it and the touch left a circle of grime on my finger. One of the upstairs windows had been boarded up; the other was broken; a piece of grey net fluttered through the hole.

You won't get no joy there, said a voice behind me, They've up an' left.

The woman leaned in the doorway of Number 4. Her eyes grew wide when she saw my face,

My God, Mary!

She put her hand to her chest as if in pain: this old woman was Mrs Riley, more than thirty years on. She looked at me properly, took in my face, the sight of my hand. I needed no other introduction.

~

Mrs Riley came back with a torch and kneeled down at the front door of my mother's house. For a second I thought she was about to say a prayer, but she put her shoulder against the wood and jammed her hand inside the letterbox. She brought out a long piece of dirty string with a key attached. The shiny edge jutted towards me like a blade.

I'll show you what's what, she said – and turning suddenly to face me – You won't *find* nothing! Nothing worth having! As if I had accused her of this empty street.

You used to have to pull it, I said, making a waving motion. But the lock clicked in immediately.

She had that fixed *years* ago, she said, pushing open the door to my home.

thirteen

It's cold in here, the gas has been turned off. The cupboard under the stairs is full of plastic sacks, all bulging and squashed in a heap, leaking bits of fabric and sharp points through the holes. Mrs Riley shines the torch like a searchlight, angling the ray against the underside of the stairs, and the way the light splashes on the back wall makes my stomach lurch. There's a cardboard box filled with odd shoes, broken china, lumps of coal. I take a corner flap and drag it out of the way, holding my breath, pushing back the cupboard door where I see the pattern of my mother's fingerprints blackening the wood. A red eye in the corner blinks lazily at me; it's the electricity meter, a new digital version. A scurf of orange plaster-dust runs along the cable beneath. I remember when the meter used to take shillings. I would sit in here and watch the dial go round, counting the seconds until the red edge returned.

Mind out, look, let me do it, Mrs Riley says, pushing me aside.

She hands me the torch and crouches in my place. I stand behind her, casting the beam over the pile of bags deep in the recess.

Will you keep that light still!, she cries, It's like the black hole of Calcutta!

She bends low, presses her face into the bags, finds the gas tap.

That's it, she says, Should be on now.

~

The gas fire when it's lit fills the living room with the stink of dust. There's a bed under the window where there used to be the table piled with washing, and *True Crime*, and my crayoning books. Mrs Riley sinks gingerly onto the bed, inspecting the grime on her hands. Next to her is a tea-towel, its red words running along the edge: Irish Linen.

Use this, I say, passing it to her.

Can't use that. Can't use that for anything now, girl. That was for laying her out.

She looks at me steadily. She wants to tell me something but I'm not going to ask. I see women like her at the library, their faces lit up as they read out the obituaries, sitting at the long table with their scarves tied under their chins and the newspapers spread out in front of them. They bring flasks of tea and foil parcels of sandwiches. It's like an outing. Mrs Riley is one of these old women. Perhaps my mother was too.

She's turning the tea-towel in her lap, stroking out the creases as if she's stroking a cat; long slow sweeps of her hand.

Is it yours? I ask, guessing.

Oh aye.

She folds it over, rolling, unrolling.

You can get three for a pound at the market. Not this sort, mind!

Turns her head and looks at the pillow.

Pretty woman, your mother. Even at the end.

She catches up the torch and heaves herself off the bed, places the tea-towel carefully on the coverlet. It rests in the corner of my vision; it means something else now.

You rolls it up, see, she says, her voice confidential, You rolls it up nice and firm, and you puts it under the chin? Stops jaw-drop.

The back of her hand reaches up and flitters at the folds of skin hanging from her neck. She bares her dentures in a sparkling grimace.

There's nothing worth having, she says again, No money. Nothing.

I'm here to bury my mother, I say, seeing her out.

When she's gone I slam the door, pull and slam it again so hard the wall vibrates and the light bulb rocks in the centre of the room, throwing its shadows all over.

~

There's nothing worth having, Mrs Riley, but I'm listing what there is. An inventory in my head; cataloguing, cross-referencing. It's what I'm good at. Here's the living room with the bed, the tea-towel, an armchair, a television set perched on the table in the corner. Next to the gas fire is a brass coal scuttle wedged with magazines: *Word Search*, *The Puzzler*, *Take A Break*. A biro gathers dust in the corner of the hearth. On the mantelpiece is a scuffed blue spectacle case. I cannot touch any of it. No pictures on the walls, no ornaments over the fireplace, no lampshade to soften the light. A month ago – two weeks ago – my mother breathed in this space. She moved through it, watched television at night with the sound down low, a magazine in her lap and a pen in her hand. What did she do, at the end? At the end she made a start; putting things in order, tidying. Perhaps she was waiting for us to come back.

In the kitchen now. I sit on the last step of the stairs, nodding at the table with its two upright chairs pushed in tight to the edge, the bath with its lift-up lid, the cooker with the Toby Jug resting crookedly on the ring. It used to sit in the centre of the table. There were places for things. The Jug went there, with the pens in for my father to run a ring around the horse he would bet on, for my mother to write her IOUs. It brings back Luca, drawing out a biro to scratch my name before she carves into my skin; and Fran, her blue tattoos. It brings me right up to my mother again, standing in the yard with her hands over her face. That time, the Jug had money under it.

~ ~ ~

You're not goin' an' that's final!
Rose waits until she hears Terence's footsteps receding down the path. She sits quite still, listening to the shink, shink of the wall-clock. It's in the shape of a teapot. She saved the coupons for it. It says ten past ten. She crosses the kitchen, opens the door of the freezer and takes out a packet of peas. She holds them to the swelling on her face.

I am, she says to the teapot-clock, Try an' bloody stop me.

~

Rose lives in a crescent on Pontcanna estate. All the houses look the same: box-square semis with a rectangular patch of mud at the front. The wide picture windows show the whole world what's inside, which is nothing out of the ordinary.

Rose makes her way into the hall, bends down, slides her hand behind a loose edge of stair-carpet. She fumbles, hooks her fingers under the stair-rail, pulls out her money. No need to count it – she's taking the lot. She carries it back into the kitchen. She hasn't got an envelope and she can't find an elastic band. She holds the notes in her fist, looking for her purse, and then she blinks slowly and laughs out loud: Terence will have taken it. The teapot-clock says ten to ten. Rose picks up the packet of frozen peas, now slippery wet and melting, and rips the bag with her teeth. She empties them into the sink, running hot water on the clusters of icy peas and poking them down the plughole until she can't be bothered any more. She stuffs the notes into the Bird's Eye packet and puts it in her shoulder-bag.

C'mon, Parsnip, she says, We're goin' on our hols.
The dog that has been lying silently under the table, watching

Rose's movements with a hopeful shift of the eyes, leaps up and points his nose at the back door.

Rose walks across the estate. In the distance is the Shopping Village with its Chinese take-away, the chemist glowing golden from behind its portcullis, and the new-brick outline of The Cricketer's Arms. The carriage lamps on either side of the entrance spark with orange rain. It's falling heavily now. The dog stops to shake himself, pulling up Rose on the other end of the leash. She hears the sound of pub-laughter drifting on the night, warm and male and slightly threatening. There are two youths crouching on the floor of the bus shelter.

When's the next one due? asks Rose.

They shrug at her. The younger boy has a cigarette curled like a glow-worm in his fist. He sucks importantly on the end. The other puts his head round the edge of the shelter and nods into the distance

S'yer now, he says.

Rose sees the lights of the Hopper Bus appear at the top of the road. She clutches her bag tight to her side. She'll get a taxi at the terminus to take her the rest of the way.

~ ~ ~

The bulb on the landing doesn't work, but I can tell by the slant of light falling down the stairwell that the door to my old bedroom is open. I'm not afraid of that. A prickle of air behind me, like my father's breath, chases me flying up the stairs. I wait in the darkness until the banging of my heart subsides. I can see the bed and the wooden chest beneath the window. Safe now.

I drag the lamp as far as it will stretch, running the flex under the bed and across the floorboards. The shade is nowhere to be found; no lampshades anywhere. I imagine my mother under all this bald light. I try to pull the chest nearer to the lamp, but it's too heavy, and when I lift the lid, it's full to the brim – with old clothes, slices of flint, a dirty nest of straw. I run my hand over the fabric and the shiny cuts of stone, pulling at the nest until it opens up its secret: a glazed chalk fawn in two crumbling halves. There's a memory here but I can't fathom it. A twist of pale straw breaks between my fingers.

On the top shelf of the corner cupboard I find two folded blankets. When I shake them out they're craggy with damp, but anything is better than the idea of using the bed downstairs. I put my cup of water on the floorboards, unwrap the gift of chocolates and eat a few. I wasn't prepared at all: I expected the phone to be connected, a Late Shop open, central heating, a fridge that worked. Not this dereliction, this hollowness. Not Mrs Riley and her sly remarks. Somewhere, bouncing off a house further down the street, is the metallic hiss and bang of music. The window sticks as I push at the sash, then slides up with a terrifying clap. I can only see the car parked on the pavement; it takes me a minute to realize that the music comes from there. The two bodies in it are still enough to be dead. A curl of smoke rises from the driver's window.

The noise is louder in the dark. I stare up at the ceiling as the grey light spreads, trying to ignore the smell coming from the pillow, the damp of the blanket, the ache of this house. The lightbulb clicks as it cools, rain shudders on the window, footsteps clip along the street and suddenly stop. A sound at the front door, a scrabbling at the letterbox, a change of air. Someone is inside.

Who's there? a voice shouts up the stairs, Who is it? nearer and nearer until the woman is standing in the doorway and I'm holding out the lamp-base like a club, ready to fight. I look at the woman and she grins at me. Her hair's wet and curly round her face, her white puffa jacket is soaked, her leggings stained a deeper black on each knee. Behind her, a wiry lurcher shivers on the landing.

Bloody hell, says the woman, Talk about Little Orphan
Annie!
Her eyes squint away from the bare bulb,
    Couldn't you find a hotel then, Dol?
I know that tone; I know this woman now.
    Rose, is all I can manage, Rose.

                        ~

I sit up, rest my shoulders against the cold back wall. It's like
I've never been away. Rose's sudden appearance doesn't help.
She searches in her handbag for a tissue, then the pockets of
her jacket where she finds a grey crumple of toilet paper. In
the lamplight, the bruising on her cheek looks like dirt. She
blows loudly into the paper, balling it up and pressing it into
the corner of each eye. If I didn't know better, I'd say she
was moved.
    Well I never, she says, dispelling my illusion, Little Crip's
come back.
Studying her face is like looking in a convex mirror. Rose is
broader across the bridge of the nose, her skin a shade darker
with a smooth thickness to her chin and neck. The blueish
stains beneath her eyes aren't bruises: I've got them too. She
has the same mouth, turned down at the edges. Our mother's
did that: she always said it was disappointment that caused it.
Rose helps herself to the chocolates while she tells me her
history; about Terence and the Forces, where they travelled,
and Brian and Melanie, her two grown-up children. She bites
into a hard centre, inspects it closely and then feeds it to the
dog.
    They bloody well hated their father, she says, running her
tongue around her gums, An' now, he can do no wrong,
like? Iss all, 'Aw, poor Dad! Give him a break' – I ask you!
Anyway, that's me. Not much to tell is there?
Her mouth settles into its u-shape. I begin to think my
mother was right; disappointment is inherited.

Where's Terence now? I ask.

Rose grins at me. She peers inside her bag and takes out the packet of peas full of money. At the sound of the rustle, the dog gets up off the floor and sits to attention in front of her. He puts a determined paw on her knee.

I've left him to fend for himself for a bit. Get off, Pars! It'll do him good – That's the last time *anyone* hits me.

The phrase comes too easily; she's used it before. There's a lull where we stare at the dog. Rose has told me her life; she's galloped over the years between us as if they were matchstick fences. I can see she expect me to do the same; she folds her arms over her chest, her lips go tight.

And now you've turned up. Out of the blue!

I tell her about the letter I received from the social services. She shifts her weight to one side of the bed.

They never told *me*, she says, They never told me, but they told Celesta, didn't they? So she rings when I'm at work and she gets Terence. 'Tell Rose her mother's died and the funeral's on Friday.' Just like that – 'her mother' – not 'our mother'.

You never came to see her? I ask.

Who? Mam? Oh aye, she says, I tried now and then. Reckoned she didn't know me. She was in and out of Whitchurch like no one's business. Not that *you'd* know anything about it.

Whitchurch Hospital. The railway tracks running along the back; the rain; the gravel; the last time I saw my mother. Rose is trying to blame me.

I was sent away, I say. Even to me, it sounds like an excuse.

Yeah, Dol. But there's no law against coming back, is there?

I have no answer for her. Everyone got sent away. Except my father – he simply ran. Rose is worrying at the squashed ball of toilet paper, tearing it into smaller and smaller pieces. They fall from her lap on to the floor, where the dog licks at them as if they're flakes of snow.

Dad?

No.

I ask about Fran and Luca. Rose shakes her head. She bends down to stroke the dog, notices the cup of water beneath the bed and stretches over to get it. She holds it out in front of the dog's muzzle and he laps obligingly, splashing blobs of moisture on her wrist.

All I know is Celesta's doing alright. Family business, two sons to look after her. She's rich now old Pippo's gone to that big pop factory in the sky. Very posh, our Cel.

Rose breaks into a sudden, bitter laugh. Just like my mother's.

She doesn't want to know *me*, that's for certain, she says, looking me up and down, So – no offence, Crip – I can't imagine she'll be glad to see *you*.

fourteen

Celesta's not in the mood for seeing anyone. Dinner is ruined.

Ungrateful sods, she says to the kitchen as she scrapes the potatoes, the meat, the congealed jelly of gravy into the bin. She hears the phone ring and ring, and the answering machine cutting in just as she lifts it up.

There is a distant echo on the line, a faint Hello, and then nothing except her own recorded message booming in the empty hall. She untangles the coiled rope of the receiver. It wasn't her boys at all. It was a woman's voice; it sounded like her mother. Celesta stares at the sweaty beads of her palm print on the handset.

~

At the other end of town, Louis and Jumbo Seguna stand outside their new restaurant. Once every minute, an arc of white beams sweeps across the room, falling out on to the pavement and speckling them in a queasy rash. It's supposed to look like moonlight on the ocean waves, but to Jumbo it looks cheap; it reminds him of Christmas tinsel and school discos. Louis is rather proud of it; he likes things that glitter.

What's the *matter* with it, he cries, It looks alright to me! Jumbo gazes up at the wide glass frontage; there's so much he doesn't like, he hardly knows where to begin. He could start with the name; etched across the plate glass in bold lettering are two words: The Moonlight. Jumbo takes his father's fob-watch out of the pocket of his waistcoat and holds it up in the dance of dark and light,

We're late, he says, Mamma's going to kill us.

The two men face each other. There's only five years to separate them, but Jumbo has the middle-aged look of his father; the round belly, a premature splash of baldness on the top of his head, the rolling walk. In contrast, Louis is as smooth as a cat.

Tell me what you want changed, he says, And I'll see what I can do.

All of it. The window, the lighting. That bloody name.

It's Retro, says Louis, Historical! You should see the original place, Jum—

Jumbo stops him. He has no interest in Louis's haunts, in hanging about street corners talking to the Old Boys about Old Times. This is not the clientele he wishes to attract. He's looking for smart money, Bay money. His mother's feelings play only a small part in his objections, but he'll use any means now.

It will really upset Mamma, he says.

She okay?

Why don't you come and see for yourself? says Jumbo. But he knows by the way Louis is fidgeting that he won't be facing their mother tonight. He doesn't offer him a lift.

Give her my love, okay? Louis calls to Jumbo's back.

Sure, Jumbo mutters, easing himself into the front seat of his car. He can feel the red burn of a migraine jabbing at his eye. Probably those lights, he thinks.

~

In the large double bedroom at Connaught Road, Celesta stands and thinks. Her ears are filled with white noise and the voice inside her head. You don't have to go, it says, taunting her. Celesta slides back the door of the wardrobe, chooses two black outfits from the rail and throws them onto the bed:

she last wore the jacket and skirt at Pippo's funeral. She bends below the swinging clothes to the rank of shoeboxes lined up on the floor. They are labelled, each pair fitted with shiny wooden shoehorns to preserve the shape of the leather. Buried among the skirts and dresses is a hanger with a neat row of co-ordinating belts, chiming in the draught. As Celesta reaches further in, one of the belts unwinds itself and slinks to the floor. She glimpses the fall of it, uncurling like a fist. Suddenly she sees another thing: the coil of leather opening, flying through a deeper black, cutting the night in two to find the flesh and cry of a child.

I don't *have* to go, she says, crouching, No one can make me.

Celesta doesn't want to face this funeral. She doesn't want surprises.

~

Jumbo pulls into the kerb outside the house in Connaught Place and glances up at the windows. The ground floor is in darkness. Upstairs in his mother's bedroom, a thin sliver of light cuts between the heavy curtains. He points his key-fob at the car and climbs the scrubbed white steps to the door.

Celesta, lying on the bed, hears the beep-beep followed by the swish of the front door. She sits upright and listens hard, tracking the sound of Jumbo's footsteps on the tiles, the silence as they cross the carpeted dining room, a squeak as he opens the oven door. He's on his own then – no Louis. Jumbo shouts from the kitchen.

Only me, Mamma! Anything for supper?

Celesta lies back on the bed and stares at the ceiling.

It's in the bin, she says to the room.

~ ~ ~

At the end of the concourse, a small woman in a sari and a pink flapping overall is sweeping the tiles with a wide broom.

She is completely bent into her work and takes no notice of anyone. She drags her broom and her black plastic bin-liner around the airport, past the flight information desk, past the Bureau de Change and the rows of chrome seating, between people's legs, brushing the edges of the sleeping bodies snuggled like grubs in every corner. She can't possibly like all that never-ending space. There is so much floor at airports it's nearly all floor, as if to echo the vast amount of sky there is to fly across.

Luca presses the telephone tight to her ear. She's shouting something, staring at anyone who stares at her. They don't see the look she gives them; her eyes are invisible behind her sunglasses. The tannoy echoes above her head, telling her in three languages of delayed outgoing flights and of the planes which can't land. There's fog, thick as a cough, in Amsterdam. Luca is grounded.

For Christ's Sake! she shouts to everyone, Shut up!
On the back of her novel Luca has written the three numbers given to her by directory enquiries. She gets Jumbo on the second attempt, then gets cut off. There could be fifty Segunas in the book, she thinks, I could be ringing strangers all night.

~ ~ ~

Jumbo peeps round his mother's bedroom door. Celesta is curled diagonally on the bed, a black jacket bunched up under her head. He sees her hand covering her eyes and the straight closed line of her mouth. Jumbo can't tell if she's asleep or simply lying there.

Mamma, he says, Mam, there's someone on the phone – I think they want you.
Celesta rises to vertical. Her left arm is numb. A row of button marks are vivid on her cheek.

God. What time is it? she asks. She picks up the telephone on the other side of the bed, hears a distant echo and the sound of the television downstairs.

Hello? she says. Her mouth feels thick with sleep. She gives Jumbo a look.

There's no one there, she says, holding out the handset. The tone of disconnection buzzes between them.

~ ~ ~

Luca has travelled – is still travelling – all the way from Vancouver. She has left her girls in the care of the new Korean housekeeper, at their new house in the suburbs. Luca's husband is in Montreal at a razor-blade convention. Last month he became her ex. There are lots of new things in Luca's life.

She finds a seat opposite a snoring man on the bank of chairs next to a burger bar. He appears lifeless, except for the sound of air trapped in his throat, in, out, in, out. She shuts her eyes and imagines the snores as colours; green brown, green brown, and as the noise grows dimmer it changes, becomes the grating of a handsaw, up down, up down, searing its way through wood.

~

Dadda!

Luca stands in the yard and watches her father sawing through the old back door. The fire was over a month ago, but there are still cinders, blowing in the corner against the wall, twirling on a web hanging between two charred stumps of wood. Luca's feet are bare. Her mother is upstairs in the Box Room. She can't find her baby sister, but she can hear her crying. Luca picks her way carefully across the mud, putting her own tiny footprints into the massive indentations left by her father.

What you doing?

Go inside.

Da-ad . . .

Go inside! Go!

He raises the handsaw above his head as if to carve her down the middle. Luca is only two; she hasn't learned to fear him yet. He lifts her by the scruff of the neck, catching hair and the soft skin at the nape and pulling it into a scream. Lifts her with one hand and throws her through the back door where she skids on her arm and face across the concrete floor. Luca lies stunned and silent, looking at a scorched fray of linoleum curling against the skirting board. Her mother comes downstairs, steps over Luca as if she is invisible, leans against the kitchen sink. She bends her head sideways under the tap so that her eyes see but do not register her child on the floor. She takes a long drink. She lets the water run straight out of her mouth and down her cheek and into her hair. She steps over Luca a second time and climbs back up the stairs to her room.

~

Luca opens her eyes. She will not allow herself to be haunted.
Bad dreams, she says quietly, That's all they are.
She finds a bench to stretch out, checking with a wary finger the ache between her ribs. She's got pills somewhere, but she's too tired; a ragged fatigue clots her up inside. She will lie down but she will not sleep. No more bad dreams.

~

Rose is lying down too, on the bed in which her own mother died a week before, but she doesn't care; in fact she's glad. She shuts her eyes but is amazed to find them open again a few seconds later. Not seeing the ceiling with its long crack like a fork of lightning running overhead, nor Terence's punch catch her on the side of the face, nor her father standing in the garden, shaking Fran like a rag-doll in his hands. But her mother she sees again, rising from the bed in a shift of the curtains, a smatter of dawn light ghosting the wall. She sees her out there with Martineau, walking quickly along the street and turning into the alley. Rose must hide. She's hit the Jacksons' window with Celesta's ball. But they are looking at each other, Martineau holding her mother, his hands running up and down her arms. It's such a gentle thing that Rose doesn't recognize it. A negotiation is taking place. Mrs Jackson's voice comes out of nowhere, over the rooftops, caught in snatches on the wind that twists through the alley,

Fire, Missus! Your house is on fire!

So bright and high that Rose has to stop herself from joining in the song,

And your baby is gone.

~ ~ ~

Rose or the dog is breathing heavily; I can't tell who from up here. The effect is tantalizing, like the hiccups: just when you think it's over, another note drags itself through the air. It makes the space between the sounds seem bigger. I fix on the chest under the window. The nightmares rise and fall like gulls on the horizon; something is being unearthed.

fifteen

Drink, says Rose. We'll need drink. Put that down.
I'm making a list. Bread, butter, ham, tomatoes, dog food.
And cake.
Cake? I say, not expecting this addition.
I *like* cake, she says, Anyway, there's no rule is there,
saying No Cake at the Wake?
She's teasing me. She leans over, takes my pen, underlines it
twice.
I must have got the habit from Mam, I say, She used to
make lists all the time.
Did she now? says Rose tartly, Well, I don't think it's
genetic. Tea. For those who don't like whisky. Put that on
your list.
We've been circling like this for half an hour. Every time I
mention the past, I feel a stony resistance from Rose. This
morning when I got up, she was already at the kitchen table,
eating chocolates, dipping her finger in and out of the plastic
tray to gather the flecks. She wore a strange expression – full
of glee or spite, I couldn't tell which. It put me on my guard:
more than thirty years on, I still couldn't trust her.
I've just had words with Old Mother Riley, said Rose,
Doesn't want the dog in her vegetable patch. Even though
he's a Parsnip.

She let out a loud laugh and shook the tray of chocolates at me.

Montelimar or Turkish Delight? she offered.

I wanted to talk about the funeral arrangements. If the social services were trying to find us, I wouldn't be the only one to come back. I didn't know who to expect, but Rose was living here; she must have had some idea. She skidded round my questions.

I'll be there, she said, beaming, And Mrs Riley; the old girl's looking forward to it. Celesta will do the decent thing, I reckon. She wouldn't miss the opportunity to buy a new hat.

Surely there'll be others? I said, Luca – Fran?

Rose made the same ducking motion that she did last night. No reply. I forgave it then. But something came clear this morning, finding myself in my old room in the bed with the dip in the middle and the dawn light leaking through the curtains. It was a reflex: I looked for Fran.

Rose pulls the scrap of paper towards her and holds it, long-sighted, at arm's length.

Neat, she says, sounding surprised, as if the lack of one hand meant the other would be useless.

Why shouldn't it be?

Dad used to call you The Sinister.

As she says it she contorts her body, pulling her arm up into a claw and leaning to the left. It looks obscene, like a caricature from a silent movie. She's doing me, at five years old. Then just as quickly she composes herself, hunches over the list and retraces each word; colours in the letters. An embarrassed flush creeps up her neck. I hold my voice steady.

Do you think we'll see him?

Rose speaks calmly. It's worse, somehow, than shouting.

You think he's gonna turn up, do you, just because she's died? Just because *you* finally decided it was time to come home? I've been here all my life, Dol. If Dad wanted to show, he'd have done it before now.

I came back, I say, not meaning to sound defensive.

Oh aye, she says, Not before time. And for what, exactly? She raises her head at last. It reminds me of Mrs Riley; *There's nothing worth having.* I had been asking myself the same question all week. There were so many things I wanted. Packing my bag, sitting on the train, lying down last night and listening to Rose's snoring, I thought I would find someone I could say it to.

I want to lift my mother's head from the track. I was only five, I couldn't do it then. I want to stop her at the moment she turns and walks away from me, burning like touchpaper in this house. There's hammering, and darkness, and a high wailing sound which lives inside my head. I want a cure.

None of this could be shared with Rose. She was making herself perfectly clear; her past wasn't mine, and I couldn't be part of it. Her likes and dislikes were written in the slant of her eyes: she despised Celesta and my mother; she admired Luca. Marina, my father, Fran, they were dismissed with a flick of the head. And me – I was still Crip. Couldn't be trusted to make a list: left-hander with no left hand. It was damning.

~

I get a cup from the dresser and rinse it in the sink; the tap-water smells like a swimming pool. Through the kitchen window I can see the yard and two wan dahlias leaning over Mrs Riley's fence. At the bottom of the garden, squatting in the uncut grass, is the rabbit's cage in a camouflage of ivy and moss. The water leaves an acid taste in my mouth.

What's he up to? says Rose. She thinks I'm watching the dog. I'm working out a way to persist.

Mam had friends, I say.

Rose makes no reply. She draws a series of loops on the paper.

What about Eva?

You've left it a bit late for all that, she says, exasperated now, I've told you who's coming. There won't be no one else.

The clouds give up a wedge of sun, filling the kitchen with light. Rose sits back and admires her handiwork. The list is illegible now, a forest of swirling lines and winding snakes. I'm thinking about a crucifix and an inky stain spelling FRAN. I'm thinking about tattoos.

I want to find Fran.

Well you won't, she says, finally, You can't find what isn't there, Dol! Try Eva, if you're really that bothered – see for yourself if she wants to come.

Rose sighs heavily, folds the list, tears off the bottom edge. She writes down the address.

~ ~ ~

Elgin Court is on the same road as Whitchurch Hospital, separated by a mile of chestnut trees shedding splotches of light on the path. Lizzie Preece brought me this way when we came to visit my mother. The ground was barbed with fresh green cases, split like wounds. She said we could look for conkers on the way back, but we never did, because after that there was my mother, sneaking me through a break in the fence and on to the railway line at the back, and after that there was the search party, the pelting rain, my mother waving me goodbye with one hand pressed to her mouth. That is how she comes to me, putting the piece of flint to her ear as if she might catch the sea in a stone; feeding me berries that tasted of nothing. It seemed as though we had walked for miles. We sat on the black grass of the embankment and looked at the tracks. My mother took something from her pocket.

I've got us a present, Dol.

Hundreds and Thousands. The packet had a picture of a

clown on the front. I licked my finger and dipped it into the rainbow of dots.

Enough left for a trifle, she said, folding the packet carefully and stowing it away, Shall we go home and make one?

I thought she meant our home.

For hours afterwards, sitting with Lizzie Preece, waiting for my new mam and dad to arrive, I would find the tiny beads of sugar in the gaps between my teeth. Crunching, like a bit of gravel or stone.

My mother would have been seventy-two this year; Eva must be near the same age. Too young to be in a home.

~

All the women wear brown stockings and floral print dresses. All the men are asleep. The room is large, low-ceilinged and open-plan, with armchairs evenly spaced to form a semi-circle. It looks like a hotel foyer, but the television in the corner is a giveaway: no sound, a strike of sunlight dissecting the screen. A tiny woman peers at the close-up faces of people arguing. The rest of them sit in their chairs, taking turns to sigh. While I'm waiting, I study the residents. There's no sign of Eva's peroxide bun with its streak of nicotine running up the side: these women are pastel rinsed, woolly permed. One of them wears a fur hat in jealous auburn which she habitually checks with her hand. If any of them is Eva, I tell myself, it's bound to be her. I'm wondering if giving me this address was one of Rose's peculiar jokes, when there's a clack of heels behind me, and a high, sing-song voice in the style of a breezy hostess.

Hello there! Dolores! How lovely to see you.

Now *this* is Eva. She is a dazzle of mismatched colours: translucent shadow, blue as a baby's eye, is smeared across her lids. There's a straight orange gash where her lips should be, horsey yellow teeth behind them. Framing her head is a helmet of silver hair. She wears an acid yellow suit, and lots of jewellery; chains and lockets do battle at her neck, a set of bangles clatter on her wrist.

We'll have tea in the conservatory, Mrs Powell, she says to the care assistant at her side, When you've got a minute. Eva raises her eyes to heaven. Can't get the staff, her look says. She sweeps ahead, throwing her arm out to show me her domain. A long corridor with a series of doors, one open to show its narrow bed, chintz curtains and covers, a mirror screwed to the wall. Then straight on into the conservatory. It's a new addition, the palms and vines are young and green, but the foliage is sparse; there isn't enough of it to soften the edges. Every pane of glass gives up a harsh, clean light. It's like being in a birdcage; the smell is baking wood.

Eva clips smartly across the tiles, sits on a sun lounger and crosses her legs. One very thin gold chain cuts a little too tight into her ankle. It's all colour – Eva, the floral lounger, the creeping ivy behind her head, the stained wood soaking up the sun, as if in retaliation against the muzzy creams and dim browns of the sitting room. It's hot in here but Eva doesn't notice; she squashes up close and covers my hand with hers. There's nothing about her face or her smile or her chatter that reminds me of the Eva I knew; I want an ocelot fur with its bottle of rum peeping from the pocket. I want a charm bracelet with its little boot, pixie and spinning heart. It feels like a cheat.

I can't spend too long, Dear, forgive me. This place is so busy – never-ending! Poor loves. Now, how are you? As I talk she blinks rapidly at me, her sky-eyes full of concern. She bends closer: I think she expects me to kiss her, her face is so near mine. I can smell her powder, and underneath, another scent. Sharp, unplaceable. I tell her about my mother. She nods vigorously. Closer still, as if to suck the breath from my mouth – so close, I can see the raddle of lines on her face, her forehead prickled with sweat, and her hairline, a fraction too low.

Nasty shock, she says. Suicide. On top of everything else. The gas oven, the railway track. It was my fear too, so I'm prepared for her assumption. But this isn't how it was.

She died in her sleep, I say, repeating what I'd heard.

They never do, Eva whispers loudly, It's just what people like to think. Take it from me, she nods confidentially, They always know when their time's up!

The heat of glass all around us, a zigzag of yellow and green, her hands on mine: it's beginning to stifle. The assistant comes with a tray.

I've brought some biscuits, she says, winking at me.

Very good, says Eva.

She releases my hand to pour the tea.

Will you come to the funeral? I ask.

Of course! she says, Would I miss that? No!

Eva takes a biscuit from a little plate. They're custard creams; the edges are blunted and the criss-cross patterns are worn, as if they've been fingered, re-used.

At your age, it's weddings, she says, prising open the two halves of the biscuit, But for me, it's all funerals.

She presses the square flat against her mouth and begins to lick the cream. A faint crust of icing, sticky on her lips.

Now your mother's gone. There'll be none of us left soon! I ask her who is left. She frowns, blinking slowly, rhythmically, as if there's a body count going on in her head.

You could try The Moonlight, that's still going she says, and with a coy smile – You might find *someone* there! An old friend!

Eva lifts her cup, sips the tea and pulls a face. She clatters it down in the saucer.

No sugar! she says, Bugger!

I thought there might be some family, I say, I'm looking for Fran.

Eva cranes her neck over the fringe of the lounger and shouts into the hallway,

Mrs Powell, you've forgotten the sugar! Sorry, love, she says, sitting again. Sweat gathers in the creases of her forehead. She puts up an orange fingernail and scratches beneath the hairline. The helmet of hair shifts slightly to the left.

Frank? she says, mishearing me, Oh, well now, *he* won't show; not now they've found Salvatore.

She reaches for another biscuit. Puts the edge to her mouth. Licks the corner. Licks the air out of the room.

You won't remember him, poor old Sal. Buried in the mud all that time. Can you imagine!

But I do remember Salvatore. Cooking, singing, smuggling parcels of cold meat under his jacket. Then gone like my father. The mention of either name would bring the house down.

She waited, you know. Thirty-odd years.

Carlotta, weaving the pips of her rosary through her fingers while Salvatore curled like a fishbone under the silt.

Got away with it, your father.

Frankie on a boat to a sunny place.

They're calling it murder.

The red of Eva's tongue on the edge. A smell of iron, smell of heat.

There's none of us left now. No one. There's no sugar! she shouts, No sugar!

Unbearable heat in here.

Let me out.

~

Eva clings to Mrs Powell as she is led back through the hall. They turn into a narrow corridor where I wait, breathing the cool air, taking it in.

Mrs Amil's gone to have a lie down, says the assistant on her return, She gets a bit tired.

She holds out a purse, covered in sequins and seed pearls.

She said to give you this.

sixteen

Luca flies through the morning sky and as she flies she's dreaming. The light flooding in at the porthole window doesn't disturb her; she wears a mask made of pale blue gel which is supposed to cool the delicate skin around the eye. It's a sight that makes the cabin staff smile: with her head wrapped in a green paisley scarf and her bug eye-wear, Luca looks like a creature from the depths. The rattle of the drinks trolley brings her to the very edge of waking. She re-adjusts her mask so that a crack of sunlight filters in around the sides, catching the red rim of her lashless lids, transforming the light into slivers of rust.

~

Fran's bed has been empty for three whole days but the sheet with the bloodstains still lies folded on the floor. Dolores is curled like a cat in the well of the mattress, the bit where their mother should be and where Luca can still find the scent of her if she breathes in and out against the rumpled sheet. Luca tries to frame herself around her sister, but she's too hot; her body is liquid with the heat of sleep. She listens through the silence for any sound of her mother, lying sedated in the Box Room. Carlotta went home earlier, after a wild exchange with her father that left him biting his knuckles with rage. From downstairs comes the sound of the television on low, and her father, moving about in the kitchen.

Then it's blacker, later, the street-light outside their window is off, and perhaps it is this that wakes her, or the shadow of someone standing in the room. Luca is not afraid. The hand that slips beneath the blanket at the foot of the bed is cool and familiar. It takes her foot and strokes it, lifts it gently so now there are two hands cupping this one hot foot. Slips along the edge of her ankle, holding it by the heel while the other hand caresses then separates the little toes as if to count them. Then takes the smallest toe and jerks it quickly so the brittle crack of the joint is lost beneath the cry that comes from Luca's mouth. Quickly again, cracking the next toe and the next, while Luca squirms in pain and lashes out her other foot against her sister. Dolores moans and shifts over to the far edge of the bed. The hands are moist from this quick work. They can feel the tremble of shock rippling under the child's skin. And then a quiet laugh, a comforting sound, a nice sound even, as if this pain is a gift brought noiselessly to a favourite daughter in the safety of darkness. Kisses the arch of the foot where the skin is softest, covers it again with the blanket and goes away.

~

Luca's eyes are wide and unblinking under the mask of pale blue gel. The dreams are stacking up. She concentrates on what there is: the rattle of the drinks trolley making its way back up the aisle, the snap of an overhead locker being shut, the sharp whine of descent. These are the things she hears.

Fasten your safety belts please, we will shortly be arriving at Cardiff Wales Airport.

~ ~ ~

The New Bridge is a safe enough distance; from up here, the docks look like a picture in a holiday brochure: the Pierhead building with its clockface glittering like a second sun, the sprinkling of yachts in the bay, the dry dock filled with a wash of blue. Pretty and harmless. But I won't go near. Behind the wide parade and sandblasted stone is another place where brick crumbles, sky falls, people fall.

I twist open the clasp on Eva's purse, releasing a pocket of damp air. Inside are two old bus tickets and a photograph, spotted with mildew. It shows a wedding party: woman man, woman man, woman man, so at first I don't know who is who. But the young girl's hair is braided with flowers – Celesta the bride. The men on either side of her are the same age, same height: one of them is fat and balding, and the other is my father. He squints against the sun. He could be smiling. He could be thinking of Celesta's happiness: married to Pippo, safe at last. Behind the slits of his closed eyes I look for evidence of his own escape. I can almost see his heart thundering in his chest. The woman on his right is my mother; in her suit with the silver threads, she doesn't look much older than her daughter. A slight breeze lifts the fringe from her forehead. She raises her head against it so she looks aloof, as though she might just blow away into the sky. And behind her, Salvatore, his face cutting into the corner like a spot of sunlight on the lens. He's smiling. He knows nothing yet; he cannot see how the day will end.

Eva's purse rests on the edge of the bridge. Just like my mother, placing her white handbag carefully on the stone above the river; before my father ducked into Joe Medora's car; before Eva came and found me under the tree. And my memory which cannot be trusted and which is all I have clings to me like mud. It brings back Eva, inching a fingernail under her crooked hairline, the colours all aflame, and the conservatory, dazzling heat through every pane of glass. Her round eyes shiny as shillings.

Buried all that time. Can you imagine!

~

I can. It would have been very different then; it was a *dry* dock then. The walls would have been visible, an endless drop of brick speeded-up so fast no eye could fix it, shooting past Salvatore as he fell. I lean over the edge of the bridge and up comes the colour, roaring.

~

He looks at the moon. He follows it, tracks it as it moves across the sky. Salvatore shuts his eyes, for only a moment, he thinks, but when he opens them again, the moon has slipped away: it rests now at the corner of his vision. He follows the twisting ropes of the paint cradle as they pass above him. He could haul himself up, if he could only move. Salvatore cannot even turn his head. First the wind, then clouds heaping over the sky, rain settling on his face and clothes, chilling the inch of naked flesh between the turn-up of his trousers and his sock. He hears the shouts of far-off voices. Greek sailors, drunk and staggering over the footbridge, followed by the ssh-sshing, clacking, giggling noise of the prostitutes they will somehow smuggle aboard their ship. Another cry, of fear and glee, as one of the women leaps clear of the edge thirty feet above the place where Salvatore lies. He opens his lips to call to her. Rita, he recites, Rita, Sophia, Gina. Then quietly, Frankie, Frankie.

Frankie sits on the bottom bunk of the tiny cabin and carefully empties his pockets: front right, a roll of notes, front left, his cigarettes, scrabbling against the satin lining of his suit for the inside jacket pocket and his new papers. He lights a cigarette, places it between his lips where it will gather a long tube of ash as he rolls, unrolls, folds, and unfolds the papers with his proud black signature. Blows smoke on them. Licks the edges and rubs the parchment between forefinger and thumb, wearing the newness into age. Thinks about a different life. Tries not to think about Salvatore.

The woman stops, holds an exaggerated finger to her lips.
What now? says her friend.

I yerd some-in, she says.

Her friend takes one arm and drags her away from the drop and the low whisper that sounds like an animal moving in the darkness.

Frankie, *Habib.*

Frankie lying down now, arms crossed behind his head, staring up at the curving grille of wire a foot above his face. The imprint of a fat man. He thinks back to when he first arrived in Tiger Bay, the basement room and bed in the corner, how he'd bang his head until he learned to swerve sideways off the pillow. The ruby ring twirling out of his grasp, finding Joe Medora.

Is you is or is you ain't my baby? C'mon, Frankie!

bending the woman, like a gift, into Frankie's lap.

I ain't, says Frankie to himself. I ain't no more.

He twists the ring on his finger. A callus will appear where the gold bites new. Frankie feels a molten wash of heat tingle through him. It's relief, he thinks, excitement. He gives himself up to it; Frankie can be anybody now.

One leg bent at the knee. Salvatore thinks he must be lying on something sharp, a hard thing digging at his shoulder blades; he can't feel his right arm. He eases slightly to the left, sending the cradle on a sideways lurch. The stars swagger in the sky.

Salvatore is unconscious when he finally hits the soft mud of the dry dock below. In the morning, the water oozes through the split lock-gates – pressing mud into his clothes, bits of stones, coiled wire, a paint can knocking gently against his cheek – until the whole of the dock is filled with the sea. The ship, cutting its way gently through the narrow passage of silt, buries Salvatore for ever. The water around it is a rainbow skin of petrol blue and red.

~

My father knew what he had done. He sailed out at dawn and left Salvatore behind. Left my mother and all of us. A man can have a hundred motives, or no reason at all, to simply remove himself from the life he has made. My father would have flipped a coin and watched his fate come twirling down to earth. A sequence is forming, scuffing at the edges of my mind like a ripple on water, but there is no order to it yet. Pieces are missing, people are missing. Rose was right about my father: he won't be back. But there are others. Eva said The Moonlight was still open. If anyone is left, I'll find them.

~ ~ ~

Jumbo sits at the dining table with his mother's telephone pressed to his heart. He notices the bowl of fabric flowers in the centre of the table, each perfect leaf coated with a sticky smudge of grime. Upstairs on the landing, Celesta, forgetting what she was doing, leans into the hot space of the airing cupboard. It's warm and dark. She thinks of what it must be like to lie in there, curled up against the copper pipe with the door shut behind her. She hasn't been to Hodge's Row since she gave birth to Jumbo. But now it's possible that she will have to go back there. Her son's voice drifts up to her in angry starts. Celesta makes her way down the stairs.

What now? she says.

Louis got confused over something – you know what he's like.

Celesta stands with her arms folded across her chest.

And?

And he's messed up the menus, the advertising—

Fix it, says Celesta, nodding at the phone. She could be talking to Pippo.

Leave it to me, Mamma – her son says, knowing by the hard set of her jaw that she won't – I'll talk to him.

Celesta bends under the table. She retrieves one shoe, then the other, and pushes her feet into them.

We'll both talk to him. Come on.

There goes my surprise, thinks Jumbo, Thanks, brother.

seventeen

This can't be right. The avenue is broad and new, shimmering with trees and pavement cafes. This is not where The Moonlight should be: it should be in a side-street; narrow doors and fractured windows and the cracked slab paving as grey as a Dowlais sky. This is not the place. And then I see the three of them. They look so familiar that my memories skate into each other and I don't know what the year is, but I feel as though I'm five again and things are just about to heave to a terrible new start. Celesta is like an older version of the mother I remembered, right down to the way she stands, with one foot out at an angle and the other tapping madly on the pavement – as if there's a beat thrumming in her head that no one else can hear. She scowls up at the plate-glass window. The man beside her could be Pippo; then a second, younger man, leaning against the door of his car and waving his cigarette in the air. He is the image of my father. Celesta knows me straight away; it's as if she's been expecting me. She puts her arms out straight in front of her. The embrace is so swift, I barely feel her touch.

These are my sons, she says, and to Jumbo and Louis, This is your aunty, Dolores.

~ ~ ~

Luca can hardly bring herself to knock on the door. She peers through the crack in the curtains, sees the bed below the window, the old formica table with the television on top. The street is deserted. She looks up at the Jacksons' windows and the house next door to it, sealed with panels of corrugated iron. She wheels her case back up the street, passing a woman being dragged along the road by a dog that looks as though it's grinning. They almost brush each other, Rose and Luca. But Luca is wearing her sunglasses and an impressive scarf which is tied over her head and crossed beneath her throat. Rose notices the woman, so out of place, like a model from a magazine, nearly. But she doesn't recognize her. Luca avoids the fat woman and the thin dog. She wants a hotel. She wants a hot bath and a sleep. She'll do the funeral and then she'll go home again; her time is wasted here.

~

Rose dumps the bag of groceries on the kitchen table and takes out a tin of Butcher's Tripe for the dog. In the pantry she finds a metal plate covered in dust, a tarnished silver tray, and under the shelf, bin-bags, bulging and split like the ones under the stairs. She feeds the dog, then makes a start, upending the first of the bags on the living room floor. Rose isn't looking for anything in particular, but she remembers the jewellery. Her mother wore only a dull orange wedding ring which could have come from Woolworth's, but Frankie wore gold. Rose considers. Frankie would have taken it; could be wearing it still, for all anyone knew. She pictures the shallow glass bowl that lived on his dressing-table; the cufflinks and the tie-pin and the ruby ring, the thin spike of an earring clogged with a dirty yellow crust. Sometimes there would be a watch or an identity bracelet, or a long chain with thick links and a sovereign hanging off it. Like the ring, these things would come and go.

Inside the first sack, she finds baby clothes and children's clothes and men's suits, stuck together with a sour grey mould which flies up in a dust when she pulls at them. The dog dashes around her, poking its head into one bag, emerging suddenly, dipping his muzzle into the next one. He starts to pull at something, tugging with his teeth, his back legs bent against the weight and his claws scraping across the lino. A tangle of ties and belts and leather-hooped braces come suddenly free. The belt whips out from the bag with a noise which startles them both. Rose sits back on her haunches and looks at it. The leather is black and worn. There is a sunrise carved into the buckle, the orb and beams mouldered green at each proud edge. Unmistakable. Rose wraps the belt around her hand. It comes like an instinct. She has never beaten the dog, but this action terrifies him; a leftover memory that he can smell, oozing through the cracked leather. He crawls flat on his belly until he's safely under the bed. Rose feels the stillness of the room and the past spilling out around her.

~

She's twelve again; she's sitting in the window of the back bedroom. In the distance, a fire burns out of control, but it isn't Fran's doing. Fran is lying down in her own room, waiting for tomorrow when Lizzie Preece will come to take her to the Homes. It's been a week since the Evanses' shop caught fire, since her dad stood in the kitchen and punched Fran sideways on to the floor. Rose didn't know it then, but that was just a taster. The house has been full of people all day: Lizzie Preece with her forms, then Arthur Jackson, helping her mother through the front door and sitting her down on the chair. Her legs covered in mud. Rose was sent to look for their dad. She never found him. She left messages at The Moonlight and the Betting Office and The Bute. He never came home. But now he's here, sitting downstairs with the belt across his knees and his eyes on the door. He's shut her mother in the Box Room. No one is allowed to see her. The house is quiet.

It's not right, Cel, Rose whispers, It's not right!

Celesta slips off her bed and crouches on the floor. She sifts through the slurry of singles drifting across the floor until she finds the one she wants to play.

What do *you* know, she says, tilting the record and blowing on it, You're just a kid.

I know it's not *right*, Rose persists. She doesn't want an argument; she wants Celesta to do something. Celesta pulls the edge of her sleeve over her thumb and rubs it carefully along the vinyl.

They deserve it. This family is a bloody disgrace!
She drops the needle into place with a click and hiss. 'Under the Boardwalk' fills the dusk.

C'mon, Rose, says Celesta, Let me show you this dance! Her pink toes beat the lino as she counts herself in.

One, two, three, and – she stops – Come *on*, Rose! she says, snapping her fingers in front of her face, You can't do anything about it!
And she picks up the rhythm again.

Click. Click. Roll from the hips,
Hitch-hike right thumb, step and turn,
Hitch-hike left thumb, step and turn,
Back Step, Back Step,
Slide to the side. And Turn.

Rose doesn't feel like dancing. In her head, she goes through it once more.

The living room is in darkness; not even the blue light of the telly. Something's wrong. Rose is worried that she's stayed out too late. She never found her dad, but as she makes her way round to the backyard, she hears him, shouting. It is Fran she sees first, standing on the scrub of lawn. She has her arms up in front of her face.

Arms down! he shouts. He has his back to Rose. His shirtsleeves are rolled up, the belt is coiled around his fist.

Fran drops her arms to her sides and stands quite straight. It's military. She doesn't recognize Rose; they're only a few feet apart but everything in Fran's eyes is a bright mosaic of fear. In the light falling from the kitchen window, Rose sees the raised pink stripes on her sister's skin. Neck and arms and legs. Frankie pauses, takes a breath in, steadies himself on his back foot, breathes out. And with that breath comes the sound the leather makes as he sends it, buckle flashing, through the air. A white cry from Fran's open mouth. Another small cry, like an echo, in the distance. Frankie drags the belt back, wraps it round his fist,

Like your mother, he says.

Silence. Fran tilting, looking like she might topple.

A Liar. Just like your mother.

Aiming at her head. The sharp claw of the buckle grazes her face, cuts a thin notch of gristle from her ear. A noise like an animal. Frankie catches her up in his hands. Her body bends. So bent, Rose thinks, she must be broken. He throws her down. His fingers on her neck.

A scream.

Not from Rose, who has covered her mouth. Not from Fran, smothered beneath the weight of him. The sound stops Frankie. He crawls over his daughter's body to hide in the shadow of the wall. Fran staggers away. A moment passes before he follows her inside, ducking low as if the sky will fall and crush him. Rose is reminded of a chimpanzee at the circus.

In the kitchen, Frankie is rinsing the buckle under the cold tap. He doesn't look up, but he senses Rose at the door. He runs his finger along the brass tongue.

Fetch Dolores to me, is all he will say.

But she won't. She won't let him have her.

~

Upstairs, Fran is not crying. She rests her head against the dressing-table mirror. She has a school sock pressed to her ear.

What did you do? asks Rose.

Nothing.

He called you a Liar, says Rose.

Fran inspects the sock, turning it so that a clean piece can be found. It is polkadot blooded.

I didn't do nothing.

Let's go and tell Mamma, says Rose.

Fran's laugh is shrill.

Hah! she says, It's *her* fault!

Her ear is hot red, blue at the edge where the tine of the buckle fell.

Ow. It kills . . .

She dabs a patch of the fabric to her tongue before pressing it again on the wound. She flicks her hair over her face to cover both ears. Rose looks at the rising welts on Fran's arms.

I'm gonna tell Celesta, she says.

But in the back bedroom, Celesta is practising her steps. She doesn't want to hear.

The doctor's coming, suggests Rose, We could tell him.

Celesta freezes in mid-step.

You bloody dare! she says, He'd kill the lot of us! You tell Fran – tell her – she's not to say a word to anyone!

Celesta could change things; she's the oldest, she would know what to do.

But all Celesta will do, is dance.

~

Rose's leg has gone numb. She unfolds it from under her, tries to move, but the pain of revival is too intense. She waits for the pins and needles to pass.

~ ~ ~

It's cool inside The Moonlight, an airy space of blond wood and chrome fittings. We sit in a window seat where Jumbo brings us coffee on a polished tray – just two cups – so that Louis looks at him quizzically before he takes the hint and follows his brother to the back of the restaurant. Celesta sits on the very edge of her chair; her body is turned slightly away from me. She takes in her surroundings. Avoiding my eyes.

I was going to the *old* Moonlight, I say, It's a bit of a shock. I never expected—

The name will change, she says flatly, It wasn't my idea.

The old Moonlight still exists though? – I went to see Eva this morning. You remember Mrs Amil?

and I start to take the purse out of my bag.

I'm not interested, she says, shifting further to the side.

It's a photograph of your wedding day. Mam and Dad. Salvatore.

I don't care. Put it away.

Celesta drops her spoon, places her right hand flat on the table next to my left. Careful not to touch me. Two grown-up hands now, mine and hers. I turn my palm upwards, expose the proud edge of bone where my thumb would have been, the crescent of white flesh and the splash of purple scar tissue where the skin grafts failed. I resist the urge to bury it in my lap. She has to look at me now.

You don't mind it? she says, It doesn't bother you?

I turn my hand over again; she means it bothers *her*. I could tell Celesta about starting school and how the other children would refuse to sit with me in case they 'caught it', or how my foster mother tried to persuade me to wear a prosthesis which rubbed a channel of soreness round my wrist. But I tell her other things; about meeting Mrs Riley again and how Rose found me in the old bedroom. All the time I talk, I'm studying her face. She lets me do it, nodding slightly and fidgeting with her napkin. In shadow her complexion is smooth and brown, but on the other side, where the daylight catches it, tiny wrinkles run beneath the powdered skin.

Mrs Riley had to turn the gas on for me, I say, The

cupboard was full of rubbish! To think I used to like it, under the stairs.

Celesta narrows her eyes; she lets out a breath.

You don't remember, she says, You were only a baby.

This isn't a question but I want to dispute it. I tumble out a desperate list,

I remember learning all the books of the Bible, and how to do my buttons; you teaching me how to twist; Fran going away. Carlotta and Salvatore, and Joe Medora—

You *can't* remember Joe Medora, she says, her hands flying up as if I've just proved her point, You never met him, Dol. You can't remember Marina, for God's sake! It's only what you've been *told*. It's not the same as knowing.

I do remember Joe Medora!

Celesta says the words slowly, as if I'm a child,

You never met him.

There's something moving at the back of my mind. I'm recalling a picture of a man bending over a woman, he's covering her face with his hand and grinning madly at me out of the frame. His teeth are shining like gold. But it's an engraving from an old book I used to have. Not a memory at all.

Celesta takes up her napkin and dabs angrily at the corner of her mouth. I'm learning her gestures; this is one of ending.

I've kept my boys from all that, she says, sliding back her chair, Your lives are ahead of you. That's what I tell them. Keep facing forward.

She looks over at her sons, both of them leaning on the long counter, sipping coffee. They're watching us. Louis hurries to our table.

Go and help your Aunty Dolores fetch her bags, she says, and turning to me, You'll want to stay at ours, I expect.

It isn't an invitation, it's a summons. She would have me abandon Rose to the old house.

~ ~ ~

Louis was keen to escort me back. He loped along like a puppy, sometimes jumping slightly ahead, then walking backwards as he talked. He threw his arms wide in the air, stared at me earnestly when he made a point. I had to pull him out of the way of people moving past. Louis's voice had the quizzical timbre of the Docks; every statement had a question inside it. We veered off Bute Avenue, into a narrow road that bent into a side-street.

No, Louis . . .

I couldn't catch my breath. I couldn't explain the feeling.

But this is the quick way, he said, You'll be safe with me!

The rubbish blew along the gutter, polystyrene cups and balled-up chip-papers skittering in the wind. The developers hadn't touched this part of town; there were no proud street-lamps in civic colours, no bins with tattooed heralds. Here I was, despite myself: down the Docks. Louis wanted history, but meeting Celesta had made me wary of telling. It felt like a swamp, this past we were supposed to have shared. I gave him facts.

Five girls and then a sixth, and then a fire, and I got burnt, I said.

You got rescued! he said proudly,

I got burnt, and then – they couldn't keep it together.

He went off, your dad. I've heard all about it.

He described events he had only been told, his hands moving quickly in front of his face. They were gilt-edged stories – of a vice ring, a murderous feud, a child sold into prostitution.

This place – it's a *little* world, right? he said, cupping his hands together as if he had captured a moth, And Mam didn't want us to know? She sent us to private school? But people round here – he let his imaginary moth free into the air – They knows us. You hears talk. When Dad died, she was all for going somewhere else, but Jumbo says—

When did your dad die? I asked.

Must be two years, nearly. Kept on going 'til the end, him and Jumbo. The Dynamic Duo!

Louis stopped. There was a bitterness in this reference which told me everything: about Celesta, living here all this time, the rumours never quite going away, but changing, altering imperceptibly over the years. A small fire is an inferno, a burnt hand is a horror story, and a falling-out between old friends is murder. No wonder she didn't want to talk about the past. My own recollections seemed drab by comparison. But Louis was like me – curious, wanting. I clung to it; I told him things I couldn't tell my sisters; Celesta's distance, Rose and Luca's petty cruelty, Fran's kindness. How she was there in the dark, reaching her hand across the bed to hold mine. A bent figure in the dawn light silently folding her soiled sheets; the sense of failure seeping from her. And the fires, those scraps of glass, tattoos. Small acts of torture, third degree damage.

Louis' eyes narrowed.

Fran, he said, Fran. How old would she be now?

I didn't have to think.

Forty-five.

And you don't know where she is? he asked.

Not a clue.

I could ask around, like. I knows some of the old boys.

And suddenly, as if he'd remembered something, he grinned at me.

Hey, Aunty Dol, look at this.

He unbuttoned the front of his shirt and pulled it to one side. A tattoo of a dragon on his breast. I couldn't imagine why anyone would want to be scarred, but Louis was pleased with it.

Fran had her name written here, I said, putting out my right arm, And a crucifix here – offering my left.

Home-made, yeah? he said, taking my left wrist and holding it fast. The double meaning made us laugh. He didn't let go. I didn't let him go.

Will you come to the funeral, Louis? I asked.

He looked blank. So this, too, was something Celesta wasn't sharing.

Our mamma's – your gran's – funeral. It's tomorrow.

Aw no, he said, Aw no.

He turned his head sideways, like a pigeon eyeing a crumb. He was deciding.

I'm going, he said, We'll all go.

And he linked his arm through mine.

Nearly there, *Aunty*, he said, grinning again, Wasn't so terrible, was it?

~

I made him leave me at the top of the street. He was reluctant, kept turning round as I waved him away, shrugging his shoulders in hopeful challenge.

You sure? he shouted, You sure now? I'm useful, me! Good in a crisis!

Celesta wouldn't want him in the house. And I didn't know how Rose would react.

~ ~ ~

She is kneeling in the centre of the room, surrounded by bin-bags and baby clothes, shoes and coat-hangers in two sloping mounds. It looks like a jumble sale. From under the bed, only the grey paws of her dog are visible; he lies as bored as a corpse. Rose looks up at me – her eyes are guilty, embarrassed, as if I've caught her in some terrible act. She smells of sweat and there's a black crease running down her forehead. She has the face of a child.

I've been sorting all afternoon, she says, inspecting her hands. She holds both palms out to show me; her fingertips are sleek with newsprint.

It's mostly rubbish. I'll put it out for the binmen.

I've been to see Eva, I say, And I've met Celesta and her boys.

She's mad, her, Rose mutters.

I don't know who she means.

Did you know Dad was wanted for murder? I ask. I'm level with her now. She won't escape this time.

Oh aye, she says, sliding a knot of clothes back into the bag, And rape an' pillage and daylight robbery. Have I missed anything? Do let me know – leaning close to me, her voice high in mimicry – And I'll put it on my list.

I'm not joking, Rose.

No. You're gullible. Believe anything, you would.

She sits back on her haunches. The sunlight has sunk away; her face is blue in the gloom.

People get blamed for all sorts – Laddered your tights? – *that's* the Gaucis' fault – Break a fingernail? – *blame* the Gaucis! He did a lot of bad things, Dol, she says, raking up the mass of belts and hangers from the floor, He beat the living daylights out of us, he left us without a penny and he ju████████ off. That's the worst crime there is, if you ask me.

She stuffs the clothes into the bags, grabbing handfuls, pressing her weight on them.

You don't *need* to go looking for what he did, Dol. It's right here, she says.

She gathers the plastic bag and ties a knot in the top.

Or haven't you discovered that yet – Sherlock?

And then she tells me about finding his belt. This is all she is prepared to share. I can't remember it, but something turns in my stomach as she talks. Slippery, wet.

Anyway, I thought you might want these. Or shall I bin the lot?

A pile of photographs is heaped across the lino. I bend over to study them: pictures of Celesta as a child, countless men in suits, the smiling faces of women; and a portrait of four small children sitting upright on a couch. Our names have been written in biro above our heads: Rose, Luca, Fran, Dol, with corresponding arrows.

So she wouldn't forget, probably, says Rose.

It's Fran I want to see; leaning into me with her arm round my shoulder and her eyes lit up, the slight blur of a blink. One thin wisp of hair is stuck at the corner of her mouth, which is open, about to say something. I can't remember what it was. A joke perhaps, to make me smile for the camera.

My mother's handbag lies open on the floor next to Rose. Out of its mouth spill other stories: a faded newspaper picture of two men; a child's rosary tarnished with age; a worn wooden dice. Nothing is revealed to me. Old recipe cards of meals I've never tasted, Christmas cards from people I never knew. Nothing more of Fran.

Here, Rose says, bending over the pile, There's a good one of you.

The cream paper backing shows through where the surface is cracked; the edges are round with the wear of constant holding. Two small children. The older one wears a button-up plastic raincoat with a white trim, the collar skewed at the neck, as if she's dressed herself or been forced into it in a hurry. Even though the photograph is black and white, you can tell her hair is red – it flies up off her head like a firestorm. She carries a patent-leather bag slung diagonally across her chest, she grips the strap, stares venomously at the lens. She looks like a bus conductor: *Give me the correct fare, or else.*

The baby next to her is crying. It holds both fists in the air like a prizefighter. It takes me a moment to realize that the baby is me. I study the photograph closely. I put it so near to my eyes that the tiny left hand becomes a blur of off-white, no more than grains on a surface. On the back of the photograph, my mother's nervy script says,

Luca, age 2, with ~~Dellores~~, ~~Dorlores~~, Dolores, 3 wks.

I am crossed out and re-spelt, as if she hadn't got used to this latest child.

It's me, I say to Rose.

Aye, she grins, *All* of you.

The ghost pain flexes. I've never seen my hand before.

eighteen

In films, the funeral is always held in a lush cemetery surrounded by trees. And it's always raining. The camera cuts to a close-up of some leaves, or a blur of tree trunk, and then pulls back to show a figure in black, standing apart from the other mourners. If this person is a man, he'll be drawing steadily on a cigarette; if it's a woman, she'll have her hands folded over her midriff and raindrops twinkling on her veil. It occurs to me, sinking into the slow mud track that will lead us to my mother's grave, that I've never been to a funeral before. It makes me feel lucky.

We follow the priest and the pall-bearers. Their eyes are cast down on the acid yellow pine of the coffin; they hold it straight-armed, low at their sides. Each one has a black tie strung around the collar of his shirt. Apart from their corporation gloves and their weathered faces, they could be mourners.

My mother's burial plot is situated on the slope of a hill overlooking a recycling depot: I can just make out the name Peruzzi through the mist. In the distance there's a dim outline of a housing estate. The cars on the road below the cemetery wall don't drive slowly, despite the evidence of death above them and poor visibility in front. There's a curve at the bottom with an unexpected set of traffic lights; intermittent sounds of screeching break the silence. On the opposite side of the road is a shanty of flower-stalls. The names are all different but the flowers are the same. A man in a suit parks on the pavement below and dashes out across the traffic, risking his life to get a last-minute wreath for someone dead. He's no one I know. I look around at the headstones; the tended ones have lilies stuck in vases, but mostly the flowers are grey and broken with age. I'm watching for mysterious people hiding in the undergrowth, but there's no undergrowth at all here. No one unexpected has arrived.

We are a straggling assortment; me and Rose in a strained mix of dark grey, Mrs Riley looking like the Queen Mother in a coat of painful blueness, a rusting brooch pinned askew on one lapel; and Celesta, tiny between her two dumbfounded sons. She is immaculately dressed in black, with a broad-brimmed hat that is so big, it's almost a boast. The long chain of her handbag glitters in the dull light. Jumbo repeatedly checks his combed-over hair with a tentative hand. The mist concerns him; droplets fall from an even sky. Louis breaks from his mother's side when he sees me, moving jerkily over the sloping grass. He reaches the brow of the hill and lights a cigarette, kicking at the sulky turfs with a polished shoe.

Aunty Dol! Are we in trouble or what!

His eyes switch from me to Rose and back again. He bends close to my ear, conspiratorial,

Mamma's mad. You should've come home with me last night. Did I get some flak!

I stayed at the house with Rose, Louis – didn't you tell her?

I gesture to Rose. It's clear they know each other, but they don't speak. Rose scratches nonchalantly at her chin, examining the sky, while Louis stares at the sharp red point of his cigarette.

Here we go, he says, flicking it away into the grass.

Father Tomelty begins with a pause, searching over our heads for full attention. His mouth stays open. We shuffle, Jumbo coughs nervously, and then we turn and follow the direction of the priest's gaze. A woman in a black headscarf and sunglasses. She crabs slowly up the hill, as if she's being reeled in on his wide, unblinking stare. She clutches one gloved hand to her breast, puts out the other to me as she reaches the graveside.

My God. That hill is a Killer! she says, in a stage whisper. Someone unexpected *has* arrived: she might be in disguise, but there's no mistaking Luca.

~

I can't look at the coffin and I can't look into that hole. I study the downturned heads of all the people pretending to pray in this moment's silence for the soul of Mary Bernadette Gauci née Jessop. Celesta takes shy glances at Luca from under her hat, and Rose grins at her from the opposite side of the grave before the priest catches her eye and she stops abruptly. Father Tomelty's voice veers between a shout and a whisper. From behind me comes a sharp whiff of cigarette smoke: the corporation men are standing at what they consider to be a respectful distance. I'm like them; I don't feel anything. I'm just waiting for it to be over. I don't know who is alive now, and who is dead. I think about my list, tucked neatly in the pocket of my holdall. At least I can tick off Luca.

She stands close; she smells of fresh Chanel and chewing gum. Luca's lipstick is flame red against the parchment of her skin. Suddenly she nudges me, so brief and quick it could be accidental. I take a sidelong glance; she whispers from the corner of her mouth –

Sunday School—

and fixes her eyes on Rose.

~

Sunday School with Father Stoke, who had one leg shorter than the other from getting polio as a child, and whom Rose christened Father Slope the minute she noticed the way he walked. The gobs of chewed-up bible clinging to the back of his cassock; his eyes swimming like giant fish behind the thick glass of his spectacles; he gave us milk out of little bottles and sandwiches filled with beef paste. But we had to pray before we could eat. He'd put us in two facing lines, standing just like we are now over the grave of my mother, our stomachs rumbling in anticipation as he addressed the Almighty Father.

Dear God in Heaven,

Yes? a little voice would cry, as if it came from the ceiling. And he would look up, amazed. It was Rose's trick. He always fell for it.

~

Luca nudges me again, and this time I catch the almost imperceptible nod of her head. Mrs Riley is finding it difficult to keep awake. Her eyelids droop, her head wilts on her neck, almost touching Rose's shoulder before she catches herself up with a judder and a wide-eyed blink at the priest. Rose has her hands clasped over her stomach, eyes closed, eyebrows raised to the sky in two pious arches. She reminds me of Friar Tuck. Her bosom heaves under her coat so at first I think she's weeping; but she opens her eyes and winks broadly at us before resuming her holy stance. There's a low snigger in the priest's pause. He throws a clot of earth on to the lowered box. A muffled Ouch! from below. More earth. Then a pantomime moan. Father Tomelty crosses himself with a sharp flourish and Luca does the same, pinching her nose with her gloved hand. She turns her head to one side but the laugh still escapes her, ripping through her like an explosion, meeting Rose's smothered snorts, and Louis's and mine. And suddenly we are all laughing, embarrassed and raucous under the cold eyes of the priest, the dank air, the drops of mist falling from the sky.

~

Luca is the first to bolt; no sooner is the final Amen sounded than she's careering away on her stiletto heels, raking the mud, fleeing as if the Devil himself were giving chase. But it's only Rose, her coat blown open like a bell, who puffs behind her.

Lu, let up a minute! Wait for me!

When she catches Luca, they link arms. Their laughter falls out over the sloping graves and wilting weeds. I feel a jealous exclusion. For a short time, Rose was mine, and there was a moment at the graveside when Luca put out her hand and I felt I could claim her too. Now they've got each other again. Celesta fusses ahead of me, trying to placate the priest; she'd like to distance herself from all of us, even her boy Louis. He stays at my side. He has a look of mischief about him.

Who's that then? he says.

Luca.

Oh aye, he says, I've heard of her.

We're standing at the lip of the hill, watching the traffic below. The cars look like toys, all lined up and revving at the lights. The greyness of the day is flat, peaceful. Louis surveys the scene.

It's a shock like, seeing everyone again? he asks.

I can't hide my disappointment.

This isn't everyone, I say, There are lots of people I won't be seeing.

Like your dad, he says quietly.

No. Like Fran.

We can try, he says, We can still go and have a look-see.

He makes our excuses.

We're just gonna pop to The Moonli— the restaurant, Mam. Pick up some gin.

Celesta eases herself into the back seat next to Rose and Luca, pinching her coat round her in an unconcealed show of distaste.

We're off home, Dol, shouts Rose through the window, Bring some snacks, okay?

We watch them leave. Mrs Riley smiles and waves at us from the front seat of Jumbo's car. They could be a family on an outing. We wave back.

Now Aunty Dol, says Louis, Are you ready?

~ ~ ~

He is appalled that I don't know where I am. For Louis, the change in the city has been a gradual process, years of roadworks and cordoned-off streets, digging machines and noise and dust, the stink of tarmac smoking the air. To me, it's all new, and all the same; identical rows of red-brick terraced houses, their doors open to let out pushchairs, children's bikes, cooking smells. Tin Street, Zinc Street, Silver Row. I'm thinking about precious metals as we turn into Platinum Place. Louis pauses here.

Look, he says, pointing me in the direction of a cutting overgrown with brambles and weeds, We can get across yer. If you're not superstitious, like.

A leap of black iron spanning the railway. This is Devil's Bridge. To the left a tangle of tired backstreets; to the right, the docks spread out, the threads of the tracks cutting and crossing like the lines on a hand. Directly beneath us, curving away like a serpent, is The Arlies. I have never been on top of the arches, only underneath. A noise of banging, metal on metal, comes from one of the lock-ups in the distance, bouncing out of focus across the air.

We used to play here, I say, When we were little.

Louis grins at me,

We did too! he says, They're lived in now. Squatters and that.

~

He leads me further in, cutting his path to the heart of the Docks. We're passing a dingy row of shopfronts when he gestures to the other side of the road – there's a grocer's shop, a tailor's with a dirt-encrusted grille, an amusement arcade with its shiny purple paint and fake prizes in the window. Louis looks at me expectantly.

What? I say, What?

I follow his gaze. I have to remind him that my memory belongs to five-year-old. It's a child's bubble of street names and people's names. Not the real thing. He's pointing at a hand-painted sign above a doorway: Tino's Fruit and Veg. It still means nothing: but now there's something about this place that presses down on me. The lack of proper daylight, that smell of closed-in darkness. Something I can barely feel.

I'll show you, he says, crossing the road. He pushes the door wide, but I hold back, pretending to examine a crate of oranges on the pavement. Mould closes round them like frost. An old man sits in the entry, surrounded by boxes of vegetables in various stages of decay. Louis talks quietly to this shadow while I shiver on the pavement; the wind is carrying rain. Behind the grille of the tailor's shop, the top half of a mannequin leans sideways in the window. The face is empty and the eyes are blank. The head rests awkwardly in the corner of the frame, a smirch of fingerprints grazing its cheek. A fizzing starts up in my chest.

Come on, I shout to Louis, Let's go back.

He leans out of the doorway, gives me a wry look.

I thought you wanted to meet some people, he says, not unkindly. He grips the shoulder of the man sitting on his upturned crate.

Do you remember Dolores Gauci, Mr Tino?

The old man puts out his hand. There is grime beneath the fingernails and the knuckles are grained with dirt, but the hand is strong still, as massive and open as the day it lifted the baby from the fire. He lets out a tiny, breaking sigh of recognition.

Of course, says Martineau, beckoning me close, Let me see you.

~

The 'grocery store' is not what it seems. There's a narrow set of stairs at the far end of the hall, with a soft light shining down from above, as if the roof has been peeled off. Martineau fetches a key from a hook and lets us in to a long room. The only light in here is from a plate-glass window facing out on to the street. Windolene has been rubbed across the lower half in pale pink swirls. Someone has written a message with their fingertip. It takes a moment to decipher.

The MoonLigHt OPen foR BuS nes

So this is what Eva meant – Martineau is her 'someone'.

My eyes are slow to adjust; Louis and Martineau move like shadows in front of me, easing themselves past the round tables dotted at random in the aisle. At the far end is a counter nailed with rough formica. A single bottle twinkles darkly on the top. Martineau lines up three tumblers.

Sit, he says, Sit, please.

Louis drags a stool to the bar, and I climb up into the soft blue half-light.

It's a sad day for you, Dolores, says Martineau. He pours a measure of liquid into each glass. A scent of aniseed. His fingers drum the formica; he is looking for something.

Ah! he says, ducking. He fetches a lemon from beneath the counter. This he quarters, squeezing the juice into the drinks.

I keep the *good* fruit in here, he smiles, pleased at his joke. We raise our glasses. The drink looks cloudy and cool; it has a sharp, numbing taste.

Dolores is interested in the old times, says Louis. There is a shine on his face as he studies Martineau. It is a vision of romance, and it frightens me. I can see in Louis the cut of my father, swinging down the street with his hat in his hand, success pealing off him like a song. Of course, Louis has been here before. He's heard Martineau talk. But I'm not interested in old times. I want to know about scattering a family like grains of rice: about Marina, my father, Fran; about what it means to burn.

You want to know about the fire, of course, Martineau says, reading my thoughts.

Yes. I'd like to know everything.

He looks at me steadily over the rim of the glass; his eyes are rheumy with age or drink, a tobacco-coloured yellow shot through with bloody flecks, but his lashes are long and black: they look unreal.

Everything, he echoes quietly, shutting me from his sight. He shrugs, and smiles again.

Dolores, he says, I don't *know* everything.

In the dimness of The Moonlight, his voice feels parched. He hunches over the counter and he tells me what he *does* know.

~

All Martineau has to do is collect the debt. He's had a few jobs since landing in Tiger Bay – dock-hand, hotel porter, night cleaner, barman – and problems with each one. This latest job has nothing to do with working behind the counter or washing the lipstick-smeared glasses or pouring drinks. Occasionally he will be called downstairs to evict a drunk or scare someone into paying for the rum they've had too much of, but mostly he just has to stand at the bar, elbow to elbow with Ilya the Pole, who is not a friend of his and whose smell he does not like.

There's not much room behind the counter of The Moonlight: the stove next to the wall leaves only a narrow gap, just enough, at a pinch, for two small people. When Salvatore works his shift, no one else can fit in; he rages if they even try. But now here's Martineau and Ilya, both men vying for that extra inch of space. They stare out across the empty booths towards the far door, or down into their cut-glass tumblers, saying little, waiting like dogs for their master to return.

They don't have to stand so close; one of them could simply walk around the bar and slide onto a stool — and they would both have room. But then Ilya and Martineau would have to face each other: one would have his back to the door; the other, control of the sticky drinks bottles stashed under the counter. Neither of them wants to give up this territory. Martineau is taller and wider, his jacket stretched tight across his shoulders as he leans on the bar. He looks at the door, blinks up at the clip of footsteps passing the window, swirls his brandy. He's waiting for instructions. He's very, very bored.

It seems like an age before Joe Medora finally arrives. He puts his hand inside his jacket, takes out a slim notebook and pushes it across the counter.

Collection, Martineau. You do it.

This is a departure; collecting is normally Ilya's job. He brags about the way he threatens this person, cajoles that one, and laughs when he tells of certain women who can't pay but who are willing to treat him nice — and how he simply raises the amount the following week. Mary Gauci has become one of these women.

Sweet, said Ilya, kissing his fingers to his lips, So sweet.

Martineau knows her; pretty and exhausted and with so many children; her plain clothes and the way her head is bent to one side when she walks. The last time he saw her was only a few weeks ago. That was his first job for Joe — to move the Gaucis out of the rooms above The Moonlight. Mary stood surrounded by bulging paper bags and half-filled crates. She had one child balanced on her hip while the rest darted in and out of the doorway, holding up various items and shouting. Are we taking this, Mam? Is this ours?

Too many children to count, and they all looked so alike. Frankie was nowhere to be seen. Trying to help, Martineau picked up the first thing he saw: the sea-chest, heavy in his arms. From inside there came a muffled mewling.

It's the Babby, said Mary, swiping away the hair from her head, Be careful, now.

He carried everything tenderly after that, as if all their sticks of furniture concealed a living thing.

He hasn't seen her since, but Frankie is still around; wearing a good suit and standing drinks at Tony's Top Cafe, pretending that nothing has changed. Martineau thinks it would be nice to see Mary again.

Ilya obviously thinks so too.

That's my job, Boss, he says, snatching at the notebook. Joe Medora gives him a sidelong look.

I told you to leave Mary Gauci alone. But no. So now you have a different job.

He takes the notebook from Ilya and gives it back to Martineau.

She owes *rent*, he says, Collect it.

~

It's early afternoon by the time Martineau reaches Hodge's Row. Up until now, he's had a very profitable day. Perhaps it's the newness of his face, perhaps the size of him, but the people he must call on disappear into their houses for a second, coming back with folded squares of money, or a watch sometimes, or a ring. He takes whatever is offered, writing deliberate notes in the little book Joe gave him. His pockets are bulging with back rent and interest and gold.

But now here's Mary, standing in front of him, clutching an old biscuit tin. A smut of coal dust on the side of her nose. She's talking so quickly that he can't follow what's being said, but he knows by her eyes that she doesn't have the money. She's looking beyond him at the house opposite. She swears, turns to go back inside.

Quick now, come in, she says.

Except the door is locked to her. She pushes against it, swears again, like a laugh, he thinks, coming out of her so quickly. Mary leads him along the street, pressing into the wind.

He's taken the money, Tino, what else am I supposed to do? she shouts, turning her head once, twice, so that by the time they reach the alleyway, Martineau understands perfectly *what else* she is supposed to do. What did Ilya say about Mary? *Sweet.* Not to Martineau – to him, Mary is desperate. She takes his hands, presses them to her face, moves them down her body. Martineau grips her tight to stop her. He will not take payment this way. She looks into his eyes, pleading with him, almost angry, and then, he thinks he is saved: from around the corner comes a woman's shout; then another, more urgent than before. A small child he almost recognizes breaks from the edge of the Square, hops like a bird into the bushes, and disappears. Another, smaller child watches a curling flame of blue.

~

Something is wrong with Martineau's story. He stares down at his drink, mouth open, trying to find his way back into the tale. He rehearses the words silently over his lips.

It was a miracle to find you – he points his finger at me – Don't forget this. *It was lucky.*

He stretches his hand out flat on the counter, showing me the lifeline, and another, parallel track, across the palm. Two lifelines.

Lucky for you? I ask, unconvinced by this display. But he hasn't finished his story. He's telling me this so that I'll store it up for later. For when I've heard the rest.

~

He puts the biscuit tin on the counter; the spotlight in the ceiling turns the metal into silver. Frankie's hat sits left of the bar, so Martineau knows he's up there with Joe. He checks the money he has collected, sorting out the notes and coins and jewellery and making a careful tally, and all the while his hands are shaking. He's working out a way to tell Frankie about the fire. Already, he's considering the possibilities; Ilya did it for spite, or Joe did it, someone else he doesn't know – or no one else. Martineau does not feel sorry for Frankie. After seeing what Mary has to do, he would like to kill him. He pours himself a drink, drains the glass, pours another. He notices that the cuffs of his shirt are a good two inches shy of his wrists, and that they are grimed with soot; the hairs here are singed into little black stubs. Martineau is reminded of the woman's coat – what was her name? Eva! – and how he had been tempted to touch it. Turning his palm over at the memory, he finds the gash, swollen and specked with grit. He licks a brandy tongue along the wound.

He will have to wait a whole month before Eva contacts him.

~

They've gone doolally over at that house, she says, Some-one should be checking on them.

She sits in the booth, drains her second glass of rum, pulls the hem of her skirt over her knees. It rides up just the same whenever she leans towards him. He can smell her perfume and he loves it. His lack of words invite her near. Come closer in, the silence says.

You're a family friend, aren't you?

Martineau doesn't answer. He *feels* as though he is. He lowers his voice so that he won't be overheard,

Salvatore's wife goes over, he says, She looks after them.

That Carlotta? Another fruitcake, Eva says, They'll lose those kids if they're not careful. The state of the place!

She won't stay for another drink, but as she gets up to leave, Eva turns and touches his arm.

See you soon, she says.

Martineau will pay the Gaucis a visit.

~

The state of the place. No one answers when he knocks, so Martineau slips round the corner and in through the busted back door. The yard is strewn with pieces of timber; some new and pale, others charred black. He sees the long handsaw resting on a makeshift bench, a nest of gleaming nails in a crush of paper. The last time he was here, it was Mary standing there, holding her baby and howling at the sky. Now it's Frankie, his shirt off, his body sweating in the cold air. He is building a cage.

What's it for? Martineau asks.

For rabbits, says Frankie.

It's big, says Martineau, trying to draw him out.

For rabbits, insists Frankie.

He wanders up and down the track of mud, picking over the scorched scraps and talking rapidly in his own language. Martineau knows Maltese, but not this ribbon of words from deep in Frankie's throat. He watches as the other man nails one strip of timber on top of the other. There is no method, despite the appearance of busyness. Frankie's knuckles are split with hammering. A skeleton is taking shape: on the front of the cage Frankie has positioned an oblong doorframe, the hole covered with a grille of wire. The edges sit proud of the roof, sharp as spears. Frankie bends them flat with the heel of his hand.

How is Mary? asks Martineau, How is the baby?

Frankie purses his lips. The mess of dialect spills out of him,

Il demone, Martineau. Sinistra. Sinistra. La Diavola.

Inside the house, Martineau finds Rose and Fran and Luca still in their nightclothes. They sit one behind the other on the stairs, like sentries. Luca is on the lowest step. She cuddles her knees and blinks up at him.

You can't come in, says Rose, her voice like water, It's cursed.

Fear ripples off them like a heat haze. Fran starts to wail,

We can't let anyone in, Mister, she says, We're cursed, we
are. We got a hex!

~

There is a pause into which Martineau sighs deeply. This is
not a story about a fire.

This here, he says, trying to explain, Your skin here—

He puts his open palm an inch from my face, as if to cover it,

Was blown up – full of water. Martineau lifts his glass; a
perfect ring of moisture trembles on the counter. He puts his
finger on it, opens the circle and drags a smear of liquid in a
line towards me. As if he is drawing a map.

The eye closed, and the hair all burnt.

Louis is looking at me. He doesn't like the telling either now,
but we're both stuck here in The Moonlight, in Martineau's
story.

But you could see that it would heal, it would get better,
he says. But this—

He pauses; he can only show me the rest. Martineau pulls his
arm up crookedly, bending his hand into his breast. Just like
Rose did yesterday morning.

Held like this you see,

The fingers upturned, bent into a claw, his body coiling into
itself. It looks like something withering in a blaze. A desperate
act of protection.

This is how you were. Frankie thought – Martineau
spreads his hand like an offering – A devil had come into his
house.

He drains his glass and places it carefully back on the bar. The
light on him is opal.

They were afraid, he says.

Then I know.

Afraid of *me*.

He was a superstitious man, Dolores. He was a stupid man.

~

The telling is finished. I want to ask him more, but there's a thickness on my tongue, dirt in my mouth. I reach for my glass but it's empty. I don't remember drinking it. Louis shifts abruptly off the stool.

Sorry, Mr Tino, we've got to get back. We'd better, Dol, he says, avoiding my look, They'll be missing us.

Martineau follows us through the bar. At the door, he bends his head so that it touches mine.

I'm sorry, he says, gripping me tight and then letting me go.

~ ~ ~

Louis walks with me to the inner harbour. He hugs his body as if he's cold, but it's warmer outside than it was in The Moonlight. A sticky breeze frets the surface of the water. He presses a knuckle to the side of his face, chewing agitatedly on his cheek.

He's upset you, Aunty Dol. Sorry.

He is creased with hurt.

He's just telling a tale, Louis, I say, Forget it. There are worse things.

We look out over the bay. The Bute East Dock is beautiful, a wash of wide sky split in two by a line of yellow stone. In the distance, the harbour lights glow on. They look like a series of suns. A bird swings across the sky.

I'll make it up to you, Aunty Dol, he says.

No more searching, Louis. Let's go home.

He nods in agreement, but there is a look about him: secretive, sly.

Sure, he says, I've got some stuff to do first, like. Something I needs to check. I'll catch you back at the house, okay? He moves quickly, as if he can't wait to be away from here; perhaps he is more like his mother than he knows.

nineteen

Celesta lets out a cry of dismay.

Where did *you* go? We've been waiting! – she looks over my shoulder into the street – And where the hell is Louis?

I've been down the docks. And I've seen Martineau—

She silences me. She holds her hand like a knife between us. Chops air. Celesta won't let me pass through the door until she's said her piece.

I've told you, Dolores, I won't have it. You think you can dig up whatever you like and just swan off again – but *we've* got to live here.

Just when I think her warning is ended, she grabs the sleeve of my coat and pulls me back into the living room. Her teeth are clenched; she would like to take a bite out of me.

I'm serious, she says finally, I Don't Do Memory Lane. Okay?

Then she turns away, smiles a white, dead-eyed, practised smile. The oldest sister. Perfect hostess.

At last, she says to the packed room, The wanderer returns!

~

An airless kitchen. Luca has positioned herself near the sink where Eva always used to stand, and she makes the same action – knocking her cigarette ash down the plughole with an absent flick of the wrist. She keeps her black scarf wrapped tight around her head, the sunglasses perched above her brow like a second pair of eyes. Close up, Luca looks tired. She has no eyelashes; the rims of her lids are scorched and flaky, her eyebrows painted in two careful brown strokes. She has sealed her lips with a deep red pencil line, as if to stop her thoughts from leaking. This family is good at make-up.

She's laughing loud as I come through the doorway.

You used to loathe the poor thing, she's saying to Rose – You torturer!

so for a moment I think they're talking about me,

I was not! protests Rose, That Jacksons' dog was a bloody nuisance. Smelly article, always howling. I *like* animals, me. Ask Parsnip!

Rose's dog has positioned his head between Jumbo's knees; every time he pushes it away, the dog slides it back. Jumbo stares into his teacup looking hot and uncomfortable. The dog, hearing his name at such volume, slinks under the table.

I'm taking it all in; the suffocating body heat; a vague smell of nervous sweat; the windows glazed with condensation. There's not enough space for anyone else. Rose and Luca, Celesta and Jumbo. And now me. We are too many for this room. I watch them talking, their mouths opening and shutting; Rose laughing, Luca bending to whisper in her ear, Celesta's eyes narrowed in a permanent, unspoken rage. She's rapping the tabletop with her long pink fingernails; drumming for Louis.

My mother had to face us, every day, in this room. I try to imagine the five, then six of us to feed, clothe, take care of. Waiting for Frankie to come back, writing her lists and notes and begging letters for something on tick.

I'm good at listing too; I'm putting things in order.

Well, we are, aren't we, Dol?

What? I say, filtering back.

A bunch of heathens, continues Rose.

Celesta is acid,

Speak for yourself.

She pulls the tea-towel off a plate of sandwiches, sniffs dubiously at them before offering one to me,

Poor Mrs Riley! And as for Father Tomelty . . .

It's Mrs Riley's red tea-towel. I could say something. I take a sandwich: it's so thickly buttered, the two triangles of bread slide between my fingers, exposing the smeared ham. When I think no one is looking, I feed it to the dog. Celesta loops the tea-towel over the back of Jumbo's chair.

Next-Door Rileys, says Rose, D'you remember, Lu?

She takes up a pose, a look of deep concentration, and her voice booms in a perfect impersonation, 'Della! Where's the bloody *Echo*?' Jumbo looks at her quizzically.

They used it to wipe their bums. Don't look at me like that – we all did! Even Mrs Airs and Graces over there, Rose says, nodding at Celesta. Celesta lifts a sandwich and takes a tiny bite out of the corner.

If you can manage not to be so crude while we're eating, Rose.

Too late to mention the tea-towel now.

They used to cut the paper into squares, I say, avoiding Celesta's grim face. Everyone looks at me. Rose's mouth falls open with surprise.

How d'you know that? she asks.

Mam used to jump over the fence and steal it from the outhouse. Said it would be good for the rabbit hutch. Warmer.

Silence. I don't know where I found this memory. Celesta inspects her sandwich, Luca lights another cigarette. Rose lifts the bottle of whisky and unscrews the cap.

Where did I see those glasses, Dol? she says, looking about her.

They're in the cupboard under the stairs. I ease myself into the gap between the boxes and the bin-bags, stretching across to the narrow shelf and the assortment of dusty glasses. I call out to Rose.

Hang on a sec, I'll pass them out.

In the corner, the meter blinks its eye. It used to be a dial; the red edge whizzing round at speed, or slow, slow, when the house was dark and quiet. The red edge of the tea-towel as Mrs Riley showed me how she laid my mother out; Eva's tongue as she licks the cream; the sliver of a ruby. Another deeper red, like bloody pearls dropping into my hand. I'm putting things in order.

~

Standing in front of the cupboard door, my mother calls up the stairs.

Rose? Fran? Then quietly to someone else, They're not back from school.

She must have forgotten our game. We were playing hide and seek. I'm here, in the cupboard under the stairs.

I'll count up to a hundred, Dol, you go and hide!

and she kissed my head and turned her back. I heard my mother moving past the cupboard and into the living room, then nothing. That was ages ago. I watched the dial on the meter, waiting for the red edge to return. I counted the numbers as far as I knew, and invented the rest.

Eleventy, twelvty, thirteenty, a hundredl

I thought she would come and find me.

Now she snaps on the lights, and the red edge starts to spin. I'm going to call out, but there's a man's voice. His words are all soft at the edges, as if they're melting. My father has this same tone when he's shaving or he's had a win. But it's not my father.

Come to me, the man says.

Frankie'll be back in a minute, says my mother. Her voice is tight.

He laughs at this. I try to see through the crack, but there's only a bit of my mother's coat. Cold air tickles the corner of my eye. They're standing very close and she sighs, a sharp upwards sound like when she pricks her finger. He makes a buried noise, leaning his weight against the cupboard so it goes very dark. He whispers something I can't understand and laughs again.

Over here, she says, moving him away.

They stop talking for a long time. Then the swishing sighing noise. She mustn't find me now. When my mother speaks, she's almost singing.

Will you let me see her? she says softly, Will you?

Running water. Something being moved on the table.

Any time. Any time you like.

You promised, she says.

Yes – we can leave whenever you like.

I can't.

An argument is starting with this man. Footsteps across the lino, the back door latch.

It's up to you, he says, It's easy.

My mother shouts at the darkness, so loudly that the whole street will know,

I can't! You know I can't!

It's cold and quiet. The red edge of the dial comes and goes. I don't think she'll ever find me. I unbend my legs and crawl out, and the room is stinging bright, full of her perfume and another smell I don't know. On the kitchen table is the Toby Jug with two five pound notes curling under it. My mother is in the yard with her hands over her face. It's as if she's still counting. I slip past, creep up the stairs; she'll know where to find me up there.

~

Come out, Dol, let me get them, Rose says quietly from behind.

I can manage.

She puts the glasses on the table: a Babycham glass with a

chip in the rim, three dusty tumblers, a schooner sticky with grease. Celesta lifts it up to the light,

Ugh. Needs a wash, she says.

It's alright this, says Rose, flicking it with her fingernail, Crystal. I'll have this.

Celesta lets out a gasp of disgust.

You could at least wait until she's cold.

She's always been cold, says Rose.

My mother sitting pressed against the hearth with a tissue up her sleeve and her face pink with weeping. This isn't what Rose means. There's a shift in everyone's breathing; time begins to open.

Not cold to *you*, of course, she continues, Her precious! They *wanted* you.

Don't start.

Made sure you were alright, didn't they? – Rose's voice is rising – What about us? What about Fran?

Celesta stands up.

C'mon, Jumbo, we're going.

Not *nice*, says Rose, swilling the sherry glass under the tap, A bit *upsetting* for you, is it?

Luca puts her hand on Celesta's shoulder.

Sit down, she says, placating, We could all do with a drink.

You didn't see, says Rose, turning on us, You didn't see what he did!

And then a voice.

I saw.

It belongs to me. I am severed in two: here in the kitchen, and there at the end of the garden, watching. It looks like a puppet show; Punch battering Judy to the ground. A quick glance passes between Rose and Luca; a small adjustment, a reckoning. Celesta sits down again.

And I know by their faces they will not yield to this. The moment when it can all be said is pulling away. Years pile up in front of me: the sign on the door saying KEEP

OUT. THIS MEANS YOU! and the times when they did things, played games in the street, and went to school together, and I was never allowed to share it. They have never let me in.

Go upstairs now, Dol, and do your puzzle.

To keep me out of my father's way. It races through my blood, feeling again the soft dusk falling in The Moonlight and Martineau speaking low: *they were afraid.*

They still are.

Celesta begins to fuss with the glasses, moving Rose aside and rinsing them one by one. She places them on the drainer.

Where's that Louis? she says in an embarrassed voice, He's a bugger, he is!

Jumbo reaches into his pocket and pulls out his fob-watch, as if looking at it will make his brother come faster. His round eyes blink slowly at the time.

Nearly half-past four, he says, sounding surprised. Celesta takes this as her cue,

We'll have one drink and then we'll be off, she warns, Louis or no Louis.

No one argues. Rose reaches over behind Jumbo and pulls the tea-towel free. She twists it inside the glass until it squeals with pain, and, mocking Celesta, holds it up to the light.

Clean enough for you?

We raise our glasses. Celesta's lips are already pursed at the rim when I offer a toast. A last try.

To us, I say, To *all* of us – wherever we are.

It doesn't matter who they think I mean: Fran, or Marina, our father, Salvatore, even Joe Medora. I'm including them all. I'm including me. I'm looking at my sisters, caught in the kitchen with their glasses raised and ready to drink. They're all so still, they could be a snapshot from a family album. I could fetch that pen from the Toby Jug and write the names in the space above their heads. I'm unlocking a door which would let us all pass through. They will surely let me do this. But Celesta won't: she closes it again.

To *Mam*, she says firmly.

Aye, laughs Rose with relief, At least we know where *she* is. Thank God.

~ ~ ~

Drinking in the afternoon has never suited me. Perhaps it's that. Or maybe it's the thought of Salvatore, sinking in the thick mud of the bay. It's defiling, being dragged into the light. The twisting action of Rose's hand as it turned inside the glass, the tea-towel squeaking round and round and the kitchen bulb shining through it, the closed-in streets, the gulls rising and falling in the distance; something being unearthed.

I stand in the yard. Sharp points of light, like silverfish, swim before my eyes.

Come on in, Dol, says Luca, It's wet.

She inches down the steps and leans against the door of the outhouse. I'm catching raindrops on my face. Inside me, something claws to get out.

It'll be the drink, she says as I heave again, On an empty stomach.

She puts an arm round my shoulder.

Not pregnant, are you? she whispers.

The cage at the end of the garden. Split skin, fur on the tongue.

Not likely, is all I can manage.

Then I can give you something. It's herbal. It'll help.

Luca is getting soaked. The raindrops on her scarf are pretty as pearls. She looks towards the end of the garden and the cage, crouching in the long grass. She doesn't like it out here.

Do you remember the rabbits? I ask, keeping her.

A short, thick-sounding No. Luca used to be a good liar.

You must! There were dozens. He'd buy them as presents—

I don't remember, she says, turning away, Understand me, Dolores, I don't remember One Single Thing.

The rain and the cage and Luca standing in the garden, denying everything. The heaving in me comes out as a shout.

Well I do! You and Rose, locking me in there. Shame on you, Luca!

She faces me. In the twilight, her own sickness shines like a jewel. Luca closes her eyes; she's tired of not remembering.

Dol, we were *letting you out*, she says.

~ ~ ~

Louis leans over the parapet of Devil's Bridge, his arms spread out on either side for support. From behind, it looks like a scene from the crucifixion. The lock-ups under The Arlies have been there for as long as Louis can remember, but he's confused now; he can't locate the spot. Curtains hang from a few of the arches, and where there are still doors, new padlocks have been fitted. Louis knows Anto and Denise by name, and most of the others by sight, but he can't be sure. Seeing Anto's lock-up, Louis drops down on to the oily mud below the bridge. He counts the rows of arches until something catches his eye. That's it − a strip of Christmas lights looped across an entry. The bulbs are different colours, green and red and smashed and blue and missing and yellow. The cable ends abruptly. It is plugged in to nothing. Louis knows he will be late back, but he doesn't care. There's something important to do. He passes beneath the string of bulbs, lifting a low hoop hanging from a nail. It reminds him of the restaurant and the gaudy rash of fairy lights. It's a mistake to call it The Moonlight, he sees that now; there is no glamour in such a thing. He'll tell Jumbo when he sees him. Louis peers inside. He is looking for a supermarket trolley filled with bags. He hopes he's got it right.

~ ~ ~

All is rusted here. The cage has a corrugated sheet for a roof, rivulets of water shiver in the folds. I catch a droplet from the edge and it sits in my palm like a wept star. There are weeds growing over the square door, ivy embedded in the joints and cracks. When I drag it away, a frenzy of woodlice scatter in all directions. The grille with its crumbling skin of rust. I half expect to see a rabbit, or a litter of pink-white babies shut-eyed and squirming. All there is, is darkness.

Rain on the tin roof sounds like a shower of stones falling from the sky. You have to be on the inside to know this.

Forgetting time was when I stared at the kitchen window, watching her move across the lit square and willing her to come out and get me. I could see her at the sink. Sometimes she would be staring into nowhere, her hands pressed over her ears. Or she'd turn on the tap and I could hear the water curling down the drain. It would run forever, like a thirst.

Punishment time was whenever I was caught, sinking against the door that shut off the stairs, listening to them. One time my mother was shouting. Take me with you, I heard her say, Take me too. She flung the door open and dragged me down, over the last wide step, then the cold graze of the flagstones on my feet and the shivery plank sinking sideways in the mud. Don't tell your dad, she was saying in a whisper that stung my head, Don't tell him. So I knew the man she was begging was not my father.

There was one other time which had no name.

I'm here because I'm safe. A smell of murder in the house, strong as burning. I can see long grass to the left and right, the mud track and the plank leading back down to the yard. The kitchen door is open and a shadow blocks the light – I won't catch its eye! Upstairs, Rose and Celesta's room is all in darkness. The Box Room blazes bright. Lightbulb in the centre of the ceiling hanging like a pear.

He was coming back down the hill, his hat pulled over his face and the rain cutting around him in sheets. He was too early; he must have lost it all. I was on lookout. I would have warned my mother, I was on my way – but as I turn the corner of the stairs I see the man. He's bent across her and her head's back on the table and her hair is swimming over the cloth, this way and that, as she turns her face from side to side. The Toby Jug is just behind her, grinning. Her eyes hold mine. She freezes, and the man turns now, looks at me, smiles. His smile is golden. His hand covers my mother's mouth and what I fear is blood is just a flash of scarlet on the hand.

There's a shout from the doorstep. Fran is guarding too, standing out in the night air and doing as she's told, but now my father has caught her. He'll catch all of us. We run like water: me and Fran past my father, his hand clutching the air at our necks, Joe Medora flitting through the living room and away into the street. But not my mother. He gets her, rending the clothes from her body like the pelt from a rabbit. Now she lies in the box room with the bare bulb hanging over her head.

He stands on the back step, waiting for Fran. If I keep very still in here, he won't find me.

~

Things surface; the rabbits and the stink of them next to me in the hutch; all bits of streaky skin; my father with his hand inside the body, the split wound like a secret and the darkness in there, the hot black closed-in smell. The heat.

He would've smothered you.

Wanted to saw *me* to bits, Dol, like a magician!

I imagine my mother upstairs on the narrow bed, her body cut in a jagged half. My father standing over her with the handsaw raised above his head, and the blood flowing out of her like a burst pipe. His shadow on the step is giant with death; he might have murdered her already. I can't tell from here: blood looks black in the dark.

Fran slides around the yard door. I want to shout, but he's too quick. He punches her to the ground. She gets up; he screams in her face.

Arms down!

And she will stand it. The belt slices air, curves back invisible, flies again. The cry of Fran as she escapes is a close sound now, squeaking, wet. Something is being unearthed. In the corner are the squares of newspaper, all clawed up; and the rabbit, turning round and round in a tight circle, her breath going quickly. A tiny bubble pops out from beneath her, then another, another, like lumps of rain-soaked flint, like rubies in the straw.

The rabbit's eye is fixed on me. These are her babies. They are new and squirming. I want to laugh. I want to run inside and tell everyone.

Look! Babies! Six new babies!

But they are covered in a purple film. It will choke them. My father, standing in the kitchen window as the water splashes in the drain, easing the evidence from the sharp tongue of his belt.

He would have smothered you, Dol!

Closed-in heat. Darkness underneath. The weight of him.

I take each of the young in my lap and slip the membrane from their heads. I will not let them choke. It takes a long time. I have to use what I can – straw, paper, hand, mouth.

The rabbit had eaten them by morning. All that was left, I showed my mother. I tried to tell her then.

I've told you before, not to interfere, she said, But you had to, didn't you? You had to interfere.

~ ~ ~

I'm kneeling with Luca in the long grass. I don't know how long she's been with me. She's holding my hair back from my face, and her mouth is pressed close to my ear; she's whispering words. There. It's gone, It's all gone.

Dusk fell when we weren't looking. It's a navy light that finds us now.

Bad dreams, Dol, she says, That's all they are. We all get them.

With her arms wrapped tight around me, we walk the plank, unsteady as a pair of drunks. I stop at the back door. I can't face the others yet. Luca's scarf has slipped down like a caul around her neck. Her head is bald. She sees me looking.

It'll grow back, she says, smiling faintly.

I used to think my hand would grow back too. I'd watch for signs. At night, I'd will the fingers to sprout, eating up the vacant space like a bloom captured on a time-lapse camera. So I know what will and won't grow back, and I know now when Luca is lying.

~

Rose sits on her own in the kitchen. The window behind her is mirror black. Me and Luca are a soaked and shivering reflection.

They've gone, Rose says, raising her whisky in salute, Celesta said to say goodbye.

She takes a sip and makes a loud sucking noise through her teeth. Tips the bottle towards us.

Tell Luca she must pop in before she leaves, says Rose, mimicking Celesta's clipped tone, That's what she said, honest!

Rose places her hand over her heart, feigns a hurt look – No message for you though, Dol. Or me. Or Parsnip.

Luca smiles. She pulls the scarf from her neck, expertly coiling it round her hand where it thickens like a bandage. Her lipstick is blurred across her mouth.

Shall we drink to the old bitch? she says.

Rose pushes two empty glasses towards us and pours an inch of whisky into each one.

Thought we already had, she cracks, raising her glass, But if I can do it for one, I can do it for two!

And this time I drink with them, and it feels warm, the whisky and the moment and being on the inside.

Feeling alright now? Better out than in, says Rose.

I don't trust my voice so I have to nod at her. Luca finishes her drink in one gulp. She wraps the scarf tight again around her head, meticulous, covering the exposed skin. Takes a tissue out of her bag and drags it across her mouth, then reapplies her lipstick with a practised sweep of the hand. She doesn't use a mirror. She looks expectantly at Rose.

Are you ready then?

They're leaving too. Rose will go back to Terence and Luca will go back to Vancouver.

Don't be a stranger, Luca says, and we all laugh. We know what we will be.

the list

I've got my holdall, a worn wooden dice, and a rosary. I'm taking the chest too. It was a bed of sorts, when I was little. It has survived a fire. There's the picture of the whole of me with an angry Luca by my side, scowling from under her firestorm hair, and the one of us all sitting on the long couch, Fran with her arm round my shoulder and her mouth open about to say something. There's nothing of Marina I can take. There is no sign of who she was, not even a photograph. But you can't miss what you've never had: it's only ghost pain.

~

I walked up the road between my two sisters, Rose's dog lunging ahead of us, Luca's smart case wheeling behind. We didn't say much. At the corner where the Evanses' shop used to be, we phoned for a cab. No one passed us; no one else on the street.

You'll be alright, Dol? asked Luca, You could come with us to the station.
I told her I needed to put things in order. I would get a late train.

Do you think they'll take Parsnip? asked Rose, I might have to walk into town.
But when the driver came he smiled and put his hand on the dog's head.